Scandal at the Savoy

RON BASE & PRUDENCE EMERY

SCANDAL AT THE SAVOY

A Priscilla Tempest Mystery, Book 2

Douglas & McIntyre

I 2 3 4 5 — 27 26 25 24 23

Douglas & McIntyre (2013) Ltd.
4437 Rondeview Road, P.O. Box 219, Madeira Park, BC, V0N 2H0
www.douglas-mcintyre.com

Edited by Pam Robertson
Cover illustration by Glenn Brucker
Text design by Carleton Wilson
Printed and bound in Canada
Printed on 100% recycled paper

Supported by the Province of British Columbia

Douglas & McIntyre acknowledges the support of the Canada Council for the Arts, the
Government of Canada, and the Province of British Columbia through the BC Arts Council.

Library and Archives Canada Cataloguing in Publication

Title: Scandal at the Savoy / Prudence Emery and Ron Base.
Names: Emery, Prudence, 1936- author. | Base, Ron, author.
Description: Series statement: A Priscilla tempest mystery ; book 2
Identifiers: Canadiana (print) 20220476411 | Canadiana (ebook) 20220476489 |
    ISBN 9781771623452 (softcover) | ISBN 9781771623469 (EPUB)
Classification: LCC PS8609.M51 S33 2023 | DDC C813/.6—dc23

To Susie Grandfield, a dedicated Savoyard
—P.E.

For Ric. Without you there, I wouldn't be here.
—R.B.

It is the public scandal that offends. To sin in secret is no sin at all.

Molière

Contents

Authors' Note

There is the twenty-first century Savoy Hotel that continues its splendid traditions of fine service into a modern era that does not always value such things. There is the Savoy Hotel that existed in the late sixties, a much different hotel back then, but certainly no less dedicated to the high standards first set out by Richard D'Oyly Carte, the Savoy's founder.

And then there is the authors' Savoy, the fictional hotel that we have created within the pages of *Death at the Savoy* and now *Scandal at the Savoy*. Our Savoy is fashioned with great fondness and endless admiration, but at the same time it is not real. It is populated by made-up characters who exist only in the world that we shaped for them. The royal, rich and famous who inhabit this imagined world live no further than the edges of our imaginations.

We have had a wonderful time living in our version of the Savoy in two novels, creating portrayals of iconic personalities as they and the hotel existed more than half a century ago. Our hope is that we may be forgiven for the occasional misbehaving movie star and the dead body that once again ended up on the premises while our backs were turned.

CHAPTER ONE

At the A Party

In the matter of the notorious, some would say scandalous, Miss Priscilla Tempest, there is the question of how she ended up at the A party in the first place.

And then there was the murder...

As far as the party is concerned, it was hosted by a pair of visiting Americans: Albert Goldman, a New York agent, and his partner, Arnold Weissman, an entertainment lawyer. They were regular summer guests at the Savoy, certainly, but even so, no one was ever quite sure what made the two of them so important. Yet somehow everyone wanted to attend the two parties they hosted in the Savoy's Pinafore Room, which took its name from Gilbert and Sullivan's fourth opera, HMS *Pinafore*.

The art deco banquet room offered a great view of the Thames Embankment, but it could comfortably accommodate no more than eighty guests, thus the necessity of two parties. The A party naturally attracted the elite of London celebrity and society. The B party, held the following night, accommodated the overflow and was for the lesser mortals.

Naturally, everyone fought tooth and nail to attend the A party.

Miss Tempest was not on anyone's A list, therefore she should never have been invited to the A party. But for reasons that were beyond her, there she was that night, accompanied by the famous playwright Noël Coward no less. Slim and lovely, her reddish-blond hair cut fashionably short, she looked particularly appetizing in her fuchsia Mary Quant dress, lavender stockings and matching chunky-heeled purple pumps.

By the time the two of them arrived, the Pinafore Room was already crowded with the sort of guests guaranteed to turn even the most jaded head.

"Except mine, of course," Noël said, passing Priscilla a glass of champagne from a tray offered by one of the waiters. "I am beyond jaded."

He took a glass for himself, downed it in a single gulp and then lifted another. Priscilla made herself sip her glass, determined that this night with this crowd she would behave.

"Beyond jaded, my bony ass," announced a small man with a noble, jutting forehead and heavy-lidded eyes. Looking at him you might conclude Sir John Gielgud should be a god or an actor. Or a bit of both.

"No one is more enthralled by this sort of thing than our dear Noël," Gielgud went on. "Thank goodness there is no piano. Otherwise, he'd soon be pounding out 'Mad About the Boy.'"

"Ah, Johnny," said Noël happily, "freshly arrived and already dipped in acid."

"Please. I bathed in it before I got here."

"Have you met my dear friend Priscilla Tempest? Priscilla, meet Johnny Gielgud, the man who, not satisfied with murdering Shakespeare from practically the moment the poor Bard dropped dead, has now taken to desecrating *my* words."

"If only they made sense, dear boy," said Gielgud with a smile. "If only they made sense." His brown eyes twinkled mischievously. "And speaking of murdering Shakespeare, here comes Larry, carrying the great weight of British theatre with a frown as usual."

Priscilla recognized the chiselled visage of Laurence Olivier, an aging beauty behind horn-rimmed glasses. And sure enough, that visage had a frown attached to it, as though he had just heard something unpleasant and was trying not to show it, and failing.

"Had a devil of a time getting a taxi over here." He glanced around, confusion replacing the frown. "What was that about Shakespeare, Johnny?"

"He says you murder him," Noël offered.

Olivier looked irritated. "Surely that's some sort of joke."

"You will discover Larry has a wonderful sense of humour," Noël said to Priscilla.

"What's that?" said Olivier.

Noël rolled his eyes and said, "You haven't met my friend Priscilla, Larry."

"What a pleasure," Priscilla said, offering her hand.

"My God, a dazzler." Olivier's eyes sparkled as he took Priscilla's hand and kissed it.

"Careful, Priscilla," warned Gielgud. "Lord Larry is a lethal combination: cad and lecher."

"Wonderful," said Priscilla. "I've had a great deal of experience with cads and lechers. I prefer the cads, but a lecher will do."

That got laughs from the three men. Gielgud looked impressed. "My heavens, Noël, your friend has a sense of humour and lovely legs to boot. You should cast her in your next production. You might even get a laugh or two."

"If only I could find an actor to read the lines properly," Noël said.

Olivier was distracted, adjusting his glasses. "Who is that?"

Priscilla turned to see her competition. Flaming hair piled high on her fine head, Skye Kane dazzled in a low-cut gown that emphasized what was drawing the attention of Larry Olivier, not to mention several other males in the Pinafore Room.

Skye towered on the arm of a small, dark, moustached man with slicked-back hair and large, suspicious eyes. David Merrick, the American Broadway theatrical impresario and regular Savoy guest, always struck Priscilla as a man who was afraid he was about to be taken advantage of, angry about it, and determined not to allow such a thing to happen.

"That's Skye Kane," Priscilla announced, automatically summoning her promotional mode. "She's one of the Savoy dancers at our nightly Cabaret which, incidentally, for the next few weeks stars the famous film actress Diana Dors."

"My, my," said Olivier in awe, his interest in Priscilla very much in the past.

"Unless my failing eyes deceive me, with her is that moustache-twirling villain out of a Victorian melodrama, enemy of all that is holy in the theatre, David Merrick," said Gielgud.

"Hated by everyone," added Noël, "right up to the moment he wants to produce one of their shows." Noël aimed a glance at Olivier. "Right, Larry?"

"He might have had something to do with *The Entertainer*." Olivier looked uncomfortable.

Skye noticed Priscilla, smiled, and waved hello. Priscilla started over, trailed by Olivier as Skye detached herself from Merrick. The two friends embraced.

"What a pleasure to see you," Skye said in the little-girl voice that could bring male admirers to ruin.

"Pleased, or surprised?" Priscilla said.

"Are you kidding? Do you think I ever expected to be here?" She jerked a thumb in the direction of the approaching Merrick. "The trick is to keep the right sort of bloke wrapped around your little finger—even if he looks as though he's about to tie you to a railroad track."

"Hello, Priscilla," Merrick said in a low, insinuating voice, his arm taking custody of Skye's waist.

"You two know each other?" Skye asked in surprise.

"Mr. Merrick spends a lot of time complaining to me when he stays at the Savoy," Priscilla explained.

"There's plenty to complain about," Merrick said. "Lucky for you there's a whole lot more to complain about at the Dorchester."

"We do try our best, Mr. Merrick."

"My advice would be to try harder," Merrick said.

"David, dear boy," said Larry Olivier, placing his hand on Merrick's shoulder.

"Should I call you Lord Olivier?" asked Merrick, working up the approximation of a smile.

"Not yet, dear boy. A bit premature. For now, it's simply Larry." His attention turned to Skye. "Tell me, who is your stunning friend?"

"I'm Skye Kane, a huge fan of yours, Lord Olivier," she said brightly. "I loved you in *The Entertainer*."

"A wonderful part," Larry said. "One simply had to spit out John Osborne's words; the piece did the rest for you."

"You might remind Miss Kane that I produced that show," Merrick said huffily.

"Of course," Olivier said. "How could I ever forget? How could you ever let me forget?"

"You always manage to," Merrick rejoined.

"I thought you were brilliant," Skye said.

Olivier looked bashful. "You are very kind. I certainly felt as though I'd rediscovered something in myself as an actor playing Archie Rice."

"Yeah, you were great, no doubt about it," Merrick said. "But that was then and this is now. I hope you're not going to ask me to bring *The Dance of Death* to New York." Merrick sounded miserable at the prospect.

"Never crossed my mind." Some of the previous enthusiasm had slipped from Olivier's voice. "Although," he added quickly,

"I must say it has been one of my signature successes at the National Theatre."

"It's not commercial," Merrick declared.

"What's not commercial?" asked Gielgud. He and Noël had joined the group.

"There you are, Johnny," Merrick said. "What have you been up to?"

"*The Shoes of the Fisherman* with Tony Quinn. I'm a pope. A role I was born to play."

"Oh dear. The thought of Johnny as a pope drives me to drink," Noël announced. "I'm in desperate need of more champagne."

"Let me get it for you," Priscilla said.

"You're such a dear. I hereby order you to accompany me to all future parties."

"You poor thing," groaned Gielgud.

Priscilla made her way through the crowd to the bar. As she worked to get a waiter's attention, she felt a tap on her shoulder. She turned to confront a man with a Roman-emperor haircut framing an intellectual's somewhat saturnine face. Not a handsome face by any measure, thought Priscilla, but arresting, framing sharp, inquisitive eyes that were only for a flattered Priscilla. The eyes belonged to the available bachelor who had taken London by storm in the past few days and who Priscilla knew to be staying at the hotel: the Canadian prime minister, Pierre Elliott Trudeau.

"I've been trying to meet you since I saw you arrive," he said. "I thought I'd come over and introduce myself. I'm Pierre. And you are...?"

"Priscilla Tempest, Mister—what should I call you? Mr. Prime Minister?"

"Why not simply, Pierre?" he suggested. He spoke in a dry, melliferous mid-Atlantic drawl, which was surprisingly seductive, she thought. Not that she could be seduced, she told herself. This evening, she was being a good girl, as Eliza Doolittle might have said, and being a good girl did not allow for seduction by charismatic Canadian politicians.

"Actually—Pierre—we have met before," Priscilla said, accepting a glass from the bartender.

"Impossible," said Pierre. "I certainly would have remembered."

"The last time you stayed with us," Priscilla said.

"Ah, so you work here at the Savoy."

"You were totally uninterested."

"I must have been preoccupied. I believe I had just been elected and I was still in a daze. That's the only reason I can imagine for not showing more interest. Thankfully, I've settled down a bit and come to my senses."

His quick, knife-edge smile left her somewhat weak in the knees.

Weak in the knees? Oh God, she thought.

In need of a breather from the attentions of the prime minister, Priscilla retreated to the ladies' room to apply unnecessary lipstick. She exhaled, commanding herself to settle down, reminding herself that she was a Savoy Hotel employee and therefore was obligated to deport herself appropriately. That meant resisting any of the erotic impulses she might currently be experiencing.

Finished with the lipstick, she was inspecting herself in the mirror, questioning what it was about this pixie face...attractive enough, she supposed, but hardly a face to launch a thousand ships. Maybe three or four hundred on a good day but nowhere near a thousand and certainly not enough of a face to attract a kind-of-sexy prime minister.

The bathroom door opened and in stumbled Skye Kane, her left cheek flaming, her face wet with tears. She fell against the sink for support, head down, sobbing.

Priscilla rushed to wrap her arm around Skye's heaving body. "What's wrong, Skye? What happened?"

"He hit me. We were in the hallway. The bastard hit me," Skye sobbed.

"Who? Who hit you?"

"Who do you think? That bugger David Merrick." She lifted her head to face the mirror. "God, I can't do a show tonight looking like this."

"Why did he hit you?"

"Why do men hit women? Because they can, that's why. He dragged me out of the party, wanted me to come back to his suite. In a fury because I said I wouldn't, there wasn't time."

"He mustn't get away with this. We should call the police," Priscilla said.

"God, no!" Skye looked mortified. "He's staying at the Savoy. I call the police and I lose my job. Men like him are always protected from little tramps like me, right? Isn't that the way it is?"

"It doesn't have to be," Priscilla said, thinking that she was saying meaningless words. That sadly, Skye was right.

"Doesn't it?" She returned a cynical look. "Yeah, well, let me know as soon as that changes."

Skye straightened, gathering herself. "For now, I will go to the dressing room, clean myself up, put on the brave face that's always necessary, and get ready for the show. While I'm doing these things, I will spend time telling myself to smarten up and stay away from brutes. But then that would mean I'd have to give up men entirely, wouldn't it?"

The two women chuckled, facing their reflections in the mirror. "But he shouldn't get away with what he did," Priscilla repeated.

"After he hit me; you know what he said?"

"What?"

"He said if I told anyone, he would kill me."

Morning Has Broken

A shaft of early morning sunlight seeping through the drapes awakened Priscilla Tempest to the realization that she was lying naked, inches from a sleeping form, male in gender by the look of things.

It took her another moment to realize that she had drunk too much champagne the night before and that might account for the headache starting to bang between her ears. Another moment was needed to understand that the sunlight was seeping into one of the hotel's highly desirable river suites. They would put the prime minister of Canada into such a suite.

It was an impeachable offence for an employee to sleep with a guest, particularly a guest who was a prime minister. Since she worked in the Savoy Press Office, she most certainly was an employee, and given the evidence of Pierre Trudeau's handsome, slightly pockmarked face so close to her, she most certainly had slept with him.

Had done a lot more than sleep, she recalled dimly.

Tamping down her rising panic, Priscilla rose slowly, easing away the bedcovers and keeping an eye on her sleeping companion. Across the room, she could see her clothes, neatly arrayed on an armchair, and she was thankful that whatever passion had ensued did not involve throwing her clothes around.

Not this time.

She gathered up her Marks & Spencer underwear, the lavender

pantyhose, and the Mary Quant dress, then slipped into the ornate bathroom and closed the door. Her naked reflection was caught in golden light reflecting off various mirrors as she dressed hurriedly, lamenting her careless foolishness yet at the same time unable to extinguish the thought that, for a Canadian prime minister, Pierre Trudeau was unexpectedly lively, kind of fun—and pretty damned good in bed.

What had he said? Yes, reason over passion. That was his mantra, he had explained at the bar as they discussed how he had succeeded in politics—and in life.

Well, passion had certainly trumped reason last night. Champagne might have played a part in drowning reason.

Dressed, Priscilla splashed cold water on her face, noting that in this perfect light at least, she did not look too ravaged.

Taking one last reassuring glance at herself and a deep, deep breath, she opened the bathroom door, tip-toed back into the bedroom, scooped up her purple pumps, and headed for the door. The prime minister—thank goodness!—remained an unmoving lump on the king-size bed.

Priscilla eased the door open and stepped into the hall, and jumped as she was confronted by two bulky, equally surprised dark-suited gentlemen with short haircuts—the Royal Canadian Mounted Police officers assigned to guard the prime minister. She could not remember them being there when Pierre had led her—lured her?—into his suite. Would the presence of security have made a difference? Would she have been swayed by reason rather than passion?

Probably not.

But the officers were present now. After a tense moment, they noticeably relaxed as they realized that Priscilla was not an assassin sent to slit their prime minister's throat, but merely his one-night stand.

Was that what this was? A one-night stand? What else could it be? After all, she was hardly going to marry a prime minister, even if he was rather attractive and certainly captivating. She was not going to marry anyone.

"Good morning, gentlemen," Priscilla said as everyone shuffled awkwardly and looked mutually embarrassed. She slid past, pausing to lean against the wall so she could slip on her shoes and then hurrying along the hallway, praying to whatever gods looked over the Savoy that no one else saw her. The security people were undoubtedly discreet but was anyone else? She shuddered inwardly thinking of how quickly General Manager Clive Banville, always on the lookout for a good excuse to be rid of her, would banish her from the pampered world of the Savoy, tossing her out into the cold, dreary reality of the London streets. If she could only get to the safety of the press office, everything would be fine.

She hoped.

The red lift off the Front Hall was out of the question. Who knew what prying eyes might be present? Instead, she descended the stairs at the rear of the hotel. Halfway down she encountered a man slumped on the steps. White-haired, dressed in a three-piece suit that looked as though it had seen better days, he appeared to be sound asleep. At Priscilla's approach, he jerked awake. "So sorry," he said in an accented voice that sounded German to her ears.

"Are you all right?" Priscilla asked.

"Yes, yes, fine. I must have dozed off. Most embarrassing, you must forgive me."

"Are you a guest at the hotel?"

"Yes, yes, a guest, certainly," the man said, using the railing to lift himself to his feet. His eyes behind rimless glasses were pale blue, his suit grey and pin-striped, his tie slightly askew. At first glance, he resembled a university professor a bit down on his luck, shabbily dressed, in need of a shave and haircut. Vaguely she wondered what he might be doing at the Savoy—and then immediately dismissed the thought. *Everyone* was welcome at the Savoy! Even if they could use a good barber.

He offered a hand as he said, "Hans Kringelein."

"Priscilla Tempest," Priscilla said, taking Hans Kringelein's rather soft white hand. "I work here at the hotel."

The old man's face lit up. "Do you now? Isn't that marvellous? Must be quite an honour."

"Is there anything I can help you with?"

"No, no," he said hurriedly. "I'm just waiting to check in—they tell me I am too early, that my room is not yet ready. I became very sleepy—age, I suppose. I did not want to fall asleep in that lovely lobby area so I came in here."

"Do you mind if I ask where you are from, Mr. Kringelein?"

"Not at all. I am from Itzehoe. That's in Germany. Do you know it?"

"No, I'm afraid I don't."

"There is a most famous hotel there, the Dithmarscher Hof, where I worked for many years."

"Welcome to the Savoy, Mr. Kringelein," Priscilla said. "Why don't you come with me? I'll see if they can hurry your room so that you're not having to sit in the stairwell."

"That's most kind of you."

Priscilla accompanied him down the stairs and along the hallway past the press office and into the Front Hall. Vincent Tomberry, the assistant reception manager, was on duty. He bestowed upon Priscilla and Kringelein the haughty, distracted gaze he reserved for the less-important personages in his life. "Yes, Miss Tempest, what is it I can do for you?"

"This is Mr. Hans Kringelein," Priscilla said. "He has just arrived from Itzehoe in Germany and is very tired. He needs his room as soon as possible. I'm hoping you can accommodate him, Mr. Tomberry."

Tomberry's cold eyes gave this new arrival the once-over and did not particularly like what they saw. "It is very early," Tomberry announced.

"Nonetheless, I have assured Mr. Kringelein that at the Savoy we do everything that is necessary to ensure the comfort and happiness of our guests. Am I not right about that, Mr. Tomberry?"

Tomberry cleared his throat. "Yes, of course." He gave Kringelein another look, this time apparently deciding that he had found something more to his liking. He forced a smile. "Why don't you leave Mr. Kringelein with me? I'm sure we will be able to accommodate him in short order."

"I do not wish to make a fuss," Kringelein protested.

"It's no fuss at all," Priscilla said. "At the Savoy, there is no such thing as a fuss when it comes to our guests."

Kringelein took Priscilla's hand in both of his. The gratitude shone from his old, lined face. "You are so very kind, Miss Tempest."

"Not at all, Mr. Kringelein. You're in excellent hands with Mr. Tomberry. I'm in the press office if you need anything."

"*Danke*," Kringelein said gratefully.

CHAPTER THREE

The Summons

Having done her good deed for the morning, Priscilla hurried back across the Front Hall and into the welcoming safety of the Savoy Press Office in Room 205.

Her assistant, Susie Gore-Langton, of the monied, aristocratic Gore-Langtons, was of such a pedigree that it had been decreed by the gods she should be provided with naturally blond hair, a body to die for and an aversion to arriving anywhere on time.

This morning, Susie had actually beat Priscilla into the office and was getting off the phone as she entered. Her eyes grew large at the sight of her boss. "You're *wearing* the same clothes you wore *yesterday!*" she exclaimed, as though this was unimaginable and yet here it was—*imaginable!*

"Don't ask," Priscilla said, ducking past into her office. She felt better once she was behind her desk. The three telephones that were her communication with the outside world were, thankfully, silent for the moment. She needed coffee—badly. She pushed at the waiter button, one of three. The other two, housekeeping and valet service, were rarely used in the press office.

Susie stuck her head in the door. "And you're not wearing makeup!"

"I never wear *that* much makeup," Priscilla protested.

"But you're not wearing *any*..."

"Go away, Susie," Priscilla said.

Susie smiled one of her Cheshire-cat smiles. "You were bad last night, I just know it. "

"Susie!"

"I'm going. But it's only a matter of time before you tell me what happened. Meanwhile, you should know that the Rajah of Faridkot has arrived with three wives, a fleet of cars and four bodyguards."

"Rajah that," Priscilla said.

"Rajah comes from the Sanskrit word for 'king,' incidentally," Susie reported. "Maharajah from the word for 'great king'."

"You've done your homework, Susie—bravo."

Encouraged by Priscilla's compliment, Susie added, "Harinder Singh, that's the rajah's name, will be meeting with the Queen."

"Will he be bringing along his three wives?"

"That I don't know," Susie said.

"The Queen is so democratic," said Priscilla. "You don't have to be a great king to meet her, you merely have to be a king."

"I am told further," Susie went on, "that Harinder Singh does not wish to speak to the press and we are to make certain his wishes are accommodated."

Susie moved aside to make way for Karl Steiner, the floor waiter assigned to the press office. He bore lifesaving coffee on a silver tray.

"Karl, my hero," Priscilla proclaimed.

"I thought it might be an emergency," Karl said, setting the coffee on the desk in front of her.

"Whatever would make you think that?"

"As I have often suggested to you, madam, there are no secrets at the Savoy."

"Karl," Priscilla said with a straight face, "I have no idea what you're talking about."

"Of course not, madam," Karl stated solemnly. "If you require anything else, please ring."

Karl faded, leaving Priscilla to gulp down the coffee—which provided a quick jolt but also made her feel even more jittery than before.

She put her cup aside, fretting that if Karl knew what he shouldn't know, then it was almost certain others also knew what they shouldn't know.

Damn!

Did she really think she could slip away unnoticed from what was probably the summer's most prestigious cocktail soirée with the prime minister everyone was talking about?

Ha!

Priscilla forced herself to think rationally about what had happened—that yes, there might be certain unsubstantiated rumours making the rounds among the Savoy's staff, but those same staff members were nothing if not discreet. The chances of her indiscretion becoming public knowledge were slim.

That is what she told herself, anyway.

She sipped more coffee, beginning to feel less like she had recently been up having sex all night.

Her telephone rang. There, she thought, the business of the Savoy Press Office resuming, taking her mind off whatever nonsense had occurred the night before. Old news—on with the day!

"Priscilla, good morning, it's Percy Hoskins from the *Evening Standard* calling."

Priscilla's heart sank. "Yes, Percy, I certainly know who you are; I know only too well who you are."

"That's no way to respond to the love of your life," Percy said merrily.

The love of her life? Priscilla thought to herself. Maybe in another life, but certainly not in this one.

"The love of my life I never hear from," Priscilla said.

"I called two weeks ago. You never returned my call."

"Because it had been a month before that since I'd heard from you."

"We're both busy, luv, careers to pursue and all that—but you know I'm mad about you."

"What is it, Percy? As you point out, we both have careers to pursue."

"Okay, listen. I'm hoping you can help me here. Pierre Elliott Trudeau, this new Canadian prime minister everyone's so fascinated by."

"What about him?" Her stomach began to tighten.

"He's here for a Commonwealth Conference and staying with you, right?"

Priscilla's stomach began to sink. "Yes, that's correct. The Commonwealth Conference. We also have the Australian prime minister with us."

She had not slept with him. Not yet, anyway.

"Half the eligible women in London are not after the Australian prime minister," Percy pointed out.

"And they are after the Canadian guy?" Priscilla thought she was doing a fine job feigning ignorance.

"Definitely. All London is atwitter, as they say."

"Is that what they say?"

"Apparently our Canadian bachelor PM showed up at a posh party last night where he was swept off his feet by a comely young thing."

"I wouldn't know anything about that," Priscilla said, the words choking in her throat.

"I was hoping you could help me with a name for this woman."

"Why would I do that, Percy?"

"Because you love me."

"Ah, but you see? I don't love you."

Priscilla hung up the phone and closed her eyes, immediately wondering if she had acted too hastily. Perhaps the best way to keep Percy at bay was, in fact, to love him.

Except, she didn't love him.

Shit!

Susie stuck her head in the door. "Do you know anything about the woman Pierre Trudeau was with at the party last night? I've got a reporter from the *Daily Mail* on the phone."

"Why would I know anything about who the prime minister was with?" Priscilla snapped.

"Weren't you at the same party?"

Ah yes, Priscilla thought, the party—the party that, like so many other parties, she should never have attended.

Too late now, though. The party had been attended. The trouble had started. The tragedy of her life unfolded further...

The ringing telephone drew Priscilla out of her reverie.

"Miss Tempest, please come to the bandstand immediately," ordered the tense voice of Major Jack O'Hara, the Savoy's head of security. "It is most urgent."

CHAPTER FOUR

Showgirl

They know!

As she made her way past the Front Hall, down the stairs to the Restaurant, Priscilla was certain everyone was hearing the loud, panicked thump of her heart. A sickly young woman with great legs and bad judgment, born to screw up her life.

But if management *did* know, then why would Major Jack O'Hara call her to the Cabaret? Why would she not be drummed out in General Manager Clive Banville's office, the Place of Execution, where her misdeeds ordinarily would be punished?

But this was Canada's prime minister, for heaven's sake! Mr. Banville would want to stay as far away from scandal as possible. Therefore, Major O'Hara would conduct the inquisition in a place where he was certain not to be disturbed at this time of the day—*the bandstand!*

Reaching the deserted Restaurant, Priscilla crossed the dance floor. In the evening the floor rose on a hydraulic lift to become the stage for a nightly Cabaret. Major O'Hara bolted suddenly from behind the bandstand, giving her a start. He looked grim, the way executioners tended to look as they were about to spring into action. All he lacked was the axe with which to take off her head.

"Miss Tempest, there you are. Come with me."

"Please," Priscilla began, "I would just like to—"

"No questions," Major O'Hara snapped. "Follow me and do as you are told."

Major O'Hara performed a perfect parade square about-face, as befitted an ex-military man, and marched off, with Priscilla scurrying after him.

They entered a narrow hallway flanked by cubicle-like dressing rooms. Clive Banville came out of the dressing room at the end of the row, his face grey and drawn. "Miss Tempest," he said in a choked voice. "I'm afraid we are going to need your assistance this morning."

"Yes, of course, sir," Priscilla said, not quite believing what she was hearing.

"This is a most unfortunate duty—"

Oh damn, Priscilla thought. Here it comes, the axe dropping...

"—inside, please..." Banville indicated the dressing room he had just exited.

She paused, wondering what any of this had to do with being fired. "I'm not certain—"

"Miss Tempest, please!" O'Hara said angrily. "Do as you are asked."

Banville moved aside to allow her to enter.

"Make sure you do not touch anything," warned Major O'Hara.

Priscilla pushed the door open further and stepped into the dressing room. The light from the hallway illuminated the body crumpled against a makeup table, its mirror outlined in light-bulbs. Skye Kane was still in costume from the night before, her long showgirl's legs stretched out at an awkward angle. Her lavishly red hair was dishevelled, mascara smeared. She stared with glassy, unseeing eyes at a world she would never see again.

Priscilla's hand shot to her mouth too late to stifle a loud gasp. Major O'Hara had moved to stand directly behind her. "Can you identify this person?" he asked in his crisp, military voice.

"Skye Kane," Priscilla managed to say, hardly able to breathe.

"Then you know her?"

"Yes. She's one of the Savoy dancers in Diana Dors's show."

Major O'Hara directed her back out into the hall where Banville waited anxiously. "Well?"

"A showgirl," O'Hara reported. "One of our dancers. Skye Kane, by name. Is that correct, Miss Tempest?"

Priscilla nodded.

"How well did you know this person?" Banville gave her a sharp look that assured her knowing a dead person at the Savoy was not a good thing.

"Not well," Priscilla said. "I've gotten to know her the last few weeks since Miss Dors opened here. The two of them are—were—friends."

Banville closed his eyes. His mouth tightened. "Damnation," he said. "I don't suppose this is some sort of accident."

Major O'Hara considered the possibility before shaking his head. "Doubtful," he stated. "I'm no expert but there is a slight blue discolouration on Miss Kane's neck."

"What does that mean?"

"It could mean a lack of oxygen, which would indicate that she was strangled to death."

"Oh God," Banville groaned. "More scandal at the Savoy." He opened his eyes again. "As if we don't have enough trouble with Miss Dors." He sighed. "How shall we handle this?"

"We must not further delay calling in the police," Major O'Hara said. "Otherwise, it begins to look suspicious."

"Why would it look suspicious?" Banville sounded suddenly angry.

"It might appear as though we're trying to cover something up."

"We have a dead showgirl in a dressing room at the Savoy. How the devil could we cover that up?"

For a moment, nobody said anything. The three of them stood awkwardly together, the hallway seeming to press in on them.

"Very well," Banville said in a resigned voice. "Call them in. Call the damned police!"

Miss Dors Is Questioned

"Skye was one of the eight Savoy dancers who open and close the show," Diana Dors was explaining.

With her white-blond hair, flawless makeup and voluptuous figure—this morning hidden beneath a black trench coat—even under these terrible circumstances Diana managed to personify the movie sex symbol the former Diana Fluck had worked so hard to become. A pale goddess surrounded by a mob of plain-clothes detectives.

"What happened last night after the show?" Priscilla recognized the stolid Scotland Yard copper's face, the piercing eyes and firm jaw of Detective Chief Inspector Robert "Charger" Lightfoot.

"What happened is what usually happens," Diana answered. "We all get out of our costumes, tell each other lies about how good the show was, and then go home and fall dead tired into bed."

"And last night how did Miss Kane seem?"

"I talked briefly with her before the show. She seemed fine," Diana said.

She spotted Priscilla and broke away from the detectives to embrace her. Around them the Restaurant had filled with uniformed bobbies. "Oh God," Diana cried holding tight to Priscilla. "Isn't this the most horrible, awful thing imaginable?"

"It's dreadful," Priscilla said consolingly. "Do you have any idea what happened?"

Diana dropped her voice to speak into Priscilla's ear. "The police are saying Skye was murdered—*murdered!* Can you believe it. And, and—"

Her words were lost in a flood of tears.

"What? What is it, Diana?"

"They want to know where I went after the show! Can you imagine?" She embraced Priscilla again, her tears damp on Priscilla's face as she whispered, "I know who did this. I know—"

"Who?" Priscilla asked.

But then Inspector Lightfoot was hovering, offering a large, white handkerchief that might have been mistaken for a flag of surrender—but to what? The charms of Diana Dors? It wouldn't surprise Priscilla in the slightest.

"Are you going to be all right, Miss Dors?" Lightfoot asked solicitously.

"Yes, yes, I'm fine, Inspector, thank you." Diana was using the handkerchief to carefully wipe at her tears so as not to disturb the makeup. "This has been a terrible, terrible shock, as you can imagine..."

"Yes, of course." The inspector's deeply creased face was the picture of sympathy. "I think that's all for now, Miss Dors. I can have one of my men drive you home if you like."

Diana smiled wanly. "No, that's fine, Inspector. I have a driver."

"Thank you, Miss Dors. We will be in touch."

Diana threw her arms around Priscilla dramatically for a final embrace before swaying away, the eyes of the policemen in the room following her out—to ensure her safe exit, of course.

As soon as Diana was gone, the inspector reluctantly turned his attention to Priscilla. "Well, Miss Tempest, here we are again."

"Your favourite suspect is back," Priscilla said gloomily.

"Yes, unfortunately. As I recall, you were also involved the last time we had to deal with a murder at the Savoy."

"I didn't kill Miss Kane if that's any consolation," Priscilla said.

Inspector Lightfoot looked at her in a way that suggested he wasn't ruling out that possibility.

"But you were one of the last persons to see her alive, Major O'Hara tells me."

"Not necessarily. Skye performed in the Cabaret show after she left the party that we both attended."

"Was Miss Kane alone at this party?"

"No, she was escorted by the American theatrical producer David Merrick. He's a guest here at the hotel."

"I see." Inspector Lightfoot was now busily scribbling into the notebook he had produced. "And how did Miss Kane seem to you?"

How did she seem? "Not good," Priscilla said. "Not good at all."

"And why was that?"

"She was in tears when I saw her in the bathroom. She said that Mr. Merrick had become angry because she wouldn't return to his hotel suite with him. Skye said he struck her and then threatened her life if she said anything."

"You say this man Merrick *struck* Miss Kane?" If Inspector Lightfoot wasn't interested before, he was certainly interested now, eyes alight, nostrils flaring as if scenting prey.

"That's what Skye told me," Priscilla said, beginning to doubt she should be quite so forthcoming with damning information about one of the Savoy's regular guests.

"And then Mr. Merrick said what?"

"According to what Skye told me, he said he would kill her if she said anything about being hit."

Lightfoot continued his scribbling. When he finished, he looked up sharply at Priscilla. "What happened after Miss Kane left the bathroom?"

"I returned to the party." That part was certainly true enough. "I assume Miss Kane went off to prepare for the Cabaret show later that evening."

"And what about this Merrick chappie?"

"I suppose he had left because I didn't see him."

"What time did you leave the party?"

"I'm not certain. Around ten o'clock, I suppose."

"And where did you go then?"

Oh God, Priscilla thought. How was she supposed to answer? The truth? *I went back to the suite of the prime minister of Canada, allowed him to undress me, and then spent the night not getting much sleep?*

No! Not the truth! Anything but the truth!

"I went home," Priscilla said. The lie slipped out easily enough.

"And you were alone?" Inspector Lightfoot asked.

A little lie was not enough, apparently. One little lie would soon beget another one. At least she could try to dodge a bit. "Why would you want to know that?"

"If you were with someone, that person would enable us to verify your story."

"Why would you have to verify my story?" Was it her? Or was this becoming steadfastly more complicated?

"Then we could discount you as a possible suspect."

Priscilla's stomach had twisted into a knot. "Here we go again, Inspector. You think I killed Skye Kane?"

"I didn't say that."

"But that's what you're implying." Priscilla was using the most indignant tone she could muster on short notice, partly because she was anxious to avoid the truth, and partly because she resented being labelled a murder suspect yet again.

"One more question, if you will, Miss Tempest." In the wake of her frown, he added: "Please..."

"What is it?"

"Did you know that Miss Kane was previously involved with a person named Mr. Reggie Kray?"

"You mean the gangster?" Now there's a surprise, she thought.

Inspector Lightfoot nodded. "And further, her friend Miss Dors had also been dating Mr. Kray and had learned of his relationship with Miss Kane and was very angry and jealous. Were you aware of any of that?"

"Is it all true?"

"I'm asking you, Miss Tempest."

No trouble with the truth here: "As far as I know, Diana and Skye are—were—friends. I don't know anything about the things you just described to me."

"Very well, Miss Tempest," Inspector Lightfoot said brusquely. "Thank you for your time. We will be in touch."

Priscilla groaned inwardly. The last thing she needed right now was the possibility of Scotland Yard staying "in touch." That was never a good thing, as she knew only too well.

Orgies!

"It's all over the hotel!" exclaimed Susie as soon as Priscilla entered 205. "Someone's dead in one of the Cabaret dressing rooms—*murdered*, they say! A nightmare!"

"Yes, I know," Priscilla said. The day wasn't half over, and already she was exhausted.

"I'm getting calls from reporters demanding information," Susie continued in the panicked voice she adopted when faced with a crisis. "I don't know what to say!"

"Tell them the Savoy is always concerned for the safety of its guests and employees but at the moment we have no further comment."

"The safety of guests and employees, right-o," Susie repeated with relief.

Two of Priscilla's three desk phones were ringing shrilly as she entered her office and sat down. She ignored them. Susie stuck her head in the door. "I almost forgot. Mr. Banville wants to see you."

Priscilla passed a hand over her aching head.

"Also," Susie added, "some jokester saying he's the prime minister of, I think, Canada has been calling you."

"What?" Priscilla stopped massaging her forehead.

"He's called a couple of times. It must be some sort of prank, right? I mean, why would the prime minister of Canada be calling you?"

"I'll take care of it, not to worry." Except there was *plenty* to worry about, including the numbing sadness of Skye Kane's murder.

Susie, noting the expression on her boss's face, delivered one of the uncertain looks she kept at the ready when working with Priscilla. "What are you up to, anyway?"

"Just answer the phones and don't ask questions," Priscilla ordered, rising from her desk.

"Right-o." Susie put her head down as more phones rang. Priscilla, exiting 205, was pleased to see Susie was picking up.

The bobbies in the Front Hall looked out of place, glancing around nervously at their unfamiliar surroundings. More than a few official eyes fell on Priscilla as she made her way up to the general manager's office. None of the officers chose to arrest her for murder.

Not yet, anyway.

Sidney Stopford, known as El Sid, was the keeper of the gate outside General Manager Banville's office. The wisp of a moustache, crawling along his upper lip, twitched as he flashed a gleefully malicious smile. "He's waiting for you and, as usual where you are concerned, he's not happy."

"I'm always fascinated by how someone like you becomes such a nasty little bastard, Sidney," Priscilla said.

"Having to deal with people like yourself, Miss Tempest," answered El Sid with satisfaction.

Priscilla inhaled deeply, ignoring her throbbing head, and opened the door to the Place of Execution, a.k.a. Clive Banville's expansive office.

Ordinarily, Banville could be found seated ramrod stiff behind his massive desk, preparing to pronounce judgment on a hapless Priscilla. However, today he stood with Major O'Hara near the tall window that allowed in just enough grey London light to make the pair look particularly ominous.

"Ah, there you are Miss Tempest," Banville said in that imperious tone that, to her ears, always suggested trouble was on the way.

"Mr. Banville," Priscilla said in her best obsequious-employee voice.

"Not a very good morning, is it?" Banville replied, despite the fact she had not bidden him good morning. It had become an article of faith since Priscilla arrived at the Savoy that when summoned to his office, the general manager never asked her to sit down.

"Dreadful morning," Major O'Hara agreed.

"Yes, yes, it is," added Priscilla. "Very sad, indeed."

"Once again this institution must deal with unfolding scandal," Banville went on mournfully. He moved away from Major O'Hara, closer to Priscilla so that he could give her the sharp glance that suggested she might be responsible for it.

"I'm sure that with you at the helm, sir, the Savoy can weather any storm."

"Yes, well, good of you to say, Miss Tempest." Banville, to Priscilla's relief, actually seemed somewhat mollified by her statement. "However, there are matters that need to be addressed and I believe you will be able to lend a hand."

"Anything I can do, sir." She chanced a quick glance in O'Hara's direction. He stood watching her with the measured, distracted air he might bring to inspecting a corpse.

Banville cleared his throat and hesitated as though searching for the right words. "Miss Dors." He seemed to pounce on the name, hoping to take it by surprise.

"Good point," interjected Major O'Hara while Priscilla wondered how good the point could be since it had yet to be made.

"Major O'Hara informs me that he has received intelligence— heard rumours, I suppose—not placing our Miss Dors in the most positive light. These rumours at the best of times would not have gone unaddressed. However, they are of particular concern in the wake of the death of Miss Kane." He cast another sharp glance in Priscilla's direction. "Do you know anything about these stories, Miss Tempest?"

"I'm afraid I don't, sir." That wasn't quite true. But then very little she said within the confines of the general manager's office was quite true. In fact, very little of what she had said so far today was true in the slightest.

"Orgies," pronounced Major O'Hara as if that word explained everything.

Priscilla looked puzzled. "Orgies?"

"Yes, an activity in which a group of naked men and women participate in various sexual acts."

Banville looked irritated. "I think we know what an orgy is, Major O'Hara."

"The point is," Major O'Hara continued, "Miss Dors appears to host said orgies at her home. There is every reason to believe Miss Kane participated in these...activities."

"And yet those two notorious—as it turns out—women have been appearing nightly at the Savoy Cabaret," said Banville in a way that suggested this state of affairs was beyond imagining.

"Sadly, that is the case," Major O'Hara acknowledged. "And now one of the women has been murdered in said Cabaret."

"My God," exclaimed Banville, "is no one around here looking out for the reputation of this hotel? How did those two ever get hired in the first place?"

"As you know, sir, the shows at the Savoy are handled by Miss Ethel Levey, our veteran booker who works out of a small office at the D'Oyly Carte Opera Company," Priscilla explained. "I'm certain Miss Levey would be anxious to remind us that Miss Dors is a very popular screen actress who, because of her film background, has been selling out her shows every night."

"I do not care," Banville snapped. "You must deal with the situation, Miss Tempest. Talk to Miss Levey. I don't want this Dors woman back on our stage."

"Sir, if I may, I would point out that for the time being, the police have closed down the area and designated it a crime scene. I think we would be within our rights to keep the Cabaret closed for the next couple of weeks. At that time, consulting with Miss Levey, we can reassess the situation."

"What do you think, Major?" Banville asked.

"Yes, for now that would seem a reasonable solution," the major answered in the gruff, officer-in-command voice he used when handing out advice. "In the meantime, Miss Tempest can deal with Miss Dors."

"Orgies," Banville muttered. "What the devil is the world coming to?"

When it became apparent neither Priscilla nor the major was prepared to offer an answer, Banville shot a glare in Priscilla's direction. "Keep a lid on things, Miss Tempest," he ordered. "Do you understand?"

"Lid on things. Understood, yes sir."

As she left, Priscilla wondered vaguely where she might find such lids.

Bird on the Wire

Her mind swirling with uncertainties as to how exactly she was to deal with Diana Dors, Priscilla no sooner entered the Front Hall than she was nearly run over by the fast-moving entourage headed by His Royal Highness, the Rajah of Faridkot, Harinder Singh. Dressed in a beautifully embroidered sherwani and wearing a turban, the rajah was a small, squat man with a very large and long moustache. The rajah's entourage consisted of his three wives in colourful saris and four burly bodyguards in threatening black.

His path inadvertently blocked by Priscilla, the rajah came to a halt.

"You must be Miss Priscilla Tempest," Singh said in a cultivated English accent.

"I am," Priscilla said, trying not to sound surprised that the rajah would know who she was.

"Your manager, Mr. Banville, pointed you out to me. He stated that you are in charge of the Savoy's press office."

"That's correct."

"He assured me that you would keep the press away."

"That is true," Priscilla said quickly. "We are working very hard at our office to do just that." As hard as it was to keep away a London press corps that couldn't care less about powerless Indian rajahs, Priscilla thought.

"Very good," Singh nodded. He turned and used a pudgy hand to indicate his wives, standing very still, their eyes lowered.

"These are my wives," he announced as if this was a revelation.

"They are lovely." What else could she say?

"My wives love jewellery," his highness pointed out. "Rajahs, you should know, have a long tradition of buying their wives very expensive jewellery. Alas, we are off today to maintain that tradition."

"Well..." Priscilla ventured, desperately thinking of the right words. "Good luck..."

Harinder Singh leaned into Priscilla and dropped his voice. "But do not tell the press."

"Mum's the word, Your Highness."

He gave her a conspiratorial wink before going off, his entourage hurrying after him.

In her next life, Priscilla promised herself as she continued on her way, she would settle for nothing less than a man dictated by custom to buy her expensive jewellery.

As soon as Priscilla was back in 205, Susie started making frantic hand gestures. "What?" Priscilla demanded, in no mood this afternoon for antics.

Susie then proceeded to mouth a word Priscilla didn't understand. She gave Susie a puzzled look and shrugged.

"I think Susie is trying to warn you that I'm in your office drinking beer," Percy Hoskins said, standing in the doorway, beer in hand.

"That's exactly what I was trying to do," confirmed Susie.

"What do you want, Percy?" demanded Priscilla. She brushed past him into her office.

In need of a haircut and a shave, eyes red-rimmed from the previous late night, tie badly knotted, his open trench coat in need of cleaning, Percy Hoskins was the walking, talking poster boy for that prowling, carnivorous animal known as the Fleet Street reporter.

As she sat down, keeping an eye on him, Priscilla was determined not to find Percy, in all his shaggy, rumpled glory, attractive. There were men who could fool you into thinking they were wonderful; Percy wouldn't fool anyone. He had "Approach at Your Peril" written all over him.

Naturally, Priscilla found it difficult to stay away.

"I want you out of here," she said in her most authoritative voice.

"You always say that, pet, but I know you're not serious."

"I am not your pet or your luv or anything else," Priscilla protested. "But I am very serious. I want you out."

"The fastest way to be rid of me is to say the name of the woman they found in a dressing room backstage at the hotel's Cabaret this morning."

"The Savoy is most concerned for the welfare and safety of its guests and employees," Priscilla intoned. "Otherwise, I have no comment."

"Not to worry. I already know who she is," Percy said with a grin, slumping into a chair.

"I doubt that very much—and *don't* sit down."

Percy didn't move. "Skye Kane, a pal of the film star Diana Dors. Two notorious ladies about town, I might add."

"I have no idea what you're talking about."

"Rumours of sex parties at Diana's place, Skye an avid participant along with some of London's best-known celebrities, not to mention a royal or two, and gangsters thrown in for good measure. Everyone fornicating like crazy. No class system in the dark when you're naked. Sex! Scandal! Murder!—and England's finest reporter breaking the scandal on the front page of the *Evening Standard*."

Groaning inwardly, having no doubt as to who Clive Banville would blame for the publication of such a story, Priscilla fought as best she could to maintain a professionally neutral expression.

"At best those are rumours, and as far as I know, there is no truth to them."

"Bollocks!" cried Percy. "I can tell by that look on your face that it's all true."

"Get out of here, Percy," Priscilla once again ordered.

"I'm on my way," Percy said. "Thank you for confirming my story."

"I have done no such thing!"

Percy was heading out the door.

"Percy! Don't you dare quote me!"

He paused, seemingly struck by a thought. He turned back to Priscilla. "There is one other thing you could help me with."

"I haven't helped you with anything—I am not going to help you."

"Help me with this and I might be able to keep your name out of the Skye Kane story."

"You really are the worst kind of bloody bastard," Priscilla pronounced.

"What I called you about this morning. The little bird who flew away with this hot Canadian prime minister bloke named Trudeau. I thought the story would get dropped. But now my editors are hearing that women can't keep their hands off this guy. Suddenly, they're hungry for the story."

"Who is saying that?" The words were out of her mouth before she could stop them.

"Little whispers in the dark," Percy answered. "What I need is a name to go along with the whispers. How about it? What have you heard?"

"I haven't heard anything," Priscilla said insistently. Too insistently?

"No idea who she might be?"

Priscilla felt her stomach falling for the umpteenth time that day. "Out!"

"Trudeau's bird and your name stays out of my story."

"Percy, you're blackmailing me again."

"Not at all. As I always say, my luv, merely trying to persuade you to help a highly regarded member of the Fourth Estate."

"As soon as that highly regarded member shows up, I'll be sure to give him a hand."

"A name, luv—call me as soon as you have it."

And Percy was gone. Priscilla breathed a sigh of relief. Another potential disaster averted—for now.

Then Susie poked her head in the door. "That prime minister bloke called for you again."

Priscilla was fighting hard to hold on to a poker face. "Did he leave a number?"

"He said he would call back," Susie said, her face clouding with suspicion. "What's up with him, anyway? Is he really a prime minister?"

"Mr. Trudeau is staying with us this week," Priscilla answered. "It makes sense that he might call the press office from time to time."

Susie did not look appeased. "It doesn't make any sense to me."

Once again, Priscilla felt her heartbeat quickening. And were those walls closing in on her? Yes, they were.

"I'll take care of it," Priscilla said aloud. "Right now, prime ministers are the least of our concerns." Well, not the least, Priscilla thought. But down on the list a bit.

"There's more," Susie was saying.

"What?"

"The banqueting manager feels his department is not getting enough exposure in the press."

50

Priscilla looked at Susie in astonishment. "The banqueting manager wants more publicity?"

"The other day, according to him, the hotel catered a luncheon featuring five hundred guests in the Lancaster Room. The luncheon was supposed to end at 2:30 p.m., which would have given the staff ample time to prepare the room for a wedding reception in honour of Lady Serena Abbott's daughter and her new husband. The luncheon, however, went overtime and did not end until 3 p.m. Lady Serena's eight hundred guests were due to arrive at 3:30 p.m. In less than a half-hour, the staff cleaned carpets, added fresh flowers, aired out the room and splendidly set the buffet table."

"I see," said Priscilla, duly impressed. "What a crackerjack staff we have here at the Savoy."

"Exactly," agreed Susie. "Our banqueting wunderkind has invoked a commonly repeated phrase here at the Savoy," Susie said.

"My name should be in the papers?" suggested Priscilla.

"No: 'The impossible we can do immediately; the miracles take a little longer.' The impossible was performed within minutes, thus the manager feels he should be celebrated in the press."

Priscilla sighed. "See if one of the women's sections might be interested. 'Culinary Miracles at the Savoy,' something like that."

"Miracles in the kitchen, dead people in the dressing rooms, got it," said Susie.

"Ha, ha," was Priscilla's response.

"Are you sure you're all right?" inquired Susie.

"Get out—perform the miracle of not asking questions."

"Something's up, I know it."

"Susie!"

Susie indulged herself in one more suspicious glance before disappearing.

Priscilla sat back, massaging her temples some more. She wished her headache would go away. She wished everyone would go away. A tragic murder, an amorous prime minister, the afore-mentioned throbbing head, and the day wasn't over. Not by a long shot. God, she thought to herself, what more could possibly go wrong?

As though on cue, her office door banged open and in barged David Merrick, thick eyebrows curled furiously over bulging black eyes. "There you are." He spoke as though he had discovered Priscilla in hiding. "I've been looking for you!"

"To say the least, Mr. Merrick, it's been a busy day. What may I do for you?"

"Do you realize what's happened to me?"

"I'm sorry, I don't," Priscilla had to admit.

"I'm a *suspect* in a *murder* case!" he barked.

"I'm sorry to hear that," Priscilla replied calmly. At the same time, the last words Skye had spoken to her resounded in Priscilla's head: *"He said if I told anyone, he would kill me."*

For all Priscilla knew she was staring into the dark eyes of Skye's killer.

"You're *sorry*? I check into what is supposedly the finest hotel in London where, incidentally, I am a regular guest, and the next thing I know, I've got Scotland Yard pounding on my door first thing this morning."

Given how her mind was working, it was all Priscilla could do to control her temper. Instead, she spoke with the courtesy a proper Savoy staff member must employ with a valued guest. Even if he was a killer. "You do understand that Miss Skye Kane has been found murdered?" Priscilla said reasonably.

Merrick looked miffed. "I don't know what that has to do with me."

"The two of you were together last night at a party in the Pinafore Room, Mr. Merrick."

"Who would have told that to the police? I'd certainly like to find out." The anger was back in his voice.

Yes, well, Merrick didn't have to look far to find the culprit. "The two of you were not exactly hiding," Priscilla ventured. "Any number of people saw you together."

Merrick wasn't paying attention. "The cops accused me of hitting her. That's crazy. I never hit her. Who the blazes would have told them that?"

Priscilla knew exactly who told them.

"What would you like me to do, Mr. Merrick?" Priscilla asked in her best helpful-Savoy-employee voice.

"What would I like you to *do*? This is the Savoy Hotel, for Christ's sake. You're supposed to take care of your guests. You're not supposed to allow them to be harassed by the police with insinuating questions and unfounded allegations."

"I'm afraid we at the Savoy, regrettable though it may be, have no power when it comes to the police and their investigation of a murder."

Merrick leaned on Priscilla's desk so that his angry, flushed face was inches from hers. "I tell you what you do, girlie. You're in charge of the press office at the hotel, are you not?"

"That's correct," Priscilla said, pulling back from him.

"Then you keep my name out of this nonsense, you understand? *I wasn't involved with that woman.* You hear what I'm saying?"

"You're not threatening me, are you, Mr. Merrick?"

"I'm making it clear what the situation is: Keep me out of it—or *else!*"

"That does sound like a threat," Priscilla said, trying to keep the frightened tremor out of her voice. "But we always do our best here at the Savoy. Therefore, I will do *my* best."

"Do what you're supposed to do: protect me. Or so help me God, I'll make sure you're finished at this hotel—which means you're finished in this town!"

"Now that really is a threat, isn't it?"

"You're goddamn right it is!"

Merrick straightened to issue a final fierce glare before turning on his heel and storming out the door. Priscilla was left struggling to reassure herself that there wasn't really much David Merrick could do to her.

Ah yes. There was the one thing. He could make good on his promise to ruin her life.

And then she got to thinking that there was one more thing. He could kill her.

CHAPTER EIGHT

Buck's Fizz to the Rescue

Throughout the afternoon, the phones kept ringing, reporters from the BBC, ITV and all the papers demanding information that Priscilla wasn't about to provide about a murder at the Savoy. If anything about the calls was comforting, it was that no one mentioned David Merrick as a possible suspect.

For the time being, anyway.

Nor did anyone demand to know the identity of the mysterious little tramp who had made the career-ending mistake of sleeping with the prime minister of Canada.

The prime minister, who, incidentally, had stopped calling. That was fine with Priscilla. Wasn't it? She shoved aside even a glimmer of the disappointment she might be feeling. A one-night stand, that's all it was. Nothing more.

After all, no possible good could come from seeing him again, particularly with Percy Hoskins and his ilk snooping around. Her stomach sank yet again. Knowing Percy and his regrettable dog-with-a-bone tendencies, it was only a matter of time before he discovered who Pierre Trudeau had been with the night before. But then she could control Percy, couldn't she? Except he would be terribly jealous.

The phone rang again. She gritted her teeth before picking up the receiver.

"Buck's Fizz time!" announced the mellifluous voice of Noël Coward.

"Noël, thank goodness," Priscilla said with relief.

"Given what's happened today, I thought you might need rescuing. Hurry to the American Bar, my dear, a Buck's Fizz awaits."

Before she could say she was too busy for a Buck's Fizz today, Noël hung up.

Failure to offer an objection, Priscilla decided, left her with no excuse but to adjourn to the American Bar. After all, she could not let down Britain's most famous playwright, and, more importantly, a longtime valued guest at the Savoy.

Besides, she badly needed a drink.

As she crossed the Front Hall, she spotted Hans Kringelein studying the William Turner landscapes displayed on the wall.

"Mr. Kringelein," she called to him.

He turned and broke into a smile. "Miss Tempest, so wonderful to see you." He hurried over to her.

"Did you get into your room all right?"

"Yes, it's fine. Small, but very pleasant. I had a nap and now feel quite rested."

"I'm so glad to hear it, Mr. Kringelein."

His smile dissolved into a frown. "But I understand there has been a terrible tragedy. A death, I am told."

"Nothing to be concerned about," Priscilla said with forced cheerfulness, not being at all cheerful about what had happened today. "The safety and security of our guests is paramount at the Savoy."

"No, no, I have no doubt that is true," Kringelein hastened to agree. "But so sad, and police everywhere. Most alarming. I hope you are okay."

"I'm fine, Mr. Kringelein, a little shaken up, that's all. How long will you be staying with us?"

"A week or so I believe, although to be frank, I am uncertain of my plans. For the moment, this old waiter is enjoying the luxury of a fine hotel, and for the first time in my life being served rather than having to serve."

"We are very happy to serve you—to wrap you in luxury during your stay."

"Most appreciated, Miss Tempest."

"You must let me know if there's anything I can do for you."

"You are so kind, and you have already done so much." Kringelein's face was beaming as he clasped her hand. "Once again—*danke!*"

Priscilla left the old man and continued into the American Bar. This was the hotel's famous watering hole, its interior created by the designer Michael Inchbald to resemble a first-class cruise ship saloon—not surprising, perhaps, since Inchbald had done the same thing on the *Queen Elizabeth II*. The bar was the de facto headquarters for arriving Americans, the evidence that they were safely in London, their favourite drinks ready to be served by Joe Gilmore, the popular white-coated, white-haired barman. As always, he had a Buck's Fizz ready for Priscilla when she walked in. "It's been a day," he said, handing her the flute. "Unusually quiet, what with all the police around."

"Bless you, Joe," Priscilla said.

"Anything for the one person I can always count on to shake things up around this staid old place." That Irish twinkle was in Joe's eye; the knowing smile was on his lips.

Oh God, thought Priscilla, as she paused to take a reviving sip of the champagne. Is that how I'm thought of around here? Someone who shakes things up? No wonder Clive Banville desired her head on a pike.

Noël, occupying his usual corner table, was on his feet greeting her with tobacco-scented, two-cheek kisses and a warm gleam in those otherwise fathomless pools of darkness he called eyes. "There you are, my dear," he said cheerily. "So good to see you. You know these two reprobates, of course."

Johnny Gielgud and Larry Olivier stood to bestow kisses. Once everyone had settled, Noël announced, "You should know, Priscilla, that by unanimous consent of its members, we have decided to hold our monthly meeting of the Gossip's Bridle Club here at the Savoy."

"The Gossip's Bridle Club? What's that?"

"You see, in medieval times, gossiping was frowned upon—a crime in fact," Gielgud explained. "Those found guilty were encased in an iron muzzle—or gossip's bridle, as it was popularly known—and publicly humiliated. Naturally, the punishment was mostly inflicted on women. They were the ones who were muzzled and then led around by their husbands on the end of a leash."

"And the bridle was only used to discipline the lower classes," added Olivier. "If you were at the royal court you were allowed, even encouraged, to gossip to your heart's content."

"We three, being inveterate gossips, have decided to celebrate that fact and thus we meet together periodically to indulge in the latest juicy tidbits we've gathered," said Noël.

"Like squirrels with nuts," added Olivier.

"Thus, the Gossip's Bridle Club, restricted to a membership of three," proclaimed Gielgud.

"Until now," interjected Noël. "Again, by unanimous consent we have elected you, Priscilla, an honourary member!"

"To our first female member," Gielgud raised his glass in salute. The others followed. Priscilla couldn't help but notice that no one had bothered to ask her if she wished to be a member. It was a given that the honour of membership in this august group was such that it could not possibly occur to her to object.

"I guess I should be flattered," Priscilla said, "although I'm not quite sure what it is I must do."

"Basically, membership requires you to sit still, drink champagne and listen to Larry prattle on about what a fine job he's done at the National Theatre," said Gielgud.

"Don't listen to a thing he says," Olivier said with a tight smile. "Although I must say the theatre has thrived under my tutelage."

Gielgud rolled his eyes. "What did I tell you?"

"The point is," said Noël, "we believe you will be an invaluable asset to our little group."

Gielgud leaned forward, his eyes narrowing. "Our first order of business today is to extract as much information from you as we possibly can about this murder at the Savoy."

Aha, Priscilla thought to herself. The penny has dropped.

"Most definitely," Olivier added. He leaned forward, adjusting his glasses. "Of course, anything that's revealed within the confines of the club goes no further than the sensitive ears of club members."

"Absolute discretion is our motto," assured Noël. "Except when we are talking among ourselves, naturally."

The murder explained why the three were so willing to add her name to the very limited club membership roll. Noël quickly guessed what his friend was thinking.

"However," he went on, "it is also a maxim of our club that the tit is for tat, and therefore we must give as good as we get." Noël nodded at Gielgud. "Johnny…"

"Yes, we all saw with our own fading eyes last night that villain of the theatre, Mr. David Merrick, squiring a comely young lady, a chorus girl in the Cabaret show here at the hotel as it turns out. Observers that we spoke to tell us on the best of authority that Merrick and his date ended up in some sort of fight. The next thing a young woman is found murdered in one of the dressing rooms. So what do we deduce from that?"

"We deduce that the young woman with Merrick is the same unfortunate found murdered!" added Olivier.

"And from that, we must further conclude that our Mr. Merrick, the Abominable Showman himself, is a prime suspect in the murder investigation," put in Noël.

"Which, given the nasty bugger's state of mind most of the time, comes as no surprise," said Olivier.

All eyes turned to Priscilla. "How are we doing?" asked Noël.

"I wouldn't say any of that is exactly giving as good as getting," Priscilla said politely.

Noël's gnome-like face brightened. "Which is to say you are already aware of most if not all of what we have told you."

"You *might* say," amended Priscilla, not wanting to give too much away, even if her fellow club members were as reliable as they claimed. Given their natures, Priscilla wasn't all that certain.

"Before you jump to too many conclusions, there is something else you should be aware of," Priscilla continued. "I've just come from being screamed at by Mr. Merrick, who claims he is innocent and had nothing to do with the death of Skye Kane."

"Skye Kane is the young woman we met last night," Noël said.

Priscilla nodded. "At this point I don't think her name is a secret. She was a friend and I'm devastated by what has happened to her."

"Despite what Merrick *claims*, what do you think, Priscilla? Did he commit this terrible crime?" Noël asked.

"I really don't know," Priscilla replied. "Mr. Merrick says he didn't do it, and right now he is making life very difficult, threatening to have me fired if anything about him shows up in the papers. Therefore, I would implore you gentlemen to strictly abide by club rules and not leak anything to the press."

A chorus of "of course nots" went up, three mature men suddenly taking on the expressions of children eager to please.

"Priscilla, I have something you may not know..." Noël had dropped the eager mien and adopted a conspirator's voice.

"Are you about to tell me of sex parties at Diana Dors's home?" Priscilla interrupted.

Noël's face collapsed in disappointment. Priscilla gave him a sympathetic smile. "I'm sorry, Noël, but Diana has been performing in the Cabaret. It's hard not to hear these things."

"Now, if we are looking for possible suspects who might attend these parties, I have the perfect candidates." Noël's face had lit with excitement.

"Tell me, please."

"The Kray twins!" Gielgud announced gleefully, swooping in to steal Noël's thunder.

"Good Lord, Johnny, keep it down," admonished a chagrined Olivier. "They'll be pulling our corpses out of the Thames before you know it."

"You mean the gangsters?" Priscilla said.

"The twins, Reggie and Ronnie," Noël explained in an effort to regain the high ground. "The worst of the worst."

"Yes, but even if the Krays do attend these parties, that doesn't mean they're suspects, does it?" asked Priscilla.

"Think about it," Noël said, dropping his voice in case anyone at neighbouring tables was listening. "Diana gave these parties at which your friend Skye was undoubtedly a participant."

"Okay," Priscilla agreed.

"Supposing Skye ran afoul of the Kray brothers and *they* had her murdered?"

Actually, that was a possibility that made sense. She thought of the question Inspector Lightfoot had asked: *Did you know that Miss Kane was previously involved with a person named Mr. Reggie Kray?*

And yet...

"There are many ifs," Priscilla said.

"Wild speculation of course," Gielgud said. "But a possibility worth considering, given the Krays' reputations."

"That's what we do here at the Gossip's Bridle Club," Olivier added. "We hear the gossip, we consider its possibilities, and we draw our own conclusions."

"Not that those conclusions ever have much to do with reality," conceded Noël.

"It keeps Larry from going on too long about his latest triumph," Gielgud said with an impish smile.

"I tell you what, Johnny," Larry shot back, "why don't we discuss your bravura performance in *Assignment to Kill*?"

"Oh, fuck off, Larry," Gielgud snarled, Olivier having struck a nerve.

"Now, now gentlemen," Noël admonished, "remember you promised to behave yourselves in front of our newest member."

"*Assignment to Kill* is a perfectly respectable private-detective melodrama," said Gielgud huffily.

Olivier made a face that everyone ignored.

"Here's another juicy piece of gossip I picked up from one of the hosts at the party we all attended last night," Noël said, changing the subject in order to lighten the mood.

"Do tell," Olivier said excitedly.

"Pierre Trudeau," Noël accompanied the announcement with a dramatic flourish of eyebrows.

"The Canadian prime minister." Gielgud leaned eagerly toward Noël. "Do tell. Is he gay?"

"Isn't everyone when it comes down to it?" Noël said. "Whatever he is, all London is prattling on about him. Canada's most charming and eligible bachelor, according to my source. Trudeaumania along the Thames!"

"Why did we not meet him?" asked Gielgud.

"Because, dear boy, I have it on very good authority that he became totally bewitched by some lovely young thing he met at the party..." As he spoke, Noël busied himself adding a fresh cigarette to his ivory holder.

"Male or female?" demanded Gielgud.

"In this case, female, I'm told." A waiter hurried over to light Noël's cigarette. "Thank you, dear boy." Noël held up the cigarette holder as if it were a torch that had just been lit.

"More interesting if it were a man he slipped out with," Gielgud said, showing mild irritation at the playwright's antics with the cigarette. "Otherwise, politicians picking up young women at parties is hardly unusual."

"Did your source give you the name of this round-heeled young woman?" Olivier asked.

"Alas, no," Noël said, balancing his cigarette on the cut-glass ashtray without taking a puff.

"More's the pity," lamented Gielgud.

"Never fear, my source is on the case. It is only a matter of time before we have a name!"

Noël's smile was triumphant. Priscilla's stomach curdled for the umpteenth time that day. Around her rose the murmur of contented, well-to-do people smoking and drinking without a care in the world. She found them quite annoying. Increasingly, she decided, she did not like happy people. Was there no end to the hells she faced?

Unless...

Unless she took things in hand and faced those hells head-on. For herself—and for Skye Kane, too.

Aloud she said, "The Krays."

Noël perked up. "What about them?"

"If one were to get in touch with the Krays, I wonder how one would go about doing that?"

"The trick is to stay away from the Krays, I would say," Larry opined.

"Why would you ever want to meet up with them?" asked Gielgud.

"If they murdered Skye, don't you think something should be done about it?"

"I hardly think you're the one to put yourself in such jeopardy, Priscilla," Larry said. "This is the sort of thing best left to the police."

"I believe Larry has a point," Noël said. "However..."

"However?" asked Priscilla.

"Not that I'm an expert on them, but I am told they like to hang about a pub they own."

"Do you happen to know the name of this pub?"

"I believe it's called the Blind Beggar."

CHAPTER NINE

Meet the Krays

Was she out of her mind?

Priscilla considered that very real possibility as she marched across St. James's Park that evening, trying to clear her head. Did she really have the nerve to visit the lion's den of Britain's most notorious gangsters?

The answer to that question was…why not? A single young woman drops into a pub for a drink. What was the harm in that? A little investigative work might satisfy her curiosity. She couldn't get into too much trouble merely having a drink in a pub, could she?

Well, she was about to find out, she decided, hailing a passing cab.

Only a blind beggar could appreciate the Blind Beggar, thought Priscilla as she surveyed the badly lit interior of the dank pub, its ancient bones creaking from hard wear and tear. The rank odour of old beer, stale tobacco smoke, and decades of sweaty, ale-swilling men who didn't bathe often enough assailed her nostrils as soon as she entered. Even the Blind Beggar's popularity was in question given that tonight the place was deserted save for the bored bartender giving Priscilla the once over as she approached.

One other soul stood at the bar, a large, bull-like figure, his big head topped rakishly by a bowler hat.

The bull-like figure pulled at his ill-fitting black suit, adjusted the bowler hat and spread a tooth-challenged smile across his battered face. "Evening, lass," he said to Priscilla in a thick Scots burr. The very size of him blocked her path forward.

"Good evening," Priscilla replied. "You're in my way, incidentally."

"Am I now? Many apologies for that." The bull raised his bowler, his face caving into a show of regret. "My name is Jack Dickson, incidentally. My friends call me Scotch Jack."

"Because you're from Scotland and you drink Scotch, I imagine," Priscilla ventured.

"Clever lass. Edinburgh born and bred. And I've been known to have a Scotch or two in my time, no question about it. What about you, my lovely? A stranger to the Blind Beggar, I imagine."

"I was just passing," Priscilla said, "and thought I'd drop in for a drink."

"Good on you, lass." Scotch Jack's eyes were dancing. "A fine decision on your part, venturing in to enjoy the pleasures of one of London's finest pubs."

"I've never heard of the Blind Beggar." Priscilla glanced around. "It seems no one else has either."

That produced another jagged smile from Scotch Jack. "A quiet night is all, and this way makes it easier to get to know the place and its fascinating clientele, myself included. Let me buy you a welcoming libation. Tonight, as it happens, I'm a Guinness man. Won't you join me?"

"I thought you said you were a Scotch drinker."

"Have to keep my wits about me. My employers are paying a visit. Wouldn't do for Scotch Jack's head to be lost in a cloud of booze. Not tonight."

"And who are your employers?"

"Famous lads, if you want to know the truth. Well-turned-out gents, men about town, celebrities."

"Now you have me intrigued," Priscilla said. And a little jumpy, she thought to herself. "Who are these famous men about town?"

"None other than the twins, Reggie and Ronnie Kray."

"I see," said Priscilla, maintaining a neutral expression, as though the names meant nothing to her. "Should I know who they are?"

Surprise filled Scotch Jack's rugged countenance. "You don't know who they are? The famous Kray brothers?"

"I guess I should, shouldn't I?" Priscilla said, deciding ignorance worked best when attending the Blind Beggar in search of information.

Scotch Jack sighed and removed his bowler, laid it on the bar, and then signalled to the bartender. "Hiya there, Sonny, sorry to interrupt your contemplation of the complexities we all face in this modern world, but do you suppose you could pour me another Guinness? And bring one for my new friend here as well."

"I swear, Jack, I can't make out what you're saying half the time, and the half I do understand don't make no sense," Sonny said, moving toward the taps.

"A dunderhead," Scotch Jack confided to Priscilla. "My suspicion is he doesn't understand one goddamn thing I say."

The door to the pub banged open and two figures were briefly outlined by a streetlight's glow before the door slammed shut and the two were lost to the pub's dimness.

"Ah, here they are now—my lads have arrived," said Scotch Jack, abruptly tensing.

Priscilla got a better look at the two men as they stepped into the weak light thrown off by the bar. They wore identical grey bespoke suits and black brogues polished to a shine. Their black hair was beautifully cut and slicked back, glistening with hair oil—Reggie and Ronnie Kray, Priscilla surmised, in all their London-gangland-princes glory.

Her heart beat like a kettle drum at Royal Albert Hall.

"Now who do we have here?" asked the taller of the two in an East London accent. "New bird for you, Scotch Jack?"

"Scotch Jack with a bird," sneered the other brother. "Wonders never cease."

For all their similarities, Priscilla could see that they were, on closer inspection, actually quite different. The sneering brother was shorter and not as handsome as his taller sibling. Also, the sneering brother appeared a whole lot scarier.

"A new friend is all," Scotch Jack amended eagerly. "Come to experience the pleasures of the Blind Beggar."

The taller of the two brothers turned to face Priscilla. "Got a name, luv?"

"I'm not so sure I should be giving out my name to two strangers who just walked in," Priscilla said, playing coy.

The taller man cracked a smile. "Don't blame you in the least. Who knows what kind of trouble a pretty girl can get into giving her name out to strangers?" He held out his hand. "I'm Reggie Kray."

And that is the kind of trouble you can get into, Priscilla thought, as she tried not to look nervous taking his hand. "The git with me," Reggie added, "that's my brother, Ronnie."

"I'm the dangerous one," Ronnie announced, thus confirming her hunch.

Priscilla kept her eyes on Reggie. "If he's dangerous, what are you?"

"I'm the one who keeps his wits about him." Reggie was not smiling when he said this.

"Good to know," Priscilla said. She was aware of Sonny, the bartender, placing two pints of Guinness on the bar.

Reggie Kray was studying her with hooded, speculative eyes. "You still haven't told us your name—and what's that accent?"

"No, I haven't," Priscilla said. "It's Priscilla Tempest. I'm Canadian."

"Canadian? Land of ice and snow, is it?" Ronnie Kray leaned against the bar, uncomfortably close to Priscilla, the discomfort heightened by his unwavering gaze. "Wouldn't go near a place like that, I can tell you."

"More's the pity," Priscilla remarked. "I suppose the country's just going to have to get along without you."

"Priscilla, from the land of ice and snow." Reggie paused to light his cigarette. "What brings you here tonight?"

"It's like I told Jack, I was just passing and decided I needed a drink."

"That's it?" queried Ronnie. "Just passing, eh?"

"Why should there be more?"

"You seem a little out of place in this end of town, Priscilla," Reggie said. "Tell me what you do?"

"I'm in...public relations." These two didn't need to know any more than that.

"Public relations, you say." Reggie offered a tight smile as he blew out cigarette smoke.

"That's right," Priscilla said.

"Could be a piece of good luck that you wandered in here tonight."

"How is that?"

"As it happens, we're in the market for someone who can handle PR for the Blind Beggar."

"Looks like you could use some help," Priscilla said. "You don't seem to have a lot of customers."

"We're more or less closed for renovations."

"I see," Priscilla said, glancing around for signs of renovations and not seeing any.

"I like the place the way it is." Ronnie somehow made the declaration into a threat aimed at Priscilla.

Reggie ignored his brother. "When the joint reopens, like I said, we're going to need some public relations. You know, get the word out about the new, improved Blind Beggar."

"I'm afraid I've already got a job."

"That's not a problem." Reggie flicked ashes into the ashtray Sonny had set on the bar for him. "You can work for us on the side."

Reggie didn't seem to be encouraging much more discussion of the matter.

"I don't think my employers would be happy about that," Priscilla said carefully.

"Not to worry. We can make them see things our way," Ronnie said confidently. "We're very good at convincing people they should see things our way."

Priscilla could imagine—and she did not like what she could imagine. For the first time since she had walked into the Blind Beggar, she felt the bravado dropping away, replaced by a far-too-familiar emotion: fear.

She made a show of looking at her watch. "It's getting late, I'd better be going." As if she was slipping away from a cocktail party with friends. Except this was no cocktail party and these were not friends.

"You haven't touched your pint." Ronnie pointed at her pint of Guinness.

"I should have said something. I'm not a beer drinker."

Reggie looked at Scotch Jack. "Jack, why don't you drive the lady home?"

"It would be my honour," said Jack.

"That's not necessary," Priscilla said hastily. Perhaps too hastily.

"Jack *will* drive you." Reggie spoke in a way that ended further discussion. If she had not seen the gangster before, she was beginning to see him now. "And," he added, "I will escort you to the car."

Priscilla chose not to object. Reggie took her arm.

"We'll see you around," Ronnie said, not moving from the bar. Priscilla could practically feel the chill emanating from him.

Outside, the coolness of the night air drew a shiver from Priscilla. At least she hoped it was the night air and not her growing fear. Reggie preoccupied himself lighting a cigarette. Scotch Jack, meanwhile, leaned against the navy-blue Jaguar MK parked at the curb.

"A word with you," Reggie's cigarette dangled from the corner of his mouth, making him look even tougher as he guided Priscilla along the street, away from Scotch Jack's jug ears.

He brought her to a stop and then inhaled from his cigarette. The breeze lifted at the stray tendrils of his perfect hair. "You got class, Priscilla," he said. "I like that."

Priscilla, taken aback by Reggie's declaration, wasn't sure what to say. What does it mean when a notorious gangster tells you you've got class?

That you don't have any class at all?

Reggie added a cloud of smoke to the night air. "Yeah, I lost my wife a year ago." His voice had dropped into a low register. Priscilla had to lean closer to hear him.

"I'm sorry to hear that," Priscilla said sympathetically. "What happened?"

Reggie shrugged and flicked ashes onto the pavement. "Took her own life, she did."

"I'm sorry," Priscilla repeated.

"I'm trying to get past it, y'know? Doing what I can."

"Sure."

Reggie abruptly threw away his cigarette and faced her. "I suppose I should be suspicious."

"Why would you be suspicious?" Priscilla felt her stomach tightening.

"You wandering in out of nowhere."

"Like I said—" Priscilla began.

Reggie cut her off with a wave of his hand. "It doesn't matter. I'd like to see you again, you know, take you out, dinner maybe."

Priscilla struggled to maintain a neutral expression, as though notorious gangsters asked her for dates all the time.

"What do you say?" More a demand than a request. Why did she suspect a gangster like Reggie wouldn't like the word no?

"You know, we've just met," Priscilla said, stalling. "And maybe you *should* be suspicious."

"You think so?"

"You don't know me. Who knows where I came from?"

In response, Reggie just shrugged. "If you don't like the idea of dinner, maybe a club, something like that."

"I thought you were dating Diana Dors," Priscilla blurted, grasping at a straw.

"Who told you that?" Reggie's face had darkened perceptibly.

"She's a client where I work," Priscilla said, thinking quickly. "You know, people talk."

"I wouldn't worry about Diana," he said.

"There is also talk about you and one of the dancers at the Savoy Hotel." In for a penny, in for a pound, Priscilla thought.

Reggie shook his head. "I like you, Priscilla. It's been a long time since I said that about anyone. You're going to get to like me too, believe me."

If you don't kill me first, Priscilla thought.

"It's late, and I have to work tomorrow," Priscilla said.

Reggie nodded. "Don't worry about those other birds. You're the one I like."

And before she had a chance to react, he took her in his arms, and for one awful moment, she thought he was going to kiss her. Instead, he smiled wryly and said, "Don't worry. You strike me as one of these birds who shouldn't be kissed on first acquaintance."

He satisfied himself with a buss on her cheek before letting her go. "Give me your phone number." Again, more an order than a request.

"I—I don't have a pen or anything," she stammered.

Reggie smiled and withdrew a small black notebook from inside his jacket pocket. "Everything that's important, it's in this notebook," he said, holding it up. He had a pen in his hand, waiting expectantly. Priscilla gave him her home number. The last thing she wanted was Reggie Kray phoning the Savoy.

He glanced up at her as soon as he finished writing. "What about work?"

"That's the best number to get me at," she said hastily.

He closed the notebook and replaced it inside his jacket. "I'll be in touch," he said.

He turned and started away, walking briskly back up the street, leaving her to Scotch Jack.

"Come along, darlin'," Jack called, holding the front passenger door open. The rumble of distant thunder startled her. She turned and there in the Blind Beggar's doorway stood Reggie, the glow of a freshly lit cigarette illuminating his face.

Watching her intently.

Not far away, the two men inside the Ford Cortina had a good view of the Blind Beggar. The view allowed the younger man to lean forward in the passenger seat and snap photos of Reggie Kray kissing an unknown young woman. An admirable-looking young woman, both men agreed, the heart-shaped elegance of her face, the tapered length of her legs.

"Reggie is upping his game," noted Detective Chief Superintendent Leonard "Nipper" Read.

Detective Eugene "Buster" Burt snapped more photos as Reggie strolled away from the woman, cocky as you please.

The woman hesitated and walked over to the car parked out front. Read watched Reggie's majordomo, the notoriously evil Scotch Jack, open the door for her.

"What's Reggie up to with her?" Read pondered aloud. He was a short man with a face perpetually about to break into a smile; a cheery English face, you might say, but at the same time world-weary at the edges. Nipper Read did not look so cheery tonight. But then he never did when he got close to the Krays.

"What do blokes like him do with birds like her? Not hard to figure, I'd say," opined Buster.

A man in his mid-thirties, Buster possessed the sort of good looks that might otherwise suggest movie-star qualities, except those qualities were diminished by thinning, colourless hair. And there was something about his eyes that Read found disconcerting. Maybe nothing to it. Still, you could never be quite sure about anyone, Read had learned over the years.

The young woman reached the car and that's when the chief superintendent noticed that Reggie hadn't gone back into the Blind Beggar. Instead, he remained in the doorway smoking a cigarette. Even from where Read sat, it was evident that Reggie only had eyes for the woman.

They watched as Scotch Jack pulled away from the curb. As he did, it began to rain, but that didn't stop Reggie from stepping into the street, throwing away his cigarette and watching the car disappear. What was that look on Reggie's face? Longing? No, couldn't be, Read thought. A cold-hearted bastard like Reggie Kray looking longingly after a woman?

Maybe...

"Get those photos developed as soon as you can," Read said. "Let's see if we can find out who this woman is, and what she's doing with Reggie."

CHAPTER TEN

When Passion Trumps Reason

It began to pour as Scotch Jack drove Priscilla along the mostly deserted slick black streets. The rain thudded against the windscreen. Scotch Jack leaned over the wheel, concentrating on the road ahead.

In the light from the dashboard, it struck Priscilla that Jack might easily be mistaken for Quasimodo in *The Hunchback of Notre-Dame*.

"I think the boss likes you, if you don't mind my saying," Scotch Jack offered as he drove. "That's a good thing. It's time he got out more."

"Which boss is that?"

"The boss who isn't crazy. You don't want Ronnie to like you, my darlin', believe me. Reggie's sane, got his feet on the ground."

"We've only just met," Priscilla repeated carefully, using the words like a shield.

"You'll be an asset for him." Scotch Jack spoke as though a relationship with Reggie had already been decided. "You are way above them other birds who been flying around him since his wife died. The two of you look good together. Yeah, this could work out."

Work out to what? Priscilla thought. A fleeting, terrifying image of her at an altar with Reggie Kray, Ronnie as best man, floated through her mind. She immediately tried to erase it but, to her horror, it wouldn't go away.

"I've known those boys since they was kids," Scotch Jack was saying. "They've come from nothing, made something of themselves, maybe not the way the posh lads would do it, but they did it their way. Gotta give 'em credit."

"But they kill people," Priscilla ventured, immediately regretting the words when she saw the sour look cross Jack's Quasimodo face.

"I thought you didn't know who they were?" An accusatory edge to his voice.

"Let's say I didn't before I met them, but I do now," Priscilla said, once again talking fast in hopes of covering up her lie.

"Tabloid lies," Scotch Jack retorted insistently. "Whatever you hear, don't believe it. They're respectable businessmen and pub owners, that's what they are. The coppers and the press, they're out to get them, that's all."

"What about you, Jack? How did you get involved with the Krays?"

"Royal Marines, lass. Commando school in Lympstone, Devon. Action in Malaya and Korea. Straightened an Edinburgh boy around damned fast, let me tell you. Toughened me up. Got me ready for these blokes. They took me in, formed me, made me what I am."

"Is that good?"

"Damned sight better than what I was, that's for sure."

They drove in silence for a few minutes, listening to the hammering rain, the labouring swoosh of the windscreen wipers.

Scotch Jack broke the stillness. "Can I give you a bit of advice, darlin', friendly like?"

"I don't imagine I have a lot of choice," Priscilla said, giving Jack a sideways glance.

"Be good for Reggie, right?" Jack's voice was gentle enough. But was it her paranoia or was she detecting a slightly

77

ominous undertone? "Don't do anything to hurt him. I wouldn't like that."

"I doubt very much if there's anything I can do to hurt Reggie Kray." Unless, Priscilla thought, she could somehow link Reggie to Skye Kane's murder.

"He's a sensitive lad beneath that take-charge exterior of his."

"He hides it very well," Priscilla noted.

"I love them two brothers, do anything in the world for 'em, but my sincere advice is that you don't get on the wrong side of either one."

"These respectable businessmen," Priscilla said, hoping she had kept the irony out of her voice.

"That's it, respectable gents." Scotch Jack had missed the irony. His smile in the pale glow of the dashboard light made Priscilla think of Quasimodo coming through her bedroom window with an axe.

Priscilla made Jack drop her off down the street from her flat. The last thing she wanted was the Krays knowing exactly where she lived.

She waited until Jack had driven off before venturing along the street to no. 37–39. As she came up the stairs to her flat, her next-door neighbour, Lady Agatha Potter-Hayes, a proud ship of a woman adorned with numerous chins and pink cheeks offsetting china-blue eyes, opened her door and peered out. "Are you all right, my dear?" Priscilla could see that she was swathed in a pink nightdress.

"Yes, fine, Lady Agatha. How are you?"

"Strange men were lurking around earlier so I was worried."

"I don't imagine they had anything to do with me."

"You, my dear, have the distinction of being the building's only resident who attracts strange men at all hours."

"Not tonight, I'm afraid," Priscilla said, fumbling for her latchkey, afraid that in fact the Krays had already discovered where she lived and were having her watched.

"I hope there's no problem," Lady Agatha called as Priscilla opened the door.

"I'm fine, thanks," Priscilla said. "Good night."

"Good night, my dear." Lady Agatha did not sound convinced, but then, Priscilla thought, who could blame her?

Stepping inside, Priscilla came to a stop and let out an involuntary gasp. Pierre Trudeau, in a houndstooth sports jacket, a gold-coloured ascot tucked below his chin, looked up from the kitchen table where he was using one of her knives to cut into a baguette. "I brought Époisses and a baguette to go along with the Châteauneuf-du-Pape."

In a state of shock, Priscilla cautiously entered the kitchen, passing through a living room strewn with the clothing she should have put away long ago, but didn't. "How did you get in here?"

"I wondered if you would remember." Pierre grinned and resumed slicing bread.

Remember what? she thought. Damn the existence of champagne. "I'm afraid I don't," she had to admit, eyeing the hopeless mess of her place.

"You invited me. Even gave me a key so I could let myself in."

He held up her spare key as evidence. Yes, now she was able to summon a dim recollection of invitations issued. What had she been thinking? The answer was all too simple, of course: She hadn't been thinking.

"You have a lovely apartment," he said, giving up on the bread and dropping the knife to pour wine into a long-stemmed glass.

"It's a bit of a mess, I'm afraid," grimaced Priscilla. "I wasn't expecting company."

"Incidentally," Pierre said, "I did phone several times today trying to confirm, but I guess you were busy dealing with the press and this dreadful murder I've been hearing about. I thought I'd take a chance and drop around anyway—a mistake?"

Pierre's presence would, she thought, account for the strange men outside her flat. The Mounties, not the Krays.

"No, no, it's fine," she said quickly.

He handed her the glass. "I understand it was a young woman."

"I'm sorry?"

"The person who was murdered in the hotel. A young woman?"

"Yes, I knew her. It was a terrible shock."

"I can only imagine," Pierre said sympathetically. Those inquisitive eyes looked more inquisitive than ever. "Do the police know anything about who might have done it?"

Priscilla shook her head. "No."

"Are you sure about that?"

Now *that* was a curious question, Priscilla thought.

"Yes," she answered, although she did have a number of prospects, including David Merrick and now the Krays. But a little voice inside her head told her not to go blabbing too much to an overly nosy prime minister.

"I am sorry about what has happened to your friend," Pierre was saying, "but it is good to see you again."

Priscilla noted that the previous inquisitiveness in those dark, rather soulful eyes had been replaced by an anticipatory gleam. He couldn't have arrived at her flat expecting to hop into bed with her—could he? No way was she in the mood for any nonsense tonight. Bad enough that seemingly every reporter in town was trying to identify the woman who had slept with him at the Savoy. Now here he was in her apartment pouring wine for her and managing to look highly attractive, even if she didn't much like the ascot. What was it with a certain breed of men and ascots? God, never mind the ascot, she thought, here was trouble, trouble and more trouble…

"Listen," she started to say to him.

"Please, have some wine," Pierre interrupted, his voice softly lilting. "I'm sure with one thing and another you've had a long, difficult day. Me too. There must be an activity less fun than a Commonwealth Conference, but right now I'm too tired to think what it might be."

Priscilla sipped at the wine, which produced a delicious warming sensation. For the first time that day, she began to relax.

Two glasses later, Priscilla was exactly where she had sworn she would not be: in Pierre's arms. What's more, there was the unfolding mystery of how her blouse had become unbuttoned, how exactly his hands had gotten onto her breasts, and why it was that his caresses felt so good, obliterating her determination to behave?

"You're forgetting," she said, issuing a small gasp of pleasure.

"What?"

"Your motto…"

"My motto? Remind me," he murmured, keeping his hands busy.

What the devil was his motto? she thought blearily, trying to think of that rather than the pleasure he was eliciting. Ah yes, that was it: "Reason over passion," she managed to gasp aloud.

"I can't imagine I said that," he murmured.

"You did."

"I was misquoted."

Still, in the warmth of the passion bubbling up inside her and reason vanishing, her better judgment flamed briefly, sending out loud signals warning that a wise woman—a good girl— would behave. Must behave.

Alas, Priscilla thought as Pierre finished undressing her, the wise woman was nowhere in sight.

She undid his scarf. "I don't think I've ever been with..."

"A prime minister?"

"Oh no," she laughed. "I sleep with prime ministers all the time. I've never been with a prime minister wearing an ascot."

They were both naked in her bedroom—how did this happen? she dimly wondered. How did it ever happen? It just seemed to...*happen*. She took time to inspect him in a way that, what with one thing and another, she had not been able to the night before. There was excitement in her voice as she observed, "My goodness, you are a *prime* minister."

Pierre chuckled as he gently pulled her down onto the bed.

He was very good. She was so bad.

Reggie Calls

Reggie Kray's huge hands were tightening their grip on Priscilla's throat as she jerked wide awake. Sitting bolt upright she was at first pleased that Reggie wasn't strangling her to death, followed quickly by surprise that she found herself alone in bed.

Rather than an early morning exit, her usual practice, a move impossible since she was in her own flat, Pierre was the one who had left silently. His absence somewhat disappointed her as she rolled onto her back, still waking up. It would have been nice to have him beside her. But what did she expect? After all this was—well, now it was a two-night stand, wasn't it?

She had slept soundly, better than she had for a long time—the sleep of a satisfied woman, she decided, stretching languorously. Then abruptly, the memory of Reggie's hands squeezing the life out of her brought her back to earth with a thud. Whatever had possessed her to visit the Blind Beggar? She must have been out of her mind—a fact which she had faced far too many times lately. Now London's most notorious gangster wanted to date her. His chief henchman was all but planning their wedding!

How she had managed a prime minister and a gangster in a single night was a tale she would tell her grandchildren. Or perhaps not.

At this rate, Priscilla thought as she stepped into the shower, she might not live long enough to worry about grandchildren, let alone what to tell them.

She put on the robe she had hanging from the back of the bathroom door and went into the living room, noting once again the disarray of her bachelor existence, reminding herself that she had to clean up the place. One simply never knew when a prime minister was going to drop by with a bottle of good wine, fine cheese and a glint in his eye.

She entered the kitchen, intending to make coffee before heading to work, when the telephone started ringing. She dashed to pick it up, wondering if it might be Pierre. Hoping it was Pierre...

It wasn't Pierre.

"Good morning, luv," greeted the cold voice of Reggie Kray. "I've been thinking about you all night."

"Reggie, I'm just out of the shower and late for work," Priscilla said, wondering if he could hear her thudding heartbeat on the other end of the line.

"When you were in the shower, were you thinking about me?"

"How could I not?" Priscilla said, noncommittally. Her mind reeled.

"That pleases me," Reggie said. "Incidentally..."

"Yes?"

"You didn't tell me you work at the Savoy."

The pit of Priscilla's stomach collapsed. She gripped the phone harder, closing her eyes, trying to think of something to say.

"Priscilla? You there?" Reggie's sharply inquiring voice.

"Yes, I told you I'm in public relations."

"But at the Savoy."

"That's right." Priscilla's mouth had gone dry.

"Which is how you know about me and Diana. She must have told you, right?"

"Uh, she may have mentioned it." Better than saying a Scotland Yard detective told her.

"Diana is shooting a movie out at Shepperton Studios today,

a real piece of shite I hear. I tell you that woman has fallen so far from what she used to be when I was seeing her."

"I didn't know she was in a movie," Priscilla said, finally landing on a sentence that had the ring of truth to it, seeing as how she really didn't know what Diana was up to.

"Tell you what," Reggie said casually. "Why don't you take a drive out to Shepperton?"

"What?" Priscilla couldn't hide her dismay. "Why would I want to do that?"

"Shepperton," Reggie said impatiently. "The movie studio. Don't you know it?"

"I know it, but I can't go out there today, Reggie," said Priscilla, desperately fumbling for an excuse. "I have to get to my office. It's a busy day. A lot of appointments."

"No, I think you better go out to Shepperton." There was an ugly edge to Reggie's voice.

"I don't understand."

"Think of it as your first job for us."

"But I can't work for you, Reggie."

"Yes, you can." That I-brook-no-argument tone was back.

"Here's the thing," Reggie continued. "Me and my brother. Like I mentioned last night, I'm the cool, calculating member of our partnership. I assess things first, take into consideration the risk factors, then form a plan and see it through. Ronnie, on the other hand, he's the impulsive one: doesn't think, loses his temper, acts, and then regrets it later."

"Yes, I can see that," Priscilla said, wondering how she was going to get off the phone.

"This latest episode is a perfect example of what I'm talking about."

"Uh, what episode would that be?" Immediately regretting she had asked the question.

"Ronnie attending one of Diana's parties, doing things he probably shouldn't have been doing with a certain well-known member of parliament. Diana, being the lying, deceitful bitch that she is, may have taken advantage of Ronnie's indiscretion."

"How would she do that?" Yet another question she shouldn't have asked.

"Diana would do it by carrying out the filming of her guests in the midst of their indiscretions. Ronnie is convinced that Diana secretly filmed him. He doesn't want that film getting out there, particularly since we have it on good authority Diana may try to sell it to certain rivals who would love to get their hands on it."

"Rivals?" Priscilla asked.

"Right buggers who don't have our best interests in mind," said Reggie. "Particularly a psycho nutter by the name of Teddy Smith. Teddy used to be one of us. Now he's an enemy trying to get his hands on the film under discussion. The point being, if there is such a film and Diana has tried to sell it to the likes of Teddy, that is not on."

"Understandable," Priscilla said, confused as to how she could have anything to do with this.

"I'm particularly concerned because the member of parliament Ronnie was with is a friend of ours," Reggie continued. "He's no good to us if the film gets out and his career is ruined."

"But I've never been at one of Diana's parties. I don't see how there's anything I can do."

"Here's what I want you to do," Reggie said. "You get yourself out to Shepperton, you get hold of Diana, and you get that film back before she shows it to anyone."

"You're kidding," Priscilla said, not bothering to hide her astonishment.

"Did I forget to tell you?" Reggie's tone was packed in ice. "Where the well-being of my brother and our business is concerned, I never kid around."

"But Reggie—" Priscilla started to say.

He cut her off. "Shepperton. This afternoon. Get the film. And don't worry."

"About what?"

"I haven't forgotten our dinner date."

As she hung up the phone, Priscilla was certain she could feel Reggie's hands squeezing her throat.

CHAPTER TWELVE

Danger Route!

Diana Dors in a diaphanous pink negligee, her white-blond hair a shiny bouffant, lay on a brass bed holding a drink while she cuddled a dark-haired man wearing a blue suit. A nearby table set for an intimate dinner for two was ignored.

Drawing closer to her bedmate, Diana declared merrily, "Oh, I went on a bender that night, I can tell you. With a fellow I met." She paused to take a sip of her drink. "Come to think of it, he looked a bit like you."

"Me?" said the gent in the blue suit with a grin.

"Hold on...*cut!*" came a cry behind the monster Panavision camera recording the scene on a soundstage at Shepperton Studios outside London.

"What the hell, Seth," Diana said in frustration.

A heavyset man with a mane of brown hair popped out from behind the camera. "I need you to poke a finger at Richard when you say that last line," he said.

He started to say something else, but it was lost in a cacophony of coughs. An assistant passed him a tissue.

The frustration was evident on Diana's round face. "Poke him? Seth, why would I poke him? I'm trying to seduce him. You don't poke a bloke you're seducing—he pokes *you.*"

Everyone except Seth the director chuckled. Seth blew his nose into the tissue, coughed some more, and frowned. "Just do it, for God's and the budget's sake, will you please,

Diana? We're losing time, and I'm at death's door with this cold."

"We need to reload," announced the cameraman.

Seth's frown deepened. "Shite. That's it, then. Everyone, fifteen-minute break." He started coughing again. The assistant passed more tissues.

Diana jumped off the bed. A wardrobe person helped her into a robe. The director approached. "Next take, you poke him, Diana. You got that?"

Diana made a face and flounced off the set, Priscilla trailing.

Priscilla had persuaded Cecil Bogans, the Savoy's veteran chauffeur, to drive her out to Shepperton, the sprawling sixty-acre studio complex where, during the day, Diana was shooting *Danger Route*. This way she could talk to Diana in person about the cancellation of her show at the Savoy.

Oh, and perhaps Diana might care to discuss any films she might have taken of Ronnie Kray being—what was the word Reggie used?—*indiscreet*.

Diana had been assigned one of the smaller trailers lined up outside the soundstage. Priscilla joined her in the cramped interior as she lit a cigarette and poured a glass of vodka from the bottle on the counter in the tiny kitchenette. She looked miserable.

"*Danger Route*. Dangerous, right enough—dangerous to my career," she said with a scowl. "The script is terrible, the director is sick, and worst of all, I have fifth billing. After Sylvia Syms and Barbara Bouchet. I mean, who is Barbara Bouchet? I sit here waiting for them to call me, smoking too much, drinking too much, getting fatter by the hour."

"You look great, Diana," Priscilla said.

"You're too kind, Priscilla. That's your trouble, you know? You're too nice." Diana fixed a wan smile and reached out to squeeze Priscilla's hand. "I, on the other hand, am becoming less nice by the day—and the drink." She held up her glass. "Sure I can't offer you one?"

"I'd better not," Priscilla said. "I promised myself I'd behave."

"I promise myself that all the time," Diana said. "However, promises are made to be broken, aren't they?"

She took a deep drink and then put the glass down and focused on Priscilla. "What brings you all the way out here?" she asked.

"As you know, the police have closed down the Cabaret at the Savoy as they investigate Skye's murder."

"I don't want to think about it, about her death," Diana said, her eyes filling with sadness. "It's all so terrible. As awful as it is, thank God for this movie. At least I've got something to take my mind off what happened—and the fact that the police think I'm somehow involved in her death. Absolute bollocks."

"The management at the Savoy has decided to close the show," Priscilla said.

"Right now, there's not much choice, is there?"

"Even after the police finish their investigation," Priscilla said.

Diana's eyes lost any trace of sadness as they hardened. Her mouth tightened. "I'm not surprised, I suppose. More bad luck. Is that why they sent you? To deliver the death knell?"

"They didn't send me, Diana, but I wanted to let you know in person."

"Nice Priscilla, even when they require you to be not so nice." Diana shrugged. "Here you are and here I am—and thank goodness for vodka." She drained her glass and then rose to the counter to retrieve the bottle.

As Diana poured herself another drink, Priscilla took a deep breath and said, "There's something else."

"What?" Diana turned with her glass in her hand.

"Skye's death. I know the police are looking into it, but there are a few things I thought I'd check out."

"Don't tell me, Priscilla." Diana said with a smirk. "In addition to feeding visiting celebrities drinks, you've decided to become a sleuth."

Priscilla shook off the dig. She could hardly blame Diana. She wasn't sure herself what she was playing at—or what she was getting herself into. Nonetheless she plunged forward.

"Did you know Skye was seeing Reggie Kray?"

"Skye was seeing a lot of people." Diana repositioned herself on the sofa.

"Then you know about Reggie?"

"For better or worse, I introduced Skye to Reggie, if that's what you want to know. Probably for worse." Diana swallowed a good deal of the vodka in her glass and then faced Priscilla. "The question is, how do *you* know about Reggie?"

"Let's say I've been in touch with Reggie and his brother, Ronnie."

Diana frowned. "That's not good, Priscilla. Anything involving the Krays is never good."

"Ronnie is worried that you may have filmed him at one of your parties."

Diana took this in as she reached for the pack of cigarettes that lay beside the vodka bottle. She extracted one and lit it with the Zippo lighter she withdrew from her robe. She inhaled deeply and blew cigarette smoke in the air.

"Now you're into an area you shouldn't get into, Priscilla." Diana's voice had gone cold.

"I'm only too aware of that," Priscilla said. "But you know Ronnie better than I do, and you understand he is serious when it comes to this film."

Diana blew out more cigarette smoke before she said, "Ronnie is crazy."

"All the more reason not to get him upset. Please tell me, Diana: Do you in fact have him on film?"

There was a knock at the trailer door. Diana called out, "Yes? What is it?"

"They're ready for you, Miss Dors," a voice called back.

"Thank you." Diana put out her cigarette, picked up the glass and drained what was left of its contents, and then addressed Priscilla. "Duty calls."

"What about the film, Diana?"

Diana smiled blearily and shrugged. "Give Reggie my best. And I do appreciate you coming out, even though I suspect you didn't have a lot of choice."

"That's not true, Diana. I like you…"

"Then be the nice Priscilla I like so much and stay out of my affairs," she said sharply, starting for the door.

Priscilla hesitated and then called after her. "Tell me this: Could Reggie Kray have murdered Skye?"

Diana hesitated in the doorway. This time her smile was less bleary, more ironic. "The Krays are capable of anything, so I suppose it's possible. Still, it's been a while since Reggie and Skye were an item, such as they ever were an item."

"How about you and Reggie?"

Diana smiled ironically. "How about me and Reggie?"

"Were you upset when Skye started seeing him?"

"If I was anything, I was concerned for her. Being involved with Reggie, as I discovered, is not a healthy situation."

"How about someone else? Anyone who might have wanted to do Skye harm?"

"The police asked me the same question."

"What did you tell them?"

"I find it wiser to tell the police as little as possible." Diana had the trailer door open and was about to step out. Then she hesitated. "I'm going to tell you something I haven't told anyone, certainly not the coppers. But I've had a couple of drinks and I do like you, Nice Priscilla."

"Tell me what, Diana?"

"For the week or so before her death she was seeing someone very powerful, she said, so it was all very hush-hush. She was quite excited about this bloke, thought he was really sexy and intellectual and all that."

"Not David Merrick?"

"That arse? God help me—no."

"Then who?"

"At first, she wouldn't say, but then knowing Skye, she couldn't resist."

"Who?"

"Promise me you won't say where you got this, okay?"

"Certainly."

"It might have been worth this bloke's while to off Skye if he felt he had to keep her quiet."

"Why would he want to keep her quiet?"

"Because, according to Skye, the bloke she was shagging is the prime minister of Canada."

Nipper Meets Charger

"How do you like your new office, Inspector?" asked Detective Chief Superintendent Nipper Read as he sat down with Charger Lightfoot inside Scotland Yard's gleaming new headquarters at 10 Broadway in the City of Westminster.

"I must say it is a bit roomier than the cubby hole I occupied in the old pile on the Embankment," Lightfoot said, pausing from the business of lighting his pipe.

What was it about senior inspectors, Nipper mused, that they all felt they had to puff away on pipes?

"Still, I do miss the old place," Lightfoot went on after finally managing to fire up the tobacco stuffed into his pipe bowl. "You felt like a real old-time copper over there. Here—" he took time to puff on his pipe, sending out blue-grey smoke signals, "it's all modern glass and steel. A bit corporate and anonymous, wouldn't you agree?"

"Yeah, but in other ways, nothing has changed," Read said. "The hard boys are still out there on the street, aren't they?"

Inspector Lightfoot nodded affirmatively, drawing on his pipe. "Hard boys like the Krays you mean. Any luck with them?"

"Let's say I am pursuing several lines of investigation that look promising," Read said carefully. Then with more passion: "But believe me, no matter what it takes, those lads are going down. It's only a matter of time."

"A couple of right villains. Disgusts me the way they parade around town, hobnobbing with celebrities the way they do," Lightfoot said.

"Most infuriating, no question," Read agreed. "But the celebrities will disappear quick enough when we put the handcuffs on them."

"If anyone can get the job done, you can, Nipper."

"Funnily enough, it's the Krays who bring me here today," Read said. "I'm hearing that one of Reggie's old girlfriends was found murdered at the Savoy Hotel."

"The showgirl, Skye Kane, that's right."

"Our information is that she and Reggie dated about a year ago, while he was seeing that actress, Diana Dors," Read said.

"Miss Dors and Miss Kane were in the show together at the hotel's Cabaret. You think Reggie and his brother are involved?" Lightfoot had the pipe out of his mouth and was inspecting it.

"With the Krays, you don't discount anything, I always say. Who are you looking at for the murder, Inspector?"

"Right now, we're focusing on an American theatre producer named Merrick," Lightfoot said. "He was with Miss Kane the night she died. They had a row at a party, according to a witness."

"What's your thinking, then?" Read asked.

"Could be that after Miss Kane had the row with Merrick, she performed with Diana Dors in the Cabaret show. Then afterwards, when she was alone, Merrick came into her dressing room and strangled her to death."

"Crime of passion," Read observed.

"Crime of anger. Apparently, this blighter has a terrible temper. A rich, powerful American from New York. If he's innocent, you would think he'd be more co-operative. Instead, we're having trouble interviewing him. He's retained a solicitor who is giving us a hard time."

"Sounds like you may have your man. Which would let out the Krays."

"Merrick is as good a prospect as we have right now, but we're also looking into a couple of other possibilities." Lightfoot replaced the pipe in the corner of his thin mouth.

"Tell me what you know about this young woman." Read stood and placed three photographs on Lightfoot's desk.

Lightfoot stopped puffing on his pipe. "My God, that's Priscilla Tempest."

"You know her?"

Lightfoot nodded as he relegated his pipe to a nearby ashtray. "She works in the press office at the Savoy. Christ, is that Reggie Kray with her?"

"It is. Taken outside the Krays' East End pub, the Blind Beggar."

"What the devil was she doing there?"

"I've been asking myself the same question," Read said.

Lightfoot kept his eyes on the photos, continuing to shake his head in disbelief. "Miss Tempest was acquainted with Miss Kane. In fact, she is the witness who provided us with the information about Merrick's row with Miss Kane."

"This Tempest woman knew Miss Kane who was mixed up with Reggie Kray," Read said. "And now it turns out Miss Tempest is connected with Reggie too."

"An interesting turn of events," Lightfoot allowed. He reached for his pipe again and with feigned nonchalance asked, "What are your thoughts, Superintendent? Any sense that the Tempest woman or Diana Dors might be responsible for Miss Kane's death?"

"A woman strangling a woman?" Read said. "Doesn't seem very likely."

"On the other hand, it doesn't take much to strangle someone. As little as four pounds of pressure and you begin to obstruct a person's jugular vein. Once that blood flow is cut off, a victim has about ten seconds before becoming unconscious. And then, what? Fifty seconds and death is imminent? You may not think of a woman using strangulation as a murder weapon, but it is certainly possible."

Read said, "Based on what you're telling me, Inspector, and what I'm seeing in these photographs, I suppose we couldn't be blamed for considering the idea of some sort of conspiracy to commit murder involving Miss Kane's former boyfriend, Reggie Kray, and his new girl, our Miss Tempest."

"I suppose that could be a possibility," Lightfoot agreed. "But I wonder what their motive might be."

"Good question. Love. Jealousy. Could be any number of things." Read tapped the photos. "Still, this could be an angle worth pursuing."

"We'll look into it further," Lightfoot said noncommittally.

Read leaned forward and said, "Very good. But as you pursue your investigation, do me a favour and stay away from Miss Tempest for the time being."

"I can do that, but why?"

"If Reggie Kray is as infatuated as I think he is, I can make use of that infatuation and this young woman."

"To do what?"

"To do what I'm sworn to do: bring down the Krays."

Read was smiling as he spoke.

CHAPTER FOURTEEN

Secrets of the Savoy

"You seem preoccupied, Miss Tempest, if you don't mind my saying," observed Mr. Bogans as he drove Priscilla back to the Savoy, navigating the Daimler through afternoon traffic.

Sitting next to him, Priscilla said, "I'm fine, thanks, Mr. Bogans." Except she wasn't. Not only had she not been successful in retrieving the Ronnie Kray film from Diana Dors, she could not be certain that there even was a film.

What was she supposed to tell Reggie Kray?

On top of that, there was what she had decided to label The Pierre Problem. In addition to the possibility that her name would soon be known around the world as the woman who slept with the prime minister of Canada, there was now the possibility that, if Diana was right, Pierre could become a suspect in the murder of Skye Kane. What was his only alibi? Why, Priscilla Tempest of the Savoy Press Office.

Ruination!

Ruination any way you looked at it.

So yes, she told herself, she was indeed preoccupied.

"Sorry," said Priscilla to Bogans. "I suppose it's the murder."

"Ah yes, the murder," said Bogans.

Priscilla shot him a look. Bogans kept his eyes firmly on the road ahead. "More secrets at the Savoy, Mr. Bogans?"

Bogans took his time answering. "One does hear things," he finally conceded.

"Such as?"

"The usual gossip and innuendo, probably nothing to it," Bogans said.

Priscilla waited patiently. Bogans kept his eyes fixed on the traffic along Brompton Road. "Like I said, gossip. The gossip one hears about the jealousy of Miss Dors when it came to her friend Miss Kane."

"What kind of jealousy?"

Bogans shrugged. "You know how it is, Miss. An older woman, age catching up, putting on a little more weight than she should. Suddenly, everyone's attention shifts to a younger woman who she comes to see as her rival. Story as old as time, right, Miss?"

"Diana was jealous of Skye Kane, is that what you're saying?"

"Not *saying* anything, ma'am. I am merely passing on what I'm *hearing*."

"Diana says she wasn't jealous, simply concerned about Skye's well-being."

"Naturally, she would say that, wouldn't she?"

"What else, Mr. Bogans?"

"What makes you think there is something else, ma'am?"

"Is there?"

More silence, deeper concentration on afternoon traffic. Then: "According to some of the dancers who worked with Miss Kane, Miss Dors was furious because a certain notorious East End gentleman had broken off with her so he could go out with Miss Kane. Then, more recently, Miss Dors was telling people that a certain prominent New York producer was going to take her show to America. The next thing she knew, that wasn't going to happen and that same producer was seen with Miss Kane. To put it mildly, Miss Dors was not happy with this state of affairs."

"That East End gentleman you mentioned, he wouldn't be Reggie Kray, would he?" asked Priscilla.

"You will never hear that name on my lips," Bogans replied firmly. "Not on your life."

"What about the producer's name? David Merrick? Would that be a name I would ever hear on your lips?"

That elicited a wan smile from Bogans. "I would be careful about evoking the name of any guest at the Savoy. The same holds true of my fellow employees, by the way. For instance, someone who might have been in a hotel suite with someone that she shouldn't have been in said suite with. I would never say anything, knowing that while there are no secrets at the Savoy, there is discretion and that discretion has allowed me to remain a loyal employee for twenty-five years now."

"Yes, one does come to appreciate the discretion at the Savoy—to count on that discretion you might say," Priscilla conceded, not wanting to hear what she was hearing. If Bogans knew, or suspected, then how many others were there who would now be giving her the knowing eye each time she passed? And if the hotel's employees knew, how long before the whispers reached the ears of General Manager Banville?

"Someone named Reggie called while you were out," Susie said when Priscilla arrived back at 205. She placed a piece of notepaper in front of her. "He left his number."

Priscilla felt even sicker to her stomach. "What did he say?"

"He said it would be a good idea to call him back." Susie arched an eyebrow. "He sounded kind of sexy in a rough sort of way. Who is he?"

"Back to work, Susie," Priscilla ordered. "And while you're at it, get hold of Ethel Levey for me. She books the shows at the Cabaret and has Diana Dors's home address."

"Why do you need that?"

"Susie," said Priscilla in the exasperated voice she reserved for her assistant, "just get me the address and don't ask questions."

"You're not going to one of those parties of hers, are you?" Susie asked in a hushed voice.

"That's a question."

"You never tell me anything," Susie pouted.

Priscilla closed her door as Susie left and then sat at her desk, massaging her temples, debating what to do. She picked up the receiver.

"You should have called me sooner," Reggie said when he came on the line.

"I just got back to the office," Priscilla said. "What do you want?"

"What do I want? Fancy that. You know what I want."

"Reggie, could I say something about your attitude, considering the fact that you want to have dinner?"

"I do want to have dinner with you," Reggie confirmed. "No question about that. But I also want that film."

"I talked to Diana. Are you certain there is a film?"

"There is a film." Reggie sounded very sure of himself.

"How do you know?"

"Because Ronnie *says* there is a film."

"But that doesn't mean there is a film."

"Yes, it does. Did you talk to Diana?"

"She says there is no film." A little white lie wouldn't do any harm at the moment, Priscilla thought.

"She's lying."

"Tell me what happens if I don't get it back."

"You will get it back." Reggie never sounded surer of anything.

"You know, Reggie, if you kill me, we can't go out to dinner."

"Tomorrow night."

"What about it."

"We're going to dinner. Eight o'clock. Scotch Jack will pick you up."

"But—"

"Meantime, get that film."

The line went dead. Priscilla replaced the receiver, lowered her head and resumed massaging her temples, trying to think of any good reason why she should ever have been born. She could not think of one.

"Hello, have I caught you at a bad time?"

She looked up to find a short, sandy-haired fellow, his open, unlined face set to an expression of endless good cheer. Susie looked frantic in the doorway.

"He got in here before I could stop him."

"You wouldn't want to stop an officer of the law from doing his duty, now would you, Miss?"

Priscilla then noticed what the cheery-faced fellow was holding in his hand: a warrant card that identified him as a Scotland Yard detective.

"Chief Superintendent Leonard Read, Miss Tempest. You sure this isn't a bad time?" His tone was kind enough, but Priscilla had little doubt that it made no difference to the superintendent whether it was a good time or bad.

"We can always make time for Scotland Yard," Priscilla said, pulling herself together.

Susie stared and didn't say anything.

Priscilla shot her assistant a look. "Thank you, Susie."

"Perhaps your assistant could close the door on her way out," said Superintendent Read, putting away his warrant card. "That way we can talk in private."

Priscilla nodded at Susie who reluctantly departed, closing the door.

"Mind if I take a seat?" Superintendent Read asked.

"Please do," Priscilla said.

Read plopped himself down. He wore a tan raincoat open to show the bow tie that went along with his three-piece suit.

"I should tell you," Read began conversationally, "I always introduce myself formally, but I'm better known to those who know me as Nipper—Nipper Read."

"Nipper? What an odd name," Priscilla said. "Why do they call you Nipper?"

"I'm not entirely sure," he said with what struck Priscilla as a slightly embarrassed smile. "Dates back to my boxing days as far as I can recall."

"Then what should I call you? Superintendent Read? Or Nipper?"

"Why don't you call me Nipper?" he said with a disarming smile. "Much friendlier, don't you think?"

"I believe I will call you Superintendent. As in, what's this about—Superintendent?"

"Yes, what is this about, Miss Tempest? Very good question." Read was abruptly all business. "It's about a matter I believe you can help us with."

"I'm not sure how I can do that," Priscilla said.

"I've been speaking to my good friend and colleague, Inspector Lightfoot. I understand you know him."

"Charger Lightfoot," Priscilla said, keeping her manner alert and professional, the way an innocent young woman like herself always should. "Do all the detectives at Scotland Yard have nicknames?"

"Ah, then you do know him."

"Only too well, I'm afraid."

"Yes, Inspector Lightfoot does have questions regarding your association with the recent murder victim here at the Savoy."

Read made it sound as though the inspector might have similar questions for nearly every citizen of London.

"Not to put too fine a point on it," Priscilla interjected, working to get ahead of where she was certain Read was heading, "I believe Inspector Lightfoot has me down as a suspect. It's a bad habit of his where I am concerned."

"I must tell you I'm not at all certain I share Inspector Lightfoot's view. However..."

"However?" The word came out in a gulp. "Oh dear. Whenever a representative of law enforcement employs the word 'however,' I know trouble lies ahead."

"I'm afraid in this case you're not entirely mistaken." Read reached into his suit jacket and pulled out three photographs, which he laid out on the desk as though showing her his winning hand.

Priscilla let out an involuntary gasp as she saw herself with Reggie Kray in incriminating shades of black and white.

"The question does arise as to what an employee at London's most prestigious hotel is doing in the company of the country's most disreputable gangster."

Nipper Read, Priscilla noted, no longer appeared quite so cheery.

CHAPTER FIFTEEN

Our Heroine!

Superintendent Read focused hardening eyes on Priscilla. She struggled to ignore his stare, her mind spinning, working hard to come up with a reasonable explanation for what she would be doing outside a pub with Reggie Kray. Never mind reasonable, anything to fill the ensuing awkward silence.

The truth? Yes, well, about the truth... A vision of Reggie's hands at her throat, bringing her life to a swift end brought the spinning in her head to a halt. No, forget the truth.

"Mr. Kray asked to see me in connection with the death of Miss Skye Kane," Priscilla answered in a formal voice. As close to reasonable as she could manage under the circumstances. Not to mention close to a semblance of truth.

"He *asked* to see you?" Read's brow was doubtfully knit. Apparently he wasn't buying her version of reasonable. "Why would he *ask* to see you in particular, Miss Tempest?"

"I imagine he knew I was friends with Miss Kane."

"And were you friends?"

"Friendly acquaintances, I would say." Priscilla pulled herself into what she hoped would be seen as a businesslike sitting position, hands clasped in front of her on the desk. Summoning the authority of her office. Never mind there was no authority in her office. "Superintendent, what is this all about? Have you been following me?"

"Not following you. But we have been keeping an eye on the Kray twins. I'd like to know what you told Reggie."

"I didn't tell him much of anything because I don't know much of anything," Priscilla answered.

"If that is the case, then why has Reggie since called you a number of times?" Read's face maintained its cheeriness but his voice had become as hard as his eyes.

"How would you know he called me?"

"We're Scotland Yard. We know such things."

"You had better ask Mr. Kray that question."

"Would you like me to tell you what I think after observing Reggie with you the other night, Miss Tempest?"

"Not particularly," said Priscilla. Her stomach now had tightened to the point where it hurt.

"I believe Reggie has taken a shine to you. The way he looked at you that night. The subsequent phone calls. I have not seen anything quite like it since the death of his wife a year ago."

"I'm sure you are mistaken."

"I don't think I am," Read said. "I'm quite certain of things."

"Then you are in an enviable position, Superintendent."

"Yes, I am, aren't I?" Read seemed pleased with himself. "And one of the things I'm sure of is the fact that you're not telling me the whole truth about your encounter with Reggie Kray."

"I've told you what I know." Priscilla kicked herself for her inability to sound sincere when lying.

"I don't think you have," Read pronounced. "For example, you have failed to tell me the part where, in addition to intending to date you, Reggie has put you in the very difficult position of having to retrieve a film that shows his brother Ronnie in what I can only describe as a compromised situation."

Priscilla fought to keep off her face what she was certain was the expression of a deer caught in headlights.

Read drew a reel of eight-millimetre film from his side jacket pocket. He dropped it on the desk in front of an astonished Priscilla. "I believe that's what Reggie wants from you," he said.

Priscilla asked, "But how—?"

"Let us simply say that Miss Diana Dors, given her situation, feels it is in her best interest to co-operate with us."

"So *she* told you—and there *is* a film."

"Yes, most definitely," confirmed Read. "Not only is the film an embarrassment for Ronnie among his gangster colleagues but it could mean a scandal that would ruin the career of a prominent member of parliament and High Anglican churchman."

Priscilla pointed at the reel in front of her. "A High Anglican churchman is with Ronnie?"

"His name is Tom Driberg, incidentally. Not much of a churchman, I'm afraid, given the fact that he is a friend of the Krays."

"What do you want me to do?"

"Give the reel to Reggie."

"I'm afraid I don't understand," Priscilla said.

"This way, the film doesn't get out and a scandal involving Mr. Driberg is avoided. In addition, it places you firmly in Reggie's good books. Exactly where I want you."

"Why would you want me in Reggie's good books?" Why would anyone want her anywhere near Reggie, let alone his good books?

"Because I am the copper who is finally going to destroy the Krays and you, Miss Tempest, will help me do it."

"Me?" was all Priscilla could gasp.

"The Kray twins are dangerous killers," Read went on, speaking with a new intensity. "They have been conducting a reign of terror for years. That pub you visited, the Blind Beggar? That's where Ronnie shot and killed a man named George Cornell in cold blood while he sat at the bar. A year later, Reggie murdered a bloke named Jack McVitie, known as Jack the Hat."

"If you know all that, surely you can arrest them," Priscilla asserted.

"Believe me, I'd like nothing better. And with your help, Miss Tempest, we can accomplish just that."

Priscilla felt sicker and sicker as the superintendent talked on. It was as though her body had been invaded by a terrible virus designed to assault her with increasing violence each time her ears received bad news. The news delivered by the various police officials in her life seemed to make her particularly ill.

Vaguely, she became aware that Read was still talking. "Reggie likes you and, when you give him that film, he will like you even more. To date, we haven't been able to plant anyone close to the Krays. You are our best hope for obtaining the sort of information we need to bring a case against those two."

"But I don't want Reggie to like me," Priscilla said, finding her anguished voice. "I don't want to have anything to do with him—or with you, Superintendent."

"I hate to say this, Miss Tempest, but you don't have a choice. You will meet with Reggie in order to return that film. After that, you will see him again, and when you do, you will do your best to discover what he and his brother are up to and then report to me."

"You must be out of your mind," Priscilla sputtered. "I can't do that."

"You underestimate yourself, Miss Tempest. I believe you can."

"Well, I'm not going to."

"Yes, you are," Read stated firmly. He pointed to the photographs. "I would hate to see those fall into the wrong hands—the press, for example, or your employers."

"You wouldn't do that."

"My suggestion is that you do not place your job at the Savoy at risk in order to discover what I would or would not do. Also, let me point out that your co-operation will help assuage any suspicions Inspector Lightfoot may have as to your involvement in the murder of Skye Kane."

Read reached over to gather the photos. "This will be strictly between the two of us. No one else need know; no one else *will* know as long as you co-operate." He laid a card down on the desk where the photos had been. "You will report to me and only me. You know better than to say anything to anyone else. The Krays have big ears so you must be very careful."

"This is insane."

"You will be aiding in the apprehension of the two worst gangsters it has ever been my displeasure to know," Read went on. "You will be doing this country an immense service. You will be a heroine."

"I don't want to be a heroine," Priscilla said. "I want to remain my same old cowardly self."

"That's too bad." Read's voice had regained its cheerful tone. "Whether you like it or not, Miss Tempest, with a bit of prodding from me, you're about to become one."

"You know, Superintendent, I think I know why you like everyone to call you by your nickname—Nipper."

"And why is that, Miss Tempest?"

"Because that way, with your boyish face, your cheerful nickname and that silly bow tie, you can deceive everyone—make them believe you are not the ruthless bastard that you truly are."

"You are absolutely right. I *am* a ruthless bastard and I *will* do what it takes in order to get the Krays."

Read was smiling as he stood. He pointed to the reel of film lying on her desk. "Get that to Reggie as soon as you can."

Superintendent Read continued to smile as he left. Priscilla stared at the reel in front of her, feeling cold and numb.

In the Cellars of the Savoy

As soon as Superintendent Read left, Priscilla, given her emotional state, feared that she would break out the waterworks.

To her surprise, she didn't. Some choking back and hard swallowing, granted, but no tears. Weeping wouldn't solve anything, she decided quickly. What's more, without the presence of threatening police officials, her stomach had begun to settle. She was actually feeling better. She was in a horrible mess, no question—in several horrible messes. At least one of those messes had been created by her decision to visit the Blind Beggar and meet the Krays. She had no one but herself to blame. Given that she was the architect of her own disaster, the question was, what to do about it? She had gotten herself into all this, now how was she going to get out?

On second thought, perhaps a good cry was not out of the question. But later, after she got some help.

When she called, Noël Coward answered almost immediately.

"As the newest member of the Gossip's Bridle Club, am I allowed to call an emergency meeting?"

"Of course," said Noël.

"Then that's what I'm doing," Priscilla said.

"How soon do you require this emergency meeting?"

"Since it's an emergency, as soon as possible."

"Done!" cried Noël with glee. "We will meet in the cellars."

"The cellars?" Priscilla was already feeling better.

"The Savoy cellars, dear girl. Where the wines are stored and secrets revealed. Be there in an hour!"

The heat from the coal-fired stoves inside the Savoy's cavernous restaurant kitchen—the more prestigious of the hotel's two kitchens—was oppressive, the noise at ear-splitting levels from the small army of sous chefs in their flared toque hats preparing the day's culinary delights.

On her way through, Priscilla paused beneath the hanging copper pans and once again could not help but be in awe of the organization conceived originally by the great Georges Auguste Escoffier himself. The kitchens hadn't changed much since his time. So fixated with cooking precisely the way he wished was Escoffier that he refused to even consider learning English, fearing he would end up cooking like the English.

Although French remained the language of the Savoy kitchens, the current maître-chef—Silvino Trompetto, nicknamed Tromps—was the hotel's first non-French chef, commanding a staff of 130, preparing 2,000 meals a day for the restaurants and banqueting. Tall and always, in Priscilla's eyes, quite regal, outfitted in his crisp white chef's jacket, Tromps greeted her with his usual warm smile and distracted nod as he prepared fresh truffles, the black diamonds of cookery flown in daily from the Périgord region of France.

At the same time, he kept a close eye on his sous chefs—the fish chef, sauce chef, roast chef, pastry chef, etcetera. Everyone worked with admirable precision. Nearby, the commis cooks busily chopped the evening's selection of fresh vegetables.

As she was about to start down the staircase to the cellars, Tromps raised his voice above the kitchen cacophony, calling out a familiar refrain: "Dining is an art, Priscilla!"

"Animals feed," Priscilla called back.

"But man *eats*," Tromps shouted in response.

"But only a guest at the Savoy knows *how* to eat!" Priscilla replied.

The staff, as usual, broke into laughter and applause, a momentary reprieve from the tension of preparing the day's dinner menu.

A staircase curved down into the cellars beneath the hotel, the former dungeons of the old Savoy Palace that extended beneath the Thames. The original stone walls had long since been bricked and painted white. Noël was already present, along with Gielgud and Olivier. The trio, cast in sinister shadow under a single light hanging from the barrel-vaulted ceiling, was seated at a small table surrounded by shelves stocked with musty wine bottles, part of the Savoy's extensive wine collection.

"You look as though you're plotting to blow up the parliament buildings," Priscilla observed.

"Don't think it hasn't crossed our minds," Gielgud said.

"Count Peter of Savoy insisted on the dungeons in the thirteenth century when he conceived his 'fayrest manor in Europe' as he described it," explained Noël as he inserted a cigarette into an ivory holder. "Incidentally, the count paid a token peppercorn in rent to King Henry III. Why a peppercorn, I have no idea."

"Noël was the count's first guest," Gielgud interjected. "He immediately found a piano and plunked out 'There's Always Something Fishy About the French.'"

"I do not go back quite that far," Noël said mildly. By now his cigarette was lit and he was adding a cloud of blue-grey smoke to the cool air. "However, I was camped at the Savoy during the Blitz when these cellars were used as an air-raid shelter. Spent quite a few hours down here, let me tell you."

"Mr. Coward, do you by chance remember playing the piano after the bomb went off?" A squat, red-faced fellow dressed in a white jacket and striped cotton trousers had appeared out of the surrounding gloom. He carried two uncorked wine bottles and four Waterford wine glasses.

"Ah, there you are, Fred. Let me introduce you to the others," Noël said. "This is my friend Fred, who has been kind enough to allow us to sneak in here today. Fred is the head cellarman at the Savoy. A very important job, let me say, keeping track of the wine that arrives regularly from all over the world."

"I'm sure I will regret asking," said Gielgud, "but what's all this about a bomb going off?"

"It exploded in the garden at the height of the Blitz," explained Fred. "I was working as a waiter in the dining room at the time. The explosion blew out the windows and sent smoke billowing through the restaurant. Diners, understandably, were thrown into a panic. Mr. Coward, however, did not panic. Instead, he leapt up and started to play a tune on the piano."

"Which must have sent everyone stampeding away, I'm sure," offered Gielgud.

"To the contrary, sir. Mr. Coward played for over an hour, calming everyone."

"Once I got started, I couldn't stop," Noël said.

"I'm not surprised," mused Gielgud dryly.

"Among the many heroic deeds I performed during the war," Noël said with a grin.

"In which you served, Noël," Olivier said. "In which you served."

Gielgud turned to Priscilla. "In case he hasn't already told you, Noël won World War II."

"I did have some help," the playwright admitted.

"Well, I'm cold," said Olivier with a shiver, rubbing his hands together. "Was this your idea, Noël? What's next? We meet in the Savoy's freezers?"

"Away from prying eyes, dear boy. Away from prying eyes. This way no one with big ears can overhear us while we attempt to help Priscilla." Noël turned to Fred the cellarman, lingering with the wine. "What do you have for us this afternoon, Fred?"

"One of your favourites, sir." Fred presented the two dusty bottles, already open so they could breathe. "Vintage 1942 Château Mouton Rothschild."

"Ah yes, indeed. Wonderful choice. Thank you, Fred."

Fred proceeded to pour the wine into two crystal decanters, careful to tilt the bottles at a forty-five-degree angle, keeping an eye out for sediment. He then poured the decanted wine into the Waterford glasses for his guests.

"Excellent," said Noël when the cellarman had finished.

"I'll leave you to it, sir," said Fred before slipping away.

"Off we go," said Noël. "We have at hand very fine wine, passable company"—accompanied by a raised, questioning eyebrow—"and best of all, complete privacy and discretion so that we are free to come to Priscilla's aid."

"Very much appreciated," Priscilla said.

"I must say, Priscilla, you do look a bit pale and not quite yourself," Gielgud sympathetically observed.

"The wine will certainly help," Priscilla said, holding up her glass as though presenting evidence of its restorative powers.

The Château Mouton Rothschild the head cellarman had poured was swirled and savoured after the four clinked glasses. "Chin-chin," announced Priscilla. "That's much better."

"Now you must tell us what's wrong and, more importantly, how we can help," Noël said.

"I'm not sure you can help," Priscilla said mournfully. "I'm not sure anyone can help."

"Of course we can help." Olivier leaned forward, his face filling with sympathy. "After all, we *are* the Gossip's Bridle Club."

"How does that make any difference?" asked Gielgud.

"We are actors, man, directors!" Olivier cried out. "We make our livings smearing on the greasepaint, hiding ourselves, slipping undercover in plain sight, solving problems, coming up with solutions when others can't. *That's* what sets us apart. *That's* why we can help!"

"Well, it wasn't Larry reciting the St. Crispin's Day speech from *Henry V*, but pretty darned good nonetheless," conceded Gielgud.

"With all due respect, Larry," Noël said acidly, "you make a living reciting words written on paper for you by other much more intelligent humans—humans such as myself. What sets you apart is *not* your ability to solve problems, but simply to remember the words written down for you."

"I would *highly* dispute that contention." Olivier was now in a huff.

A twinkle-eyed Gielgud addressed Priscilla. "As you can plainly see, we are like bickering children, unsuited to help ourselves, thus I do wonder about anyone else."

Noël disposed of what was left of his cigarette and inserted another into his holder. "I'm afraid we've gotten a bit off track. Despite what I said, I do tend to agree with Larry to the extent that, collectively, I believe we can, in our way, come to Priscilla's aid." He turned to Priscilla. "But please, tell us what your problem is and then we will put our ancient-but-brilliant heads together to come up with a solution."

"Yes, that is a very good idea." Priscilla was bursting to confide in someone, so why not in fellow Gossip's Bridle Club members within the soundproof confines of these former dungeons? After all, it was a safe bet that the walls down here in centuries past had overheard countless secrets being spilled.

"Let me see," Priscilla began, "I suppose it all started the other evening when I was careless enough to sleep with the man who picked me up at the party."

"Who picked you up at the party?" asked Olivier.

"That's not the point," Priscilla said. "The point is the next morning, as I was in the process of regretting my stupidity and fearing for my job, Skye Kane turned up murdered in her dressing room. No sooner had Scotland Yard Inspector Lightfoot declared me a possible suspect than Mr. Merrick showed up in my office, threatening to have me fired if I didn't protect him from the police, who also have his name on their list of suspects—possibly right next to mine."

Priscilla paused for dramatic effect before she continued. "That's when I decided I had to *do* something."

"What did you do?" Noël asked.

"I went around to that pub you told me about."

"Not the Blind Beggar." In astonishment, Noël's eyebrows shot up to what was left of his hairline.

"The Blind Beggar," Priscilla confirmed.

"Whatever made you enter such a dangerous nest of vipers?" asked a horrified Olivier.

"The police suspect the Krays might be responsible for Skye's death. I wanted to see for myself, find out what I could about them."

"My God," breathed Olivier.

"Tell us what happened when you got to the pub," Gielgud interjected.

"If I'm to believe one of his henchmen, Reggie is ready to marry me."

The three men exchanged disbelieving looks.

Priscilla soldiered on. "But first he wants to take me to dinner."

"Good God!" another explosion from Olivier.

"And he also wants me to retrieve a film that he says is in the possession of Diana Dors."

"What kind of film?" Noël asked.

"It was shot at one of her house parties. It stars Reggie's brother Ronnie. The word being used to describe his performance is 'indiscreet.'"

"Goodness gracious me!" exclaimed Gielgud.

"What's more, he apparently was indiscreet with a member of parliament who is also a High Anglican churchman."

"Not Tom Driberg," piped up Noël.

"How do you know?" asked Priscilla in astonishment.

"In the rougher circles I move in from time to time, Mr. Driberg is notorious," Noël responded calmly.

"But that's still not all," Priscilla went on.

"That's more than enough," said Gielgud with a shake of his head.

"As a result of Reggie's interest in me, I received a visit from Detective Chief Superintendent Leonard Read. Everyone calls him Nipper, incidentally, because apparently that was his nickname when he was a boxer."

"Nipper Read, my God," said Olivier.

"Superintendent Read has sworn to bring down the Krays and, for reasons I find impossible to fathom, he believes I can help him do so."

"But how could you possibly?" inquired Noël.

"Superintendent Read has given me the film that the Krays want. However, in return I must help the superintendent end what he calls the Krays' 'reign of terror.'"

The members of the Gossip's Bridle Club fell into a stunned silence.

Priscilla swallowed the remainder of her wine. Noël placed a comforting hand over hers before pouring more wine into her glass.

"I'm sure I'm speaking for all of us when I say that we've heard nothing here in these cellars that can't be resolved tickety-boo," Noël said. "Right, Larry?"

"My goodness," Olivier said in a soft voice. "The Krays. The personification of evil."

"Nonsense," stated Noël. "The personification of evil is the theatre critic at the *Times*. Everything else can be dealt with, including these low-level thugs."

"But the Krays, Noël," cautioned Olivier.

Noël ignored Olivier and leaned into Priscilla. "The key, I believe, is the solving of Miss Kane's murder. We do that and everything else falls into place."

"*We?*" Olivier exclaimed. He and Gielgud traded quick glances. "Are *we* supposed to solve the murder?"

"We are indeed, dear boy," Noël answered. "That way we can exonerate a fellow club member, namely Priscilla, and in the process have the time of our lives."

"*End* our lives at the hands of the Krays," mumbled Olivier.

"What do you think, Priscilla?" asked Noël. "Do you think the wicked twins are responsible for Miss Kane's murder?"

"I don't know. It's possible, I suppose," replied Priscilla. "But the police are looking at a number of suspects, me included."

"But why? Why would they strangle Miss Kane in her dressing room?" questioned Noël. "They are killers. But do they kill women?"

"Crime of passion," pronounced Olivier. "The oldest motivation there is."

"Reggie had been seeing Diana Dors," Priscilla explained. "But he dumped her when Diana introduced him to Skye. The rumour around the hotel is that Diana was very angry and jealous."

"Then is it possible Diana Dors murdered her friend in a fit of jealousy?" asked Gielgud.

"But would she have had the strength to strangle someone?" offered Olivier. "Strangulation isn't exactly the preferred method when it comes to female murderers. Is it?"

"Personally, I wouldn't strangle anyone," Priscilla said. "But that's me."

"Let's keep moving," said Noël, transformed into the ringmaster at the circus. "Let us talk about my favourite suspect—"

"Producers! Worse even than theatre critics," pronounced Olivier.

"David Merrick," added Gielgud.

"Precisely," said Noël.

"The police have questioned him," Priscilla said. "He was at the party with Skye. They had a fight and he hit her."

"Are you certain of that?" Noël asked.

Priscilla nodded. "She came into the ladies' room right after he slapped her. Her face was red and she was crying. I wanted her to go to the police but she wouldn't hear of it."

"Merrick is a cad," Noël said, "and he possesses a hair-trigger temper, but those character traits don't necessarily make him a killer."

"It does make him mad," countered Gielgud, "and mad people kill."

"He told me in no uncertain terms that he's innocent," Priscilla said.

"He's also a bloody liar," put in Olivier. "He told me he was interested in bringing my production of *The Dance of Death* to New York and later claimed he said no such thing."

"Perhaps in the case of *Death* that was simply a demonstration of good taste," Gielgud offered mildly.

"Oh, go to hell, Johnny," said Olivier angrily.

"Gladly. Except I'm afraid it's crammed with producers, theatre critics and bad actors."

"That's it then," Noël interjected, bringing their discussion back into focus. "Our list of suspects—"

"There is one more that I should mention," Priscilla said hesitantly.

All eyes were on her. "Do tell." Noël's eyebrows were again lifted high in anticipation.

"According to Diana, Skye was seeing Pierre Trudeau. She believes he could be a suspect."

"You don't mean the Canadian prime minister?" questioned Noël.

"I do," replied Priscilla.

"Good God," exclaimed Gielgud. "A Canadian prime minister murders a British showgirl at the Savoy."

"Except he couldn't have done it," Priscilla said.

"And why not?" asked Olivier.

"Because he was with me," admitted Priscilla soberly.

"You're the one!" exclaimed Gielgud.

"If he truly is a suspect," Priscilla continued, "and the police question him…"

"Then *you* are his alibi," concluded Noël.

"And I can say goodbye to my job at the Savoy."

It became suddenly and eerily silent in the cave, a sign of the depth of the trouble Priscilla now found herself in; trouble so deep that the thought of it shut down three of Britain's most loquacious personalities.

Noël pulled himself back together before the others. "Let us remain calm and not despair," he advised. "For the time being, we can assume that the prime minister would not be high on whatever list of suspects Scotland Yard might have pulled together. I mean, politicians don't generally go around murdering showgirls. At least they don't in this country; they much prefer to sleep with them."

"Yes, but remember this is a *Canadian* prime minister," cautioned Olivier. "Who knows what they are up to."

"Homicidal killers all," Gielgud said.

"Gentlemen, please," said Noël impatiently. "Let us concentrate on what is most pressing, and that is the Krays." He turned his gaze to Priscilla. "Where have you left it with them?"

"Reggie is after me to have dinner," Priscilla said.

"Are you intending to do that?"

"I don't think I have any choice."

"Yes, you are between that proverbial rock and a hard place, no doubt," Noël said contemplatively, removing the cigarette holder from his mouth. "Here's what you do then. Have dinner with Reggie; give him the film. At the same time, find out as much as you can about his involvement with Miss Kane. We will be there, standing by to rescue you in case you find yourself in danger."

"*What?*" Olivier gasped.

"My God, Larry," observed Noël, "I haven't seen you so aghast since you finished the first day shooting *The Prince and the Showgirl*."

Gielgud leaned forward to address Noël. "While I've done a much better job than Larry of suppressing my emotions, as usual, I must say I am hard pressed not to replicate his look of abject terror. I don't think I need to remind you that, a few reviews here and there to the contrary, we are actors, not bodyguards. I would never want any harm to come to Priscilla, but the fact is we may not be the best candidates to ensure her safety."

"Nonsense," said Noël dismissively. "Even a homicidal gangster like Reggie Kray would hesitate to knock off three of Britain's most beloved theatrical icons."

"If the Krays have seen Johnny in *Assignment to Kill*, or Noël in *Boom!*, they might not hesitate to put an end to them," Olivier stated. "I, on the other hand, most likely would be spared."

"My demise certainly would clear the way for that bugger Harold Pinter," groused Noël. He brightened. "Nonetheless, we mustn't underestimate ourselves. At play will be our superior intelligence and ingenuity."

"I will keep that in mind as I die in a hail of bullets," Olivier mumbled.

"Just think of the obituary in the *Times*, dear boy," Noël said. "They'll have you lying in state at Westminster Abbey."

"I will throw myself on your coffin in wretched sorrow," promised Gielgud.

"You've spent a lifetime trying to upstage me, Johnny," Olivier noted. "Why would you restrain yourself at my funeral?"

Noël's hand fell softly, reassuringly, on Priscilla's arm. "We will be there for you, my dear. Not to worry."

Priscilla studied the three famous, anxious faces arrayed before her as a single thought crowded her mind: There was plenty to worry about.

Foxy Is Concerned

Edmond John Fox, known to all as Foxy, principal secretary to Prime Minister Pierre Elliott Trudeau, and Thomas Teasdale, Tommy to his friends, the Canadian High Commissioner to Great Britain, met on a grey morning in St. James's Park off the mall leading to Buckingham Palace.

Oxford and Harvard educated, a proud External Affairs Service dinosaur and former ambassador to Germany, Tommy Teasdale was thoroughly enjoying his London assignment, including, but not restricted to, tranquil morning strolls past the park's lush gardens, Buckingham Palace set comfortingly in the background. He was not anxious to be party to anything that would jeopardize that enjoyment.

Fox, bespectacled, youthful—a wet-behind-the-ears Trudeau acolyte as far as Teasdale was concerned—huddled on a bench with the old lion of the Canadian foreign service. They sat close by a paved walkway, not far from the lake, filled this morning with young mothers and nannies pushing prams with babies—all of whom, it struck Edmond Fox, were sound asleep.

"Dozens of sleeping babies being pushed around in a London park, how curious," observed Fox.

"Yes, I suppose it is," Teasdale responded disinterestedly. "But beyond the opportunity to view parades of sleeping babies, there is a more pressing reason why I thought we should meet, Foxy."

"The conference appears to be going well," put in Fox hopefully. "You never know how these Commonwealth get-togethers will end up, I suppose, or even if they're much use."

"Yes, I've seen a good many of these things over the years," said Teasdale, keeping his eye on a fragile-looking elderly gent in a beret cap feeding the ducks and pelicans at the edge of the lake. "They are an opportunity for the British, Canadians and Australians to make promises to their African counterparts they have no intention of keeping. Everyone leaves feeling better about themselves, having accomplished nothing."

"For the new fellow on the block, the prime minister has been well received."

"Very well received," agreed Teasdale, distracted by a grey squirrel bounding toward their bench.

"And all London seems to be fascinated by his comings and goings. Lots of very good press. I believe the prime minister is considering staying on for a few more days after the conference ends. See the sights, a couple of shows, that sort of thing."

"I would advise him not to do that," said Teasdale. The squirrel apparently did not like that advice and veered off toward the safety of the neighbouring plane trees.

Fox didn't seem to like it much either. "Oh? Why not?"

"Are you aware of the recent murder of this showgirl at the Savoy?"

"It's all over the papers, hard to miss," Fox said.

"Yes, unfortunately. The young woman's name is Skye Kane. Does that name mean anything to you?"

Fox's eyebrows were now knit in confusion. "Good God, no. Why should it?"

"I've had a very discreet inquiry from a friend at 10 Downing Street." Teasdale paused, watching the elderly gentleman, so wobbly as he fed the ducks, Teasdale feared he might tumble into the lake.

"It seems Scotland Yard is investigating a number of male suitors who have recently been seeing this woman," the diplomat continued. "Looking at them as possible suspects. Among the names that came to my friend's attention, I'm sorry to say, is that of our prime minister."

Fox's knit brows were exchanged for an expression of blank astonishment. "You must be joking. Pierre's name has come up in connection with this woman?"

"It appears as though he was seeing her," said Teasdale. He watched the elderly gentleman straighten, relieved that he would not fall into the lake after all. "Now I should caution that Scotland Yard does not seriously view the prime minister as a suspect—"

"My God, I should hope not."

"However, they may decide they wish to question him."

"About what?"

"Among other things, his whereabouts on the night this showgirl was murdered."

Fox closed his eyes momentarily. "Good God," he repeated.

"What worries me," Teasdale went on, "and I assume it would concern you also, is not the possibility the prime minister would be in any way involved with Miss Kane's death, but that his name might end up in the press in connection with her. A situation, I imagine, you would like to avoid."

"My God, yes. A new prime minister, his first Commonwealth Conference, and he comes home burdened with a scandal involving a murdered showgirl."

Teasdale waited to allow Fox to digest the possibility before he said, "I'm assuming that if needed, the prime minister could account for his whereabouts on the night in question."

When Fox did not immediately answer, Teasdale frowned and leaned forward. "Foxy?"

Fox exhaled. "I can't be sure, but according to what one of his security people has told me, the prime minister was in his bed—"

"That's good," said Teasdale.

"Except that he was not there alone."

"He wasn't with Miss Kane?" Teasdale barely kept the edge of panic out of his voice.

"No, another woman, if what I'm told is correct. A young woman who works at the Savoy."

"Yes, but presumably the RCMP security people were stationed outside his suite. They would be able to verify his presence. There needn't be any mention of bedmates."

That drew more silence from Fox and more concern from Teasdale. "I am right about that, am I not, Foxy?"

"There could be a problem in that regard," Fox admitted.

"What kind of problem?"

"The two officers assigned to the prime minister did not initially return to the hotel with him."

"Why the hell not?" demanded Teasdale.

"The prime minister apparently gave them the night off. They returned to duty early the next morning and were present when the young woman left the suite."

"What time was this?"

"About seven thirty, I believe," said Fox.

"Then for all anyone knows the prime minister could have been out strangling half the showgirls in London."

"There is the young woman he spent the night with. She could provide an alibi, if it ever came to that."

"Which it won't, I'm sure. Still..." Teasdale allowed his voice to tail off.

"Still?"

"The man's a bloody fool," Teasdale stated angrily. "Can you imagine Lester Pearson putting himself at potential risk like this? Honestly, and this man is prime minister of the country."

"I've known Pierre for a long time and he's usually discreet when it comes to his affairs," Fox said. "I'm afraid exposure to so-called Swinging London, coupled with unexpected celebrity, may have got the better of sound judgment."

Teasdale shook his head. "We must deal with the situation. That's all there is to it."

"What are you suggesting, Tommy?" asked Fox.

Teasdale took a moment to look at his watch before he rose to his feet. "Let me get back to Downing Street and see where they stand with this. Hopefully, Scotland Yard will soon come up with the murderer and this will all be a moot point. In the meantime, though, I would urge you to convince the prime minister to leave the country as soon as the Commonwealth Conference ends, what? Day after tomorrow?"

"I will do my best," Fox said. Teasdale noted with satisfaction that Foxy looked paler than he did when he had sat down.

"Also, I think it would be a good idea if I have a talk with this young woman, make sure she understands the gravity of her situation and keeps quiet," Teasdale went on. "The last thing we need is her going to the press with something like 'My Night with Pierre.'"

"Damned good idea," Fox agreed. "Incidentally, the woman in question is Canadian, so you may be able to appeal to her sense of nationalism, that sort of thing."

"You say she works at the Savoy?" Teasdale asked.

"That's right. I'm not certain what she does there, however."

"And this woman's name?"

"Tempest," replied Fox. "Priscilla Tempest."

Yes, he would certainly deal with this, thought Teasdale as he left young Foxy and began trudging along the pathway. The tottering old fellow feeding the ducks had disappeared. Yes, indeed. Miss Tempest would need to be silenced. No question about that. His only concern was how to do it.

Journey into Fear

Enormous marquees promoting a curious combination of Coca-Cola, Cinzano and Wrigley's Spearmint gum lit Piccadilly Circus and the long lines stretching to Leicester Square for the re-release of *Goldfinger*. Tourists swarmed the Shaftesbury Memorial Fountain on the southeastern side of the Circus where Priscilla waited nervously, having insisted that Reggie Kray meet her here, away from prying eyes at the Savoy. She shivered despite the warm night air, surprised as Scotch Jack got out of the blue Jaguar he had parked at the curb and tipped his bowler.

"Good evening to you, Priscilla," he greeted her in an unexpectedly bleak tone. He flung open the passenger door. "Please, if you don't mind riding up front with an old villain."

"I thought Reggie was supposed to meet me," Priscilla said, sliding past him into the seat.

"Plans have changed," Jack said. No more of an explanation than that. The merrily dangerous soul she had met previously was nowhere in evidence. Jack appeared sullen and pale as he wrestled the Jag into gear and joined the swirl of nighttime traffic.

"You look like you're having a hard time, Jack," observed Priscilla, working to make the conversation that would take her mind off the distinct possibility this could end up being an even harder time for her.

"Busy times, lass, lots going on," said Jack as he manoeuvred through the traffic. "Takes it out of a fella after a while."

"So where are we headed?"

Scotch Jack managed a smile. "If I told you that, lass, then it wouldn't be a surprise now, would it?"

"I didn't know it was supposed to be a surprise."

Jack didn't respond, which worried Priscilla even more. In the shifting shadows produced by the lights from oncoming vehicles, Priscilla couldn't help thinking again that Quasimodo in a bowler hat was driving her to—what? Dinner? A rendez-vous with death? Perish that thought.

Increasingly nervous, Priscilla tried to take a breath and choked, drawing a glance from Jack. "How are you doing, lass?"

"I guess I don't like going where I don't know where I'm going."

Jack just smiled one of his Halloween-pumpkin smiles.

"We'll be there soon enough, lass. Not to worry. Scotch Jack will take good care of you."

Isn't that what gangsters told their victims just before they murdered them? Or had she seen too many movies?

"There they are!" cried John Gielgud. "That's them ahead."

"Are you certain?" Noël, seated in the back, pressed forward.

"Get over into the left lane, they're turning," ordered Giel-gud, riding tensely in the passenger seat.

"Quit yelling in my ear," snarled Olivier as he gripped the wheel and tried to move his Bentley over. A car horn blared a motorist's objection to being so abruptly cut off.

"Lord above us, be careful, man!" shouted a panicked Giel-gud. "You're going to get us killed."

"Will you shut up?" snapped Olivier. "Let me drive the bloody car."

"If you call this driving…"

"Let us all stay calm," said Noël, taking on the voice of reason from the rear. "It looks as though they're heading into the East End."

"If you're taking a lovely girl like Priscilla out to dinner, why would you take her to the East End?" demanded Olivier.

"The unfathomable mysteries of our homegrown, ill-bred gangsters," reasoned Noël.

"And we are certain this is a good idea?" Olivier was gripping the wheel, leaning forward, eyes fixed on the windscreen. "For my money, it's not a very good idea at all."

"Put it this way, Larry: We are as certain as we can be, which is possibly not at all certain," answered Noël. "However, as members of the Gossip's Bridle Club we are sworn to protect a fellow member."

"When exactly did we swear that?" Olivier demanded.

"Watch the road, Larry," Gielgud said. "They're making a right."

"Where the devil are they going?" Noël asked.

"I will tell you one thing," Gielgud said with the haughtiness that only he could muster. "They're not going to any restaurant we've ever been in."

The darker and narrower the streets—the brick walls on either side of the roadway growing higher against an increasingly dreary and deserted landscape—the more nervous Priscilla became. Not to mention scared.

"Jack, please, tell me where you're taking me." With an unintended note of anguish.

"Now you wouldn't have anyone following us, would you, lass?" Scotch Jack's eyes had fixed on the rearview mirror.

"Why would anyone follow us?"

Jack pulled his eyes back to the way ahead. "Must be my imagination," he said. "Feeling a little paranoid tonight."

"Why, Jack? What have you, of all people, got to be paranoid about?"

"Almost there," he said, dodging her question, slowing to swing the wheel so that the Jag veered into an alleyway. He came to a stop and let out a loud sound, half groan, half howl of despair—at least it was to Priscilla's ears, alarming her even more.

"Out we go," Scotch Jack announced, turning off the engine.

"This isn't a restaurant. What are you doing? What's going on?" Priscilla wasn't even attempting to hide the dread she was feeling.

"Just do as you're told—get out of the bloody car."

Her heart in her throat, Priscilla did as she was told.

CHAPTER NINETEEN

The Fighting Krays

Priscilla positioned herself directly behind Scotch Jack while he smacked his open palm against a studded green door recessed in a brick wall at the end of the alley.

After a couple of impatiently delivered blows, the door swung inward, revealing a hollow-eyed scarecrow in an ill-fitting black suit. The scarecrow grunted and then backed away to allow Scotch Jack to usher Priscilla inside. "Hey there, Kenny," Scotch Jack said to the scarecrow. Kenny grunted some more.

"Good lad, Kenny," Jack said as they made their way along a dim passage that led into a brick-walled service garage reeking of motor oil and exhaust fumes, the overhead lights revealing the silhouettes of three autos and the black hulk of a car engine mounted on a cradle.

A woman's cry echoed from somewhere at the far end. It took Priscilla a moment to adjust to the dimness. Diana Dors, wearing a deep blue evening gown, came into focus. She was tied to a chair and held upright by a big, unshaven fellow, his long hair pushed back from a bone-white forehead.

A second man in shirtsleeves, with rippling muscles out of a bottle of steroids, hovered over Diana, his fist raised. Ronnie Kray, in a black trench coat, leaned forward, watching the muscle guy intently as Priscilla called out in alarm: "Diana!"

Ronnie swung around, breaking into a nasty smile when he saw Priscilla. "There you are," he said. "Arriving in the nick of time."

Priscilla hurried forward, shouting, "Let her alone!"

"What's that?" demanded Ronnie, blocking her way.

Priscilla swallowed hard. "I said let her alone—please."

Ronnie nodded at the steroid guy, who slowly, reluctantly, lowered his fist. Ronnie was wild-eyed, his face pale and glistening, the gangster in a noir thriller come to life in this dank garage while Diana, her lovely face filled with terror, stared beseechingly at Priscilla. Her hands were bound behind her, her bosom heaving out of her gown, her face flushed and streaked with eyeliner and tears.

Ronnie addressed the unshaven fellow beside Diana. "What about it, Danny? You think we should leave Miss Dors alone?"

"Anything you say, boss," Danny growled.

Ronnie's eyes fixed on Priscilla. "I can do that right enough, I can lay off her, no problem. Thing is, though, I need what Diana bloody well won't give me."

"I don't have it," Diana cried. "There is no film—I don't have it!"

Ronnie jerked a thumb at her. "See what I mean?"

"She's right," Priscilla said. "She doesn't have the film."

Confusion, then anger, fought for space on Ronnie's face. "What's this you're talking about then? She doesn't have it? Who does?"

Priscilla reached into the side pocket of her jacket and brought out the reel of eight-millimetre film. "Here it is." She reached out her hand to Ronnie.

He snatched the reel of film from her. "What the hell?" he said. "Where did you get this?"

"Diana gave it to me at Shepperton Studios." The lie rolled out smoothly enough.

"Why didn't you say so?" Ronnie had swung back to Diana.

"She was trying to protect me," Priscilla explained quickly. "I was going to give it to Reggie tonight when I met him for what I thought was a dinner date."

Out of the periphery of her eye, Priscilla could see Scotch Jack a few paces away, looking increasingly jumpy. "Reggie's not going to like this," he mumbled to Ronnie.

"Shut up, Jack!" snapped Ronnie.

"I'm going to untie her," Priscilla said, moving toward Diana. "You've got what you want."

Ronnie studied the film reel in his hand as though not quite sure what to make of it. Diana gave another pleading look as Priscilla stepped behind the chair and saw that the actress's hands were bound with knotted cords. She began to work at the knots. Diana strained to watch, her breath coming in frightened gasps.

A loud bang at the warehouse entrance startled everyone. Reggie Kray, resplendent in a black double-breasted suit that set off his pink tie, lunged out of the darkness. "What the bloody hell?" he yelled, bulldozing his way across the cement floor.

Ronnie's mouth moved around unpleasantly but nothing came out.

Reggie slammed to a stop, confronted by the bizarre tableau set before him, shaking his head in disbelief. He turned to glare at Scotch Jack, who actually seemed to cower. "Didn't I tell you to pick up Miss Tempest and take her to the club?"

"Ronnie said orders had changed," Jack said in a faltering voice.

"Is that right, Ronnie?" Reggie was addressing his brother. "Changed orders?"

"That's right," confirmed Ronnie, thrusting out his chest defiantly. "I changed them."

"Did you? You decided to change them?"

"Maybe I didn't know you were taking the bird to dinner," Ronnie said, his voice in a lower register. "Maybe you should have said something."

"And you're beating up women now, are you? Is that what you've come to?"

Ronnie held up the film reel. "Bitch was going to blackmail me. I had to do what was necessary."

"She gave it back?" Reggie asked.

Ronnie shook his head, smiling deviously. "Your bird..."

Reggie's eyes found Priscilla. "I told you to give it to me."

"He had Diana tied up and he was ordering that muscle-bound lad over there to hit her. What was I supposed to do?" Priscilla didn't bother to hide her anger. "Ronnie is a bully who hates women. You both disgust me."

"I didn't have anything to do with this," Reggie said lamely.

"I don't have to stand here and take your shit." Ronnie's eyes flashed, his hand curling into a fist.

"Yeah, you do, Ronnie," Reggie heatedly countered. "She's right. You're goddamn disgusting." Reggie stepped directly in front of his brother. "You want to hit someone, Ronnie? Is that it? Why don't you try hitting me?"

"Don't tempt me, you bugger." Ronnie's face had darkened. Priscilla was sure he was about to strike his brother. But Reggie moved too fast for him, a blur of fists that put Ronnie down on his knees.

"You think you're tough?" Reggie said nastily, standing over him. "That's what tough is. You ever go behind my back again—"

Before he could finish, Ronnie shrieked and seized his brother around the knees. Caught by surprise, Reggie tumbled back onto the floor. Ronnie, seeing his advantage, sprang on him, attacking with his fists.

Reggie was able to fend off the blows and land a fist against his brother's jaw. Ronnie fell back and now Reggie was on him and the two of them were soon pummelling one another, wrestling across the floor, screaming curses. Scotch Jack stayed where he was, uncertain what to do. The other thugs—scarecrow Kenny, unshaven Danny and the steroid guy—drew away from the fracas as though not wanting to be caught near it.

Diana, her hands unbound, rose unsteadily from the chair. Priscilla took her arm, steadying her when she stumbled. "It'll be fine," Priscilla murmured, not at all sure she wasn't lying through her teeth. "We're going to get out of here."

As they moved across the garage toward the entrance, Priscilla glanced back and saw Ronnie roll away and rise to his knees holding a gun pointed at his brother.

"You bugger," Reggie cried. "Go on, shoot me. Shoot me! That's what you want! Go ahead!"

"Easy, Ronnie." Jack had finally found his voice. "You don't want to do this, lad. You put the gun down now."

Ronnie wasn't listening. "I'm going to shoot you," he yelled at his brother. "I'm going to do it!"

Reggie screamed, "Pull the trigger, you git! You don't have the nerve!"

Priscilla and Diana reached the exit door. Priscilla was apprehensive that Scotch Jack would notice their departure and move to stop them, but Jack and the others were riveted by the drama unfolding between the brothers.

As she reached for the latch, the door opened and Noël Coward, dressed in evening clothes, appeared on the threshold. "There you are, my dear," he said in the same manner in which he would have greeted Priscilla's arrival at the American Bar.

Priscilla was about to say something when the sound of a gunshot resounded through the garage.

CHAPTER TWENTY

Something Different

The gunshot made Noël jump in alarm and issue a yelp. Priscilla had enough of her wits still intact to push him out the door, at the same time taking Diana's hand and yanking her along.

They came into the alley as Gielgud appeared, looking vastly out of place in his perfectly tailored pinstripe suit, eyes popping in amazement. Olivier, hunched anxiously behind the wheel of the Bentley, had the motor running.

"Did I just hear a gunshot?" Gielgud asked in a shocked tone.

"We've got to get out of here," Priscilla said, pulling Diana along with her as she headed for the car.

Gielgud's eyes bulged even more as he took in Diana. "My God, is it Diana Dors?"

She managed a weak smile. "Why, Mr. Gielgud..."

"Dear me, I loved you in *The Unholy Wife*," Gielgud stated admiringly.

Diana beamed.

"Come along, Johnny," announced Noël in a voice of recovered authority. "We can discuss Miss Dors's oeuvre later. For now, we must be gone!"

"What the devil is happening?" demanded Olivier, twisting around as Priscilla, Gielgud and Diana crowded into the back. "Did I just hear a gunshot?"

"Your imagination, dear boy," stated Noël, climbing into the front. "Concentrate on getting us away from this place."

Olivier's face lit with recognition. "Goodness gracious, are you Diana Dors?"

Diana managed a nod as she exclaimed, "Laurence Olivier?"

"Miss Dors, weren't you a revelation in *Yield to the Night*," gushed Olivier.

"For God's sake, Larry, get us moving," Noël ordered.

Olivier turned back around and threw the car into gear. Priscilla saw someone emerge from the garage. Scarecrow Kenny, his mouth hanging open in incredulity, was caught momentarily in the flash of the Bentley's headlights as Olivier sped past. They turned onto a deserted street, Olivier fighting with the wheel as the car careened erratically.

"Heaven's above, Larry!" Noël called. "You're more dangerous than the Krays!"

"I'm driving!" Olivier snapped, as though that would put his passengers at ease.

In the back, Diana turned to Priscilla. "I don't know how to thank you," she said quietly. She spoke to the others. "Thanks to all of you. I never imagined I could be rescued by two of the country's greatest actors."

"Actually, you were rescued by only one of the country's greatest actors," Olivier called out as he drove.

"And one of its worst drivers," Gielgud interjected.

"Don't forget the country's greatest playwright," Priscilla said.

"Did Will Shakespeare play a part in tonight's rescue?" Gielgud asked.

"Mr. Coward! Of course!" Diana said excitedly.

"My apologies," Noël said, "I'm afraid I've not seen either *The Unholy Wife* or *Yield to the Night*, an oversight I plan to rectify at the earliest opportunity."

"Priscilla, darling, what the blazes happened back there?" Olivier asked, thankfully keeping his eyes on the road as he spoke. "We thought you were going to a restaurant."

"I thought so too," Priscilla said. "Instead, I ended up in a garage rescuing Diana and watching one of the Krays shoot his brother."

"Oh good God, you're not serious," exclaimed Olivier.

"I believe Ronnie shot Reggie," explained Diana.

"That certainly puts us into a pretty pickle, doesn't it?" Olivier groaned.

"If a Kray is dead, I'm not certain that's such a bad thing," mused Gielgud. "And let's keep in mind that tonight we've helped rescue not one but two damsels in distress. If all goes as I suspect it might, we will be able to add 'hero' to our already impressive resumes."

"Or 'damned dead fools' if the Krays find out what we've done," Olivier added.

Nobody disagreed with him.

Diana wanted to go home. Priscilla insisted she would be safer spending the night at her flat. With three famous personages of the English theatre alternately cajoling, flattering and, in the case of Olivier, outright flirting, Diana finally agreed. Priscilla's flat it was.

Olivier pulled into Knightsbridge. Priscilla directed him to park in front of her building.

"Are you going to be all right?" Noël asked as the car came to a stop.

"We'll be fine," Priscilla said. "What Diana and I need right now is a good night's sleep."

"A drink would help," Diana added.

"That definitely can be arranged," Priscilla said.

Olivier had twisted around, eyeing Diana with a *flâneur's* hooded, insinuating eyes. "If there is anything else we can do to help, you must let us know," he purred.

"Thank you, sir," said Diana with a slight lowering of her head and a flutter of eyelashes.

"Please, you must call me Larry."

By the time Priscilla got Diana out of the car amid a flurry of farewells, the victim of vicious gangsters had disappeared; a platinum Aglaopheme, the Greek Siren luring men to their doom, had risen in her place, iridescent on a Knightsbridge evening in a floor-length gown.

"Come along," Priscilla directed. "Before you do something you shouldn't."

"Getting mixed up with the Krays, that was something I shouldn't," Diana said. "I'm not so sure Sir Laurence isn't something I should."

Nonetheless, she followed Priscilla inside. As they reached the fourth-floor landing, Priscilla's dowager neighbour, Lady Agatha Potter-Hayes, peered out her door. She gasped when she saw who was with Priscilla. "Diana Dors!" she exclaimed. "Is that you?"

"It is indeed," Priscilla said, fumbling for her latch key. "Diana, I'd like you to meet my friend and neighbour, Lady Agatha Potter-Hayes."

"A pleasure," said Diana, summoning her best movie-star smile.

"What a thrill!" trilled Lady Agatha.

As Priscilla unlocked the door, she had a fleeting thought of Pierre Trudeau inside with more wine and cheese. What would she do then? But the interior of the flat was dark and, to her relief, no Canadian prime minister lurked in the kitchen. She flipped on the lights. Diana took in her surroundings. "Nice," she said.

"Thanks to the Savoy," Priscilla said. "The hotel owns the flat."

Diana flopped onto the sofa. "I am absolutely knackered."

"Being kidnapped and assaulted will do that to you," Priscilla said.

"They truly are a couple of bastards. With Reggie I might have stood a chance, but with Ronnie...well, if you hadn't shown up...my guardian angel..." Then a smile: "That drink you promised?"

"You have a choice: white wine or Stoli," Priscilla said.

"Stoli, lots of it!"

Priscilla went into the kitchen and opened the freezer where the vodka bottle occupied a place of honour. She poured vodka into two tumblers, added ice and brought the glasses back into the sitting room where Diana had stretched out on the sofa. She eagerly accepted the drink, taking deep gulps. "I don't suppose you have a ciggie."

"Sorry," Priscilla said, perching on the edge of her armchair, sipping at her drink.

Diana sat up, holding her glass in two hands. "This is a fine mess, isn't it?"

"Reggie has his film so they should leave you alone," Priscilla said.

Diana made a face. "Don't be too sure. I suppose the police have been around, that right prick Nipper Read. He must have given you the film."

"Let's just say Reggie demanded I get the film back and that's what I did. The Krays don't need to know more than that."

"Look, I don't know if Reggie is alive or dead. But if he's alive, it won't be long before he starts to think about it and begins to suspect that it was all too easy. Why would I admit to what I've been denying, filming Ronnie, and then give you the film?"

"Maybe to prevent what happened tonight," Priscilla suggested.

"Or maybe Reggie, alive, paranoid as he is, starts to think that I didn't give it to you, and that maybe the coppers got on to me. As soon as that happens..." She left the sentence unfinished, draining the remainder of the vodka. She nodded at Priscilla. "What's more, Ronnie may have the film, but he also knows that we know what's on it. He starts to think about that and decides he doesn't want witnesses. He comes after me—and you, too. That's despite what I've been hearing."

Priscilla did not like the sound of that—the sound of anything Diana was saying. "What are you hearing?"

"That Reggie is crazy about you." She punctuated the sentence with a raised eyebrow.

"Believe me, I've done nothing to encourage him," Priscilla said defensively. Nothing except show up at his pub unannounced.

"But then Reggie is crazy about a lot of women. He's crazy about me, until he meets Skye and then he's crazy about her. Now that Skye is gone, here you are to fill what he views as the empty space in his broken heart that's been there ever since his wife died."

"Is that what it is with him?"

Diana shrugged. "That's what he says. He tells you he's broken-hearted. But that's crap."

"Why do you say that?"

"To have a broken heart you need a heart to start with," Diana said. "Reggie doesn't have one."

She waved her glass at Priscilla. "Do you suppose I could have another one of these?"

When Priscilla came back from the kitchen, Diana was on her feet, out of her high heels, the gown around her ankles, naked except for gossamer panties. "It's good to be out of that," she murmured, on her tiptoes, arms raised, stretching a body the colour of ivory. "I'm getting so fat," she said huskily.

"You look great," Priscilla said.

Diana's eyes were on her as she took the glass.

"Thanks," she said, stretching on the sofa.

Priscilla resumed her seat, feeling her cheeks burning when her cheeks should not have been burning. Diana drained most of the vodka and regarded Priscilla with sleepy eyes. "Wow," she said, her voice slightly slurred, "did you hear what Lord Olivier said in the car? He likes my work. He appreciates *me* as an actress."

"He appreciates more than just your work," Priscilla said.

Diana grinned. "I don't know if I could shag him, you know, an older man. He's still kind of sexy, though... I could close my eyes and think of Heathcliff..." She laughed and finished her glass.

Priscilla decided a change of subject was in order. "When we talked out at Shepperton, you said something about suspecting Pierre Trudeau in Skye's murder. Were you serious?"

Diana took her time answering. "It's possible," she conceded. "Anything is possible, I suppose. He was seeing her the last time he was in London. Then when he came back for whatever conference he is attending, he called her—and called her a lot. She told me he was very jealous, possessive. But I don't know if that's true. From what I hear, he was seeing lots of girls. Not the jealous type, if you ask me. Why the interest in him?"

He hadn't shown any jealousy with her, Priscilla thought, slightly miffed, despite herself. And more and more it seemed she was only one in a long line of conquests. Women all over town falling into his bed. Out loud she said, "I was wondering if the police might be thinking much the same as you."

"If it is him, then he's got nothing to worry about, right?"

"No?"

144

"Come on, Priscilla. Powerful blokes like prime ministers, they get away with just about anything. The establishment protects them, particularly when it comes to women. They'll make people like us suspects right quick. But I'm willing to bet our Canadian friend gets a pass."

Priscilla tried another tack. "What about David Merrick?"

"What about him?"

"Is it true he was going to bring your show to America—until he met Skye?"

Diana smirked and shook her head. "And then in a fit of rage I strangled Skye in her dressing room?"

"That's been suggested," Priscilla said.

Diana stretched her body on the sofa and yawned. "You know what? I am too tired to rally the energy it takes to tell you how ridiculous that is. Where do you want me to sleep tonight?"

"You can have the sofa, how's that?"

Diana put her glass aside. "You're so kind, Priscilla, you really are—even if you do think I'm a killer."

"I think no such thing," Priscilla protested. Stretched out before her like this, Diana certainly did not look like a killer. Anything but.

Priscilla rose and went to the closet and got the extra duvet she used for the odd guest who wasn't sleeping in her bed. Except Diana was no longer on the sofa when she came back. Priscilla found her in the bedroom, in the bed. She had discarded the panties.

"Plenty of room," she said.

After Priscilla got out of her clothes and slipped in beside her, Diana pressed her warm body against hers and kissed her mouth. "Kind Priscilla," she murmured.

Well, thought Priscilla, this is different…

CHAPTER TWENTY-ONE

The Disappearance

Diana was gone in the morning. As was the blue evening gown and the high heels. She had, however, left the panties behind.

Movie stars, prime ministers, even the occasional rag-tag reporter, everyone was gone by the time Priscilla awoke; departing quickly, silently, as though not wanting to own up to the events of the night before. Leaving Priscilla a bit disappointed and, in Diana's case, concerned.

With the Krays out there, where would Diana go to be safe? She had left no note, no sign beyond the empty vodka glass and memories of—what could she say?—an interesting night, full of first-time adventures. Yes, that was certainly what she could say about it. A few other things as well, but she would think about all that later.

For now, she had to get to work and already she was running late. Saving stars of the stage and screen from the clutches of gangsters was one thing, but she still had to get to her day job on time.

Priscilla showered, made herself coffee, put on her favourite jersey minidress and knee-high boots, and applied makeup, studying herself in the mirror. She decided that whatever had unfolded last night, it had worked to provide her with a good night's sleep. A refreshed, rather attractive young lady, set to face whatever challenges the day might bring, smiled back at her.

Challenges such as the telephone ringing in the other room.

"Where are you?" demanded Susie Gore-Langton.

"Susie, you've called my flat, where do you think I am?" answered Priscilla in an exasperated voice.

"Okay, but it's a nightmare here and the day has just begun. All hell is breaking loose. Mr. Banville wants to see you. Mr. Merrick came around looking for you. And Percy Hoskins has phoned a couple of times."

"I'm on my way in." Priscilla could already feel her stomach issuing furious objections.

"Please hurry," said Susie in the pleading voice that always worked so effectively when it came to irritating Priscilla.

She was gathering her shoulder bag when the knock came at her door. Diana returning for the forgotten panties?

Not quite.

Detective Chief Superintendent Nipper Read was all rosy cheeks and cheery smiles in his three-piece suit topped by a fedora—the personification of the working English copper, Priscilla thought.

"Good morning, Miss Tempest. I was hoping we might have a word. Do you mind if I come in?"

"I'm really in a hurry, Superintendent," Priscilla said breathlessly. "Can't we do this some other time?"

"Won't take a moment." Read was all smiles as he stepped inside, removing his hat.

"I must say I'm a bit disappointed not to have heard from you," he said once Priscilla had closed the door.

"I did as you asked. I gave Ronnie Kray the film," Priscilla asserted.

Read looked surprised. "When did this happen, may I ask?"

"Last night," Priscilla said.

"When you had dinner with Reggie?"

"No, when I was taken to a garage somewhere in the East End where Ronnie Kray had Diana Dors tied to a chair, about to beat her to a pulp."

Read's wrinkled brow pushed the cheeriness off his face. "Tell me what happened."

"Reggie showed up, furious. The two of them got into a fight—and there was a gunshot."

"A gunshot?"

"I didn't actually see it, but Ronnie may have shot his brother."

Superintendent Read solemnly took in this news. "And what of Miss Dors?"

"She stayed with me last night. This morning, she left."

Read eyed the duvet Priscilla thankfully had left on the sofa before he asked, "And where is Miss Dors now?"

"I'm not sure, but I assume she's returned to her home." Silently, Priscilla prayed that was indeed where Diana had gone.

"We will check the hospitals, of course. But if one of the Krays was admitted overnight with a gunshot wound, I should have heard about it by now."

"Unless Reggie is dead," Priscilla said.

"Yes, there is that possibility," Read conceded.

"In that case, you won't be needing me any longer."

That returned the merriment to Read's face. "Perhaps not so fast, Miss Tempest. Let's see what I can find out about what went on between the brothers last night."

"You wanted me to hand the film to the Krays. I did that."

"Additionally, I told you I need you to provide information that would help me bring the two brothers to justice."

"I've done that too," Priscilla said. "You can arrest Ronnie for shooting his brother—or killing him, if that's what happened."

"I would not make the mistake of underestimating the Krays, Miss Tempest. Until they are sitting in jail cells or lying in a morgue, I may continue to require your help."

"I don't want to have anything more to do with them." Priscilla, standing firm in the face of police authority.

To her chagrin, her firm stand didn't appear to have the least effect on Read. "I'm sure you don't, Miss Tempest—but you will. In the meantime, I will do my best to track down Miss Dors. I'd like her to bring charges against Ronnie Kray."

"She won't want to do that." Anger was bubbling up inside Priscilla. This was all so unfair.

"She will not have a choice if she wishes to stay out of further trouble." Read carefully replaced his fedora on his head.

"The same goes for you, Miss Tempest," Read added as he headed for the door. "Depending on the outcome of this shooting incident and of our ongoing investigation, the two of you may be called upon as witnesses."

It was all Priscilla could do to stop herself from issuing a loud groan of desperation. Here was another opportunity for Mr. Banville to bring a swift end to her career at the Savoy.

The unemployed heroine who brought down the Krays.

Detective Buster Burt was about to light a cigarette when Superintendent Read emerged from the block of flats where Priscilla Tempest resided. He quickly threw the cigarette out the window. Nipper didn't like the smell of tobacco in the car and Nipper was the boss, wasn't he? Yes, sir, Nipper Read, legendary copper—what he said was the way it was done.

Nipper, who didn't even resemble a detective. He was too damned short for one thing—Buster had heard the rumours that Nipper lied about his height in order to join the force. A little goddamn gnome is what he was, with his round, perpetually sunny face and that bloody bow tie.

A gnome in a bow tie! That wasn't a copper!

Buster hated Nipper and his bow ties and his neat-as-you-please three-piece suits, hated the bugger with passion born of jealousy and envy. Not so much envy, when Buster got right down to it, as plain jealousy.

Buster dismissed such thoughts and arranged a welcoming expression as Nipper got in and closed the door. Nipper always smelled so damned clean, like he just got out of the bath.

"How did it go?" Buster asked, polite as you please.

"She says Ronnie Kray has the film."

"She's made contact with him, right?"

"Miss Tempest reports that she was taken to a garage somewhere in the East End where Ronnie was holding the actress Diana Dors against her will. Further, when Reggie arrived and saw what was going on, he was furious and the two brothers got into a fight."

"The Krays fighting? That's not like them, is it?"

"Ronnie Kray is off his rocker at the best of times. He has a hair-trigger temper to boot. Anyone gets in his way when he goes off is fair game, even his brother."

"Any idea who came out on top?"

Read had a notebook out on his lap and was writing in it. "If Miss Tempest is to be believed, it seems Ronnie ended up shooting Reggie."

"You're not serious."

"I am indeed," Read said, continuing to write in his notebook.

"Hard to believe," Buster said.

"I agree," said Read. He put the notebook away. "When we're back at headquarters, get to work and check the local hospitals. See if there were any overnight reports of gunshot wounds. They may have taken him to a hospital under another name."

"Or would they have taken him to a hospital at all?"

"Let's find out," Read said.

"On it, Chief," Buster said as he turned the car into the Knightsbridge traffic. Naturally, he would do the necessary grunt work, the boring crap that came along with being a copper. Meanwhile, Nipper Read stood by to receive all the glory.

Little wonder he hated Nipper Read.

And his bloody bow ties.

CHAPTER TWENTY-TWO

Une femme scandaleuse

Susie was beside herself by the time Priscilla arrived at 205. "*He* keeps calling for you," she gasped.

"Who's been calling?" As if Priscilla didn't know.

"Mr. *Banville*." The words whispered as though saying them too loud would mean arrest and torture.

Priscilla steeled herself. "I'm on my way."

Heart in her mouth, the omnipresent feeling of impending doom—the usual state whenever she was summoned to the Place of Execution. The first hurdle, as always, was the nasty El Sid. Sidney was a knob, no question, but he could not end her life at the Savoy. Beyond the double doors that marked the entrance to the dragon's lair, that was where the career-ending danger lay.

If Mr. Banville was at his desk, there was trouble ahead; standing, there might be trouble, but there was still a small chance of survival. At least that was her thinking, however flawed it might be.

Banville *was* at his desk as Priscilla entered, not a muscle moving, which was a bad sign—a very bad sign. She closed the door before making the long march to stand docilely before him; the unpopular court jester called to account before her liege.

"Good morning, sir," Priscilla said brightly, as though nothing in the world could be wrong.

Banville frowned and looked at his watch, an early indication that plenty could be wrong with the world. "I've been trying to get hold of you for the last hour and a half." Icicles hung from Banville's tone.

"My apologies, sir. You asked me to speak to Miss Dors. I'm afraid I became caught up with her."

Sort of the truth, Priscilla surmised. Getting caught up with Diana Dors was one way to put it.

Banville appeared unpersuaded. "Nonetheless, Miss Tempest, when you are summoned to this office, I expect you to make every effort to be here in a timely fashion."

"I will endeavor to do better, sir."

"Make sure that you do."

Banville gestured with his hand. "Please, Miss Tempest, have a seat."

The general manager of the Savoy had just asked her to sit down. That had never happened before. What did it mean? Priscilla was at a loss as to what to think. Gingerly, she perched on the chair in front of his desk, making sure not to get too comfortable in case Banville came to his senses and ordered her to resume standing.

"I am asking you to please exercise the utmost discretion with what I am about to discuss with you." The gaze he fixed on her was piercing. "What I am about to say to you must never leave this room. Is that clear?"

"Yes, sir, it is," Priscilla said, her mind in a whirl of confusion.

"Mrs. Banville," Banville pronounced, as though that explained everything and nothing more need be said. Daisee Banville, Priscilla thought, the beautiful, spoiled American wife of her boss. That was Daisee with two *e*'s, as Daisee was at pains to insist.

Banville paused to nervously clear his throat again. His gaze was no longer quite so piercing, drifting to the window on the far side of his office.

"Mrs. Banville has decided that she requires some time alone." His hand quickly covered his mouth to mask a choking cough.

"To that end," he continued, "we have mutually agreed to a separation. I have moved out of our house and, for the time being, am staying here at the hotel."

Priscilla could hardly believe what she was hearing. Why was Banville confiding his marital difficulties to *her*?

"Mrs. Banville and myself view our relationship as a very private matter and naturally we don't wish to draw any untoward attention from the press. I am hoping you will be able to manage your contacts so that this unfortunate turn in our marriage does not get into the gossip columns."

"I will certainly do my best," Priscilla said, immediately wondering how she was ever to accomplish that.

Banville cleared his throat, coughing into his sleeve. "Dear me, I'm not sure what's wrong with me today." He blinked repeatedly and, for an instant, Priscilla thought she saw a tear in his eye. No, that couldn't be. General managers like Clive Banville did not cry in front of their employees. As though reading her mind, Banville straightened, continuing to gaze out the window.

"There is more to this, I'm afraid."

"Sir?"

"I—I am informed by reliable sources that there are... rumours, scurrilous rumours, I might add..." His voice dropped away.

"I'm sorry, what kind of rumours?"

"I'm convinced none of it can be true but apparently there is talk in certain circles that Mrs. Banville has been seen in the company of the Lord Snowdon."

"Antony Armstrong-Jones, the husband of HRH the Princess Margaret?" Priscilla couldn't help adding, if only for the sake of clarity.

"Have you heard something?" he barked out, as though Priscilla should be drawn and quartered if she had.

"Nothing, sir, not a thing," Priscilla answered hastily. "I thought Mrs. Banville and HRH the Princess Margaret were good friends."

"Notwithstanding these dreadful rumours, my wife and the princess have had a falling out, unfortunately, and are no longer speaking."

"I didn't know that," Priscilla said, when in fact she did.

"I must confess to you, Miss Tempest, I am at my wit's end. I cannot go to Major O'Hara. He's far too close to the Royal Family and the sort of people who could put an end to my career if this got out. The general manager of this establishment cannot afford even a whiff of scandal. The person who runs a great hotel such as the Savoy must maintain a pristine reputation."

"I understand that, sir, but at the same time I am not at all sure how I can help."

"The requirements for an employee such as yourself are not so rigorous as they are for a person in my position. You already are—what is it the French say?—*une femme scandaleuse*."

Priscilla blanched, speechless. What had Banville heard about her that would lead him to believe she was a scandalous woman? Even if it were true—and if you looked at things a certain way there could be a modicum of truth—who would have told him such a thing?

Seeing the reaction on her face, Banville quickly waved a dismissive hand. "Please, Miss Tempest, don't be alarmed. What I say is said as something of a compliment. It frees you to help me in ways that others cannot."

Not exactly a ringing endorsement, Priscilla thought. Nonetheless, she would take a compliment from the general manager where she could get it.

"As I stated previously," he continued, "I need you to do everything you can to avoid scandal and keep my situation out of the papers. At the same time, I would like you to determine the truth of this... gossip about my wife and Lord Snowdon." He looked at Priscilla with an anxiousness she had not seen before. "Do you think you are in a position to do that, Miss Tempest?"

"I could try, sir, certainly," Priscilla said reluctantly. "If you're sure that this is how you wish to proceed."

"I must know," he said in a low voice. "If I know, then I can make decisions as to how to move forward with my life."

"If I may say, Mr. Banville—"

"I'd prefer you didn't, Miss Tempest," Banville said, cutting her off. "Right now, I'd like you to do as I ask. I understand that there are certain lectures a woman can deliver to a man in these instances, but I do not wish to hear them. Do I make myself clear?"

"You do, sir." Priscilla felt as though she had just received a slap. A light slap but a slap nonetheless.

Banville plucked a card out of his desk drawer and wrote on it. "This is a private number for my suite where you can reach me with any news if I am not in the office." He handed her the card. The previous emotion he had shown had disappeared. His face was like a block of ice. "I appreciate your help."

Priscilla glanced down at the card and nodded.

"That will be all for now," he said.

As she rose and started to leave, he called to her. "Incidentally..."

She paused at the door. "Sir?"

"Is there any reason why the Canadian High Commissioner would call me looking for you?"

Her stomach did an all-too-familiar drop. "It could be he wants to arrange some sort of press event," she ventured.

"Yes, well, he's called me. I have no idea why. But get back to him, will you?"

"Very good, sir," Priscilla said.

CHAPTER TWENTY-THREE

Canada Calling

Ignoring Susie's eagerly inquiring eyes, Priscilla closed her office door and sank onto the sofa against the wall across from her desk. Her head had renewed its pounding to make certain she understood she was once again overstressed as she attempted to grapple with what her boss had requested—*demanded?*—of her. And more to the point—and the main reason for the pounding head—the Canadian whatever-he-was was phoning Banville. It certainly wasn't to book a press event. Visions of him threatening her with exposure, the tramp—or *une femme scandaleuse,* if you preferred—who slept with the prime minister of his country—*twice!*

But then how could Banville fire her when he had just enlisted her to investigate his wife's reported infidelities? With Antony Armstrong-Jones—of all people! Was this Daisee Banville's revenge for being snubbed by her former friend, Princess Margaret? Was it even true? And how was she ever going to find out? *Une femme scandaleuse* indeed!

As she rubbed at her temples, trying to decide what to do next, one of her trio of desk phones decided it for her by starting up discordant ringing. She picked up the receiver. "Savoy Press Office," she said in the formal voice she reserved for speaking to the public. "Priscilla Tempest here. How may I help you?"

"Ah, there you are Miss Tempest. It's Tommy Teasdale calling," said the clipped, pleasant voice on the other end of the line.

"You don't know me, but I'm the Canadian High Commissioner here in London."

"High Commissioner?"

"It's a funny way of saying I'm Canada's ambassador to Britain," Teasdale clarified. "I talked earlier to your Mr. Banville."

"Yes, he told me."

Her stomach did not so much drop this time as it twisted into a tight knot. Why did she ever answer a telephone? There was never anything but trouble on the line.

Summoning her most professional voice, she asked, "What can I do for you, Mr. Teasdale?"

"It's most important that we get together for a chat," Teasdale said.

"Can we not do it over the phone?" Priscilla asked, hoping against hope.

"As a fellow Canadian, my very strong advice is that we meet in person," Teasdale said. Any previous pleasantness had evaporated.

"Yes, if that's what you would like," Priscilla said.

"Shall we say two o'clock this afternoon at Canada House?"

Priscilla dimly heard a voice from somewhere outside her body saying yes. Couldn't possibly have been *her* voice.

Oh God. It was.

Grecian columns towering toward the heavens, designed to make mere mortals such as Priscilla feel like mere mortals, flanked either side of the Canada House entrance on Trafalgar Square. Nearby, competing for attention, was Lord Nelson's fifty-two-metre-high column celebrating the Battle of Trafalgar, Nelson's victory over Napoleon's navy in 1805. In case anyone should attempt to mess with the sea lord, four bronze lions stood guard around the base of the column. Priscilla could only shake her head at the imperial majesty of it all.

Inside Canada House, a great hall fit for the passage of kings and gods, the echoing sound of her boots against marble broke the solemnity. Here was the majesty of empire in all its Greek revival glory. Curious, thought Priscilla, given that Canada was the least imperial of countries, its glories muted; a big place for what was in essence a small country, Priscilla decided.

"Impressive, don't you think?" said Tommy Teasdale, his eyes taking in the width and breadth of the hall as he shook Priscilla's hand.

"Immense definitely," Priscilla said. Teasdale dropped her hand swiftly, as if getting too close to such an interloper to these stately halls, in knee-high boots no less, was not a good idea.

"A chill runs down my spine every time I enter this place," he added.

Teasdale's snowy white hair and splendidly aged face fit in nicely here, Priscilla thought: the pin-striped god presiding over an insular, marbled world of diplomacy. Much more incongruous was his hastily adopted role of impromptu guide.

"The same fellow who built the British Museum put this place together around 1824," Teasdale explained. "The Royal College of Physicians used to be here. We acquired the building in 1923 and chiselled 'Canada' in big letters on the front. We've been banging about in here ever since."

Teasdale opened a massive oak door. "I thought we'd be more comfortable in here," he said, stepping aside to allow Priscilla into a high-ceilinged chamber, its ivory walls matching a pair of gracefully curving facing sofas. Teasdale closed the door behind him. "Please," he said, "take a seat."

Priscilla sat on one of the sofas while Teasdale settled on the other, crossing his legs, as though posed for an official photograph. "Here we are," he said.

"Yes, here we are," said Priscilla, not knowing what this was about but having her terrible suspicions.

"First of all, you should know that the prime minister has left London and returned to Canada." Teasdale spoke formally, as though reading from a prepared text.

"I trust he enjoyed his stay with us at the Savoy," Priscilla said.

A cocked eyebrow was Teasdale's only reaction. "The prime minister has been called back ahead of schedule for pending legislation that needs his attention."

"It's too bad he had to leave early." And in fact, Priscilla found herself somewhat disappointed that Pierre hadn't at least taken the time to say goodbye.

"What I've just told you, that is the story we have released today to explain the prime minister's early departure," Teasdale went on. His veteran diplomat's face hardened. "The truth is, we sent the prime minister home to avoid possible scandal."

"Scandal?" The word seemed to choke in Priscilla's throat.

"Yes, scandal, Miss Tempest." Spoken as though Teasdale had just noticed the scarlet letter branded on her forehead.

"If I may be frank—and under the circumstances, I have no choice—we acted out of concern that the prime minister's association with you was about to be leaked to the press."

Priscilla's mouth had gone dry. No words would come out. Besides, she couldn't think of words to say. Nothing appropriate anyway. No use protesting innocence since there was no innocence to protest.

Teasdale filled the silence. "Let me say that the prime minister is a single man and is certainly entitled to involve himself with whomever he chooses. Do you agree, Miss Tempest?"

"How could I not?" Priscilla managed to say.

"However, the last thing we desire is press stories concerning his liaisons. Such stories would undoubtedly overshadow his participation at the Commonwealth Conference, his meetings with Britain's prime minister and, of course, the Queen, not to mention the immense contributions to Canada's international standing he has made during the past ten days."

"That's certainly understandable."

"I believe we have successfully placed a clamp on any unwanted gossip about the prime minister's activities this past week. Yet there remains one lingering aspect to all this that has me—I suppose the word I would use is...*concerned.*"

"And what aspect is that?" Priscilla asked, feeling stirrings of irritation at Teasdale's bureaucratic tone.

"You, Miss Tempest," the High Commissioner declared, unfolding his legs and leaning forward as though to emphasize the point.

Again, Priscilla was left speechless, fighting to make sure that Teasdale didn't see her with her jaw dropped open.

"I am particularly concerned about statements you may have made to Scotland Yard detectives concerning the prime minister's possible connection to a certain Miss Skye Kane," Teasdale went on. "These statements were then recounted to certain ears at 10 Downing Street before being relayed to me. From what I'm told, your so-called revelations have resulted in suspicions on the part of Scotland Yard investigators that somehow the prime minister might be involved in Miss Kane's death."

Priscilla found her voice enough to declare, "I never said any such thing to the police. What's more, I highly doubt they would take seriously the idea that the prime minister of Canada could be a murder suspect."

"I agree that is most likely the case." Teasdale appeared to somewhat relax, leaning back on the sofa. "Nonetheless, even the hint of association with the unsolved murder of a London showgirl would create a great number of difficulties that the government, as well as myself, wish to avoid."

"Believe me, I have no desire for any of this to become public," Priscilla said.

"Then can I assume that you do not intend to go to the press with your story?"

Priscilla didn't bother to hide her dismay. "No, of course not. Is *that* what you're thinking?"

"That has been suggested as a possibility," countered Teasdale.

"Is that what Pierre—er—the prime minister told you?"

"The prime minister is unaware of our conversation today and has not said anything. I, and others here at the high commission, are acting in what we trust is his best interest."

"To be honest with you, Mr. Teasdale," Priscilla said, feeling she was now on firmer ground and therefore could more easily summon an authoritative voice, "all sorts of reporters have been trying to find out about your prime minister's activities in London. I'm amazed at how much he was able to get around. Shocked, actually."

"I'm afraid I wouldn't disagree with you," Teasdale said.

Further strengthened, Priscilla continued, "I've done my best to ensure the papers don't uncover any names, including mine. Believe me, the last thing I want is for my name to be associated with the prime minister. It would mean the end of my job at the Savoy. Now that Mr. Trudeau has returned home, I can only imagine any interest will wane, which would be good news for you, I'm sure, and certainly for me."

"What you tell me is most encouraging, Miss Tempest. I take it I have your word that you have no intention of pursuing this matter further."

"I repeat, Mr. Teasdale: It is the last thing I want." Particularly since Pierre didn't think enough of her to phone before he left. Should she be hurt? She shouldn't be. But she was. Sort of.

"Then let us pray we have both successfully done our jobs and the storm has passed."

Teasdale rose to his feet, the signal for Priscilla to do the same. He shook her hand. "Thank you for coming over. If you don't mind, it's probably better if I don't walk you out."

"No need. I can see myself out."

Priscilla had reached the door and was about to open it when Teasdale called out to her. "Miss Tempest..."

"Yes?"

"You should know, the prime minister quite liked you."

Quite liked her? Priscilla forced a smile. "He appears to have *quite* liked a lot of people while in London." To say the least, Priscilla thought.

Teasdale looked as though someone had bolted the smile to his face.

CHAPTER TWENTY-FOUR

Buster

When he said he needed to talk to them, they wanted him to come to their pub, but Buster Burt wasn't having any of it. It was then arranged to meet in the evening at an East End garage they operated on the side. That way, Buster figured, if anyone asked questions, he could always say he was there inquiring about service for his car.

He found the garage without much trouble and parked in the lane behind. He entered via a rear door into the service area, the one or two overhead lights throwing off deep shadows so that, for a moment, he failed to see the two brothers smoking near a work bench, dapper in their identical bespoke suits. The shadows played on their features so that their bruised and swollen faces looked particularly ghoulish. Reggie's arm was in a sling.

"There you are, Buster," Reggie said. Neither brother moved. Buster had to go to them.

"What happened to you two?" Buster asked.

"We ran into a wall," said Ronnie.

"Looks like it," Buster said.

"Then Ronnie shot me," Reggie said, lifting the arm in a sling as if offering it as evidence.

"Just winged him," Ronnie said with a nasty smile. "No big deal, right Reggie?"

"I don't know about that, Ronnie. Your twin brother shoots you... What do you say, Buster, is that a big deal or not?"

"My brother never shot me," Buster said. "Growing up, the prick was content to beat the crap out of me from time to time."

"A right bastard our Ronnie," Reggie said, as though this was the natural state of affairs.

"Come on, Reggie, give us a smile. I'm not such a bad bloke," Ronnie asserted.

Reggie did not smile.

Buster studied the two brothers, not sure whether they were kidding around. "You boys," he said. "I can't ever figure you."

"That's the thing, Buster," Reggie said, dropping what was left of his cigarette to the concrete floor and grinding it with the toe of one highly polished shoe. "No one can figure us. That's the way we like it."

"We can't figure ourselves most of the time," Ronnie said with a mirthless laugh.

"Except we're brothers," Reggie said. "And at the end of the day that's what counts."

"All that counts," put in Ronnie.

"Even when one of us shoots the other," Reggie said.

They both broke into brittle laughter while Buster remained stony faced, not for the first time understanding what a pair of nutters he had to deal with—and not for the first time feeling pangs of regret that he was dealing with them at all.

"Okay, Buster, you wanted to see us so here we are," said Reggie, growing serious. "Taking time out from our busy schedule to talk to a member of law enforcement." He fished a pack of cigarettes from the inside pocket of his suit jacket.

"Always willing to co-operate with our friends at Scotland Yard," Ronnie said with a smirk.

"For your information, you've also got a few enemies at the Yard, gentlemen—and as it happens, I am working with one of them."

Reggie took his time using a gold lighter to fire up his cigarette before he said, "Yeah, we're aware of Nipper. That bastard is rightly named—always nipping at our heels."

"A tosser," said Ronnie. "But he's got nothing on us."

"I wouldn't be so sure about that," said Buster.

Reggie eyed him narrowly through a veil of smoke. "What are you getting at, Buster?"

"Apparently, the two of you recently took it upon yourselves to hold a certain Miss Diana Dors against her will and threaten her with bodily harm."

"Now who would say a thing like that?" Ronnie was laser focused on Buster.

"Could be a certain bird who happened to be present and witnessed the whole thing, that's who," Buster answered. He pointed a finger at Reggie. "Someone you've been seeing and maybe shouldn't be seeing."

"Who might that be?" Reggie's tone had gone cold. If Buster allowed himself to read that tone in a certain way, he might conclude it was heavy with threat.

That made Buster nervous, but knowing he had the goods, he stood his ground: "A bird named Priscilla Tempest? Have I got that name right, Reggie?"

The expression on Reggie's face remained neutral. "I don't know, have you?"

"Yeah, I believe I have, seeing as how Nipper's got her working for him. Kind of a confidential informant, you might say. She's the one who told him what was done to the Dors bird, possibly at this very location."

Reggie dragged on his cigarette and didn't say anything.

"You have a prominent star of the screen being kidnapped and threatened, it kind of upsets everyone," Buster went on. "Not like it's someone anonymous no one gives a shit about."

Ronnie gave his brother a hard look before he snarled, "I knew she was trouble as soon as I laid eyes on her."

Reggie ignored his brother and addressed Buster: "You sure about this?"

Buster nodded. "Who do you think provided the bird with that film Ronnie was looking for?"

"Jesus Christ, the coppers had that film?" Ronnie was no longer looking so smug.

"There's more," reported Buster, suddenly feeling a lot more confident and in control. "Nipper is looking for Diana Dors high and low so she can bring charges against Ronnie."

"What do you mean, he's *looking* for her?" demanded Reggie. "Can't he find her?"

"That's the thing, she seems to have disappeared—I wondered if you boys might have had something to do with that."

"Nothing to do with us," said Reggie.

"This is a fine cock-up, isn't it?" Ronnie said to Reggie, sounding to Buster's ears somewhat lost. "What are we going to do?"

"For starters, we get on to Diana Dors," Reggie said, taking command. "Find her before Nipper does."

"What about the Priscilla bird?" Ronnie asked. "She's working for the coppers. What are you going to do about that?"

"I'll take care of her," Reggie said. He looked at the two men. "Let's get on with it."

Ronnie began moving away, but Buster remained where he was. Reggie gave him a sharp look. "What?"

When Buster didn't move, Reggie smiled knowingly. "Yeah, that's it," he said.

He reached in his inside jacket pocket and withdrew an envelope. He tossed the envelope to Buster who grabbed for it, fumbled, nearly dropped it.

"You keep a close eye on Nipper for us," Reggie ordered. "You hear anything, anything at all, you get in touch. Understand?"

Buster nodded. "That's what you pay me for, isn't it?"

"Yeah, Buster, that's what it is all right."

Buster held the envelope, liking the weight of it, but as he watched the brothers disappear together into the dimness, he began to suspect that the money in the envelope might not be nearly enough to cover what he had set in motion.

CHAPTER TWENTY-FIVE

An English Country Cottage

"They stopped him at the airport!" Susie announced melo-dramatically as soon as Priscilla entered 205.

"Stopped who?"

"David Merrick! He was trying to leave the country. Mr. Bogans drove Mr. Merrick to the airport and no sooner was he out of the car than the police arrived. Mr. Merrick yelled and screamed that he had been exonerated and allowed to leave, but they took him away anyway."

"Well, it looks like the police haven't exonerated him," Priscilla said dryly.

"But do you really think Mr. Merrick is the killer?"

"Obviously the police still suspect he is."

As soon as Susie returned to her desk, Priscilla picked up her phone.

"What do you want?" snarled El Sid when he came on the line.

"I need Mr. Banville's home address, please."

"And why would you want that?"

"Mrs. Banville has asked me to send her some information," Priscilla answered quickly.

"What sort of information?"

"Sidney, that's none of your business," Priscilla snapped, for once feeling very much in control. "How would you like me to inform Mrs. Banville of this conversation?"

"You should call Mrs. Banville." Sidney, making one last attempt to maintain control.

"Sidney, I'm calling you." Brusque and demanding. Priscilla was enjoying this immensely.

A good deal of impatient exhaling of air on Sidney's part followed. Then: "Do you want the main house or the cottage?"

The cottage? Priscilla thought. What cottage? "Better give me both," Priscilla said to him.

"She's spending a lot of time there—at the Grange."

"The Grange...?"

"Endless remodelling. It's become an obsession with her. God knows why."

"Give me that address."

"I'll bet it has to do with the renovation."

"Sidney," Priscilla said insistently, "the address."

He gave a resigned sigh. "It's not far from Chipping Campden in the Cotswolds."

The late afternoon traffic out of London was a horror, but once Priscilla got her trusty pale yellow Morris Minor convertible off Marylebone Road and onto the M40, it thinned and she reached the outskirts of Chipping Campden in two hours.

She had to stop at a pub in Blockley to ask directions so that it was nearly dark by the time she found the address El Sid had given her.

A honey-coloured, pitched-roof stone cottage with a lovely view of the rolling green Gloucestershire hills was set off the roadway and surrounded by a stone wall that looked as though it had been around since medieval times. Priscilla parked down the road and then walked back, trying to decide what to do next. Was this Daisee Banville's love nest? Or merely the country reno that kept her occupied while her husband oversaw life at the

Savoy? The cottage stood in darkness. It didn't look as though Daisee was in residence.

Standing in a lane framed by the stone wall, bursts of wild-flowers clinging along its sides, Priscilla breathed deeply, thinking that at this point she had nothing to lose—except everything. She crossed to a wooden door built into the wall. She tried the latch. The door swung open and Priscilla found herself in the back garden. Flowerpots were set along a flagstone walk. A round table surrounded by four wooden folding chairs looked out of place in the midst of this wilderness of plants.

She moved to the end of the garden. One of the cottage's casement windows had been left open. She pulled at the edge of the window frame and it opened further outward, enough so that she might be able to squeeze through. The question was, should she?

If Daisee Banville discovered her breaking and entering, this would be more than enough to send her packing—even if Daisee was sleeping with the Queen of England. But then here she was after a two-hour drive, with night falling and no one around and an open window—an inviting open window.

She pulled the casement open as far as she could and then lifted herself up to squeeze through. As she wriggled inside, she lost her balance and tumbled down onto the floor into what she saw—once she had picked herself up—was a sitting room.

A pine-beamed ceiling, a wood-burning stove set in the hearth, an easy chair the colour of pale pewter with matching cushions facing the hearth—the perfect English country cottage.

Six Windsor spindle-back chairs were pushed against a long oak table in the dining area. Not far away, a traditional country sofa and a second hearth with the necessary wood-burning stove. In the growing darkness, the mirror mounted over the mantel caught the expression of a tense young burglar in the midst of doing something she shouldn't be doing. Except, she wasn't a burglar, was she? Didn't you have to actually steal something before you were a burglar? Right now, this was merely break-and-enter; a kind magistrate, a suspended sentence, a ruined life.

Hardly a big deal.

She swallowed such thoughts and proceeded up a narrow, creaking staircase to the second floor. The master bedroom had a sloped ceiling and a king-size bed next to a small casement window. The upholstered headboard, the throw at the bottom of the bed and the night table were all done in the restrained pewter colour that probably marked Daisee's contribution to the cottage's perfectly renovated Englishness.

The casement window looked down onto the darkened laneway that was abruptly lit with light from the car now pulling into it. Wait a second, Priscilla thought. *A car pulling in?* She darted back from the window. Below, she could hear the car crunch to a stop and the motor shut down. The reflection of the headlights disappeared.

Priscilla dashed out of the master bedroom into the passageway. From below came the sound of a door unlocked, then footsteps and low feminine laughter. Priscilla held her breath. A male voice asked if there was something to drink. Priscilla couldn't quite make out the female's reply. There was more shared laughter. Light from the ground floor shot up the stairwell.

Thinking that whoever was down there might soon come up to the master bedroom, Priscilla entered a small guest room. She left the door open a crack and stood listening in the darkness to—silence.

A single window provided a view into the pitch black of the night. From here, there was no way to lower herself to the ground. She returned to the door, stepped back into the darkened passageway and crept to the top of the stairs. Sounds came from what she imagined was the sitting room. Pleasurable sounds that indicated that the couple downstairs weren't wasting time ascending to a bedroom.

Priscilla started down slowly. A loud throaty moan startled her. She stopped, listening to the heavy breathing that followed. Lovers, loving with enthusiasm, Priscilla surmised. Lovers distracted...

At the bottom of the stairs, the vestibule was the no man's land she had to cross in order to reach the front door. The sitting room, in darkness to the left, was the source of delighted gasps. Praying that lovers in the throes of ecstasy would not notice an intruder creeping toward the exit, Priscilla moved forward on tiptoes. She reached the door and tried the latch. The door eased open. Priscilla stole a glance into the sitting room.

Daisee Banville, naked on the sofa, her head thrown back, straddled her lover. In the dim light, his face was obscured.

Priscilla paused for one more look, hoping to identify Daisee's partner. Instead, it was Daisee's face, blank with passion, that turned toward Priscilla.

Daisee exhaled, her eyes widening as Priscilla slipped out the door.

CHAPTER TWENTY-SIX

The Escape Artist

Daisee saw! Priscilla thought as she hastened across the drive, skirting the parked—what was that?—some sort of sports car? Yes, a sports car, make a note of it. She stopped to catch her breath and peer at the rear licence plate: SBY 343R. Memorize the licence plate...

"Hey!" a voice called out. She caught a glimpse of a male figure illuminated for an instant in a flash of streetlight, coming toward her. "What are you up to then?"

Priscilla looked around and then headed back into the driveway past the sports car. Behind her, she could hear the voice shout something before she hopped the low wall and found herself in a dark field dropping into a moonlit shallow valley. She picked up speed, her breath coming in sharp, frightened bursts. Ahead was a grove of beechwood trees, their black tentacles reaching out for her.

She entered the wood, thick and dark, discouraging her from venturing much further even if an army were chasing her. She rested against a tree to regain her breath and stop her heart from pounding so hard. Peering back into the field, she could not see anyone coming after her.

Priscilla waited a few more minutes until her eyes grew more accustomed to the dark. The slope adjacent to the wood rose steeply. She made her way to the top, back onto the roadway leading to Daisee's cottage. No one was in sight.

Keeping to the shadows, her heart restarting its panicky drumbeat, she crept toward her car, past darkened houses. Somewhere in the distance a dog barked, startling her. Otherwise, the silence was like a wall rising around her. Silence save for the sound of her breathing.

She was certain it would wake the sleeping neighbourhood. As would the noise of her opening the driver's-side door. But it didn't. Behind the wheel, cocooned in the interior darkness, she felt suddenly safer as she started the motor. A moment later, she had the car turned around and was speeding away along the road.

Priscilla, escaping. Priscilla feeling rather exhilarated by it all. Priscilla facing danger and overcoming it.

Yes!

Except, wait...

Daisee saw... Daisee had seen *her*!

Priscilla tried to think rationally once she got past her initial panic. Daisee really wasn't in a position to say anything. *I was with my lover when I spotted Priscilla leaving my house?* That didn't sound likely. Maybe she was safe after all.

But that raised another question: Who was Daisee entertaining on the sofa? Was it Lord Snowdon? Did he take the precaution of stationing someone outside to ensure no one interrupted his assignation with Daisee?

It must have been Lord Snowdon. How could it have been anyone else? What was she supposed to tell Mr. Banville? The truth didn't seem like a great option. Besides, she wasn't *really* certain, was she?

The best thing for the time being, she decided, was to tell him nothing. If their marriage was on the edge of collapse, was she to be the person to push it over? That wouldn't do anyone any good. And suppose her boss decided to save the marriage and shoot the messenger?

She beat herself up some more as she drove along Knightsbridge two hours later, cursing the folly that placed her between the rock of Daisee's knowing that Priscilla knew and the hard place that was Mr. Banville, who did not know and perhaps shouldn't.

As she got into her building and wearily took the creaking elevator to the fourth floor, she tried to dismiss further apocalyptic thoughts. She would, like Scarlett O'Hara, worry about the apocalypse tomorrow, which, after all, was another day. She was dead tired. All she wanted was her bed and a good night's sleep, never mind cheating wives or vengeful bosses. She fumbled to get her key into the lock and then pushed open the door.

She reached for the wall light switch as she entered, except she didn't need to do that because the lights were already on to provide her with a clear view of Reggie Kray in one of her armchairs, legs crossed, holding a glass of what she assumed was her red wine.

"It's late. Where have you been?" Reggie demanded.

"I thought you were dead," she said, trying to quickly recover from her shock.

"Not a chance," he said, grinning.

"How did you know where I live and how did you get in here?"

"I'm a criminal," Reggie said. "Criminals know how to find places other people don't want them to find, and then they know how to get into those places."

"You have no right to break in here," Priscilla said, setting aside the fact that she had just returned from some breaking and entering of her own.

"You haven't told me where you've been." Reggie looked at his wristwatch. "It's after midnight." He had, much too enthusiastically, in Priscilla's estimation, adopted the role of the scolding parent.

"If it's any of your business, I was running an errand for my boss. And you haven't told me what you're doing here."

"Supposing I said that I hadn't heard from you and I was worried?"

"Why would you be worried about me?" Priscilla said.

"Or, supposing I told you I'm not happy about things I've been hearing lately."

"Really, Reggie, it's been a long day. I'm too tired for this."

With a speed that stunned Priscilla, Reggie sprang out of his chair to slap her with enough force that she screamed and was knocked back onto the sofa. She held her hand against the stinging pain of her face, the wind knocked out of her.

"You're too tired? That's tough, isn't it?" Reggie was like a dark monster hovering over her.

"What's wrong with you?" she gasped.

"That film you gave Ronnie. How's that for wrong?"

"That's what you wanted—that's what I got for you," she said, trying to hold back the tears that insisted on running down her cheeks.

"Except for one thing—Ronnie's not *in* the film."

"That's hardly my fault." Priscilla was holding her face, trying to sit up.

"That's right, I almost forgot. This is the film the coppers gave you, isn't it? How could you know what was on it?"

"I have no idea what you're talking about," Priscilla managed to say, cold fear replacing numbing pain.

"You know, I like you, Priscilla. You're the first bird I've liked for a long time. But then, like most birds, you go and betray me."

"You're wrong," Priscilla said, maintaining the lie as best she could.

"The point is, the coppers are using you to get to me with a fake piece of film and in trying to do that, they're putting you in grave danger."

"From you," Priscilla said, the pain and fear replaced by growing anger. "I'm in danger from you."

"Yeah, you could say that," Reggie acknowledged. "But Ronnie's the one you've got to watch out for. Ask me what he does to people he doesn't like. Go ahead. Ask me."

"What's he do?" Priscilla asked slowly.

"He uses a pair of pliers, see? He uses the pliers to yank out the unfortunate individual's fingernails."

"Is that what you're going to do to me, Reggie? You going to get Ronnie to pull out my fingernails?" Priscilla asked the questions with a mixture of fear and anger.

Reggie jabbed a thumb at his chest. "Me, I'm the softie. I'm as cuddly as a kitten."

Priscilla tried to imagine Reggie as a cuddly kitten. Imagination failed.

"What do you want from me?" She was sitting up now that Reggie had backed off a few paces, hopefully signalling that he didn't intend to hit her again—or get Ronnie to pull out her fingernails.

"What do you think? The film—the *real* film. Also, bring along our mutual friend Diana Dors, who seems to have disappeared into thin air after playing Ronnie and me, the coppers and maybe you, too."

"I have no idea where she is," Priscilla said truthfully.

"But you can find her. If Ronnie and me come after her, she runs away, hides in deeper places. But she trusts you; you'll have an easier time of it."

"Reggie, I can't do this." The words came out as a mournful plea. An exhausted young woman dealing with far too many threats.

"Yeah, you can," Reggie said confidently. "When it comes to doing what's needed or having to deal with Ronnie, it's amazing what people can achieve. And here's the other thing. Because I'm a nice guy and I like you, I'm going to forget that you deceived me with that bastard Nipper Read. You were under duress, I'm sure. I understand that. But now you're working for me. Okay? You don't say anything about tonight's conversation to Nipper. And you feed anything Nipper tells you back to me. Got that?"

When she didn't immediately answer, he moved closer, raising his frighteningly large hand. "Answer me! Have you got it, Priscilla?"

"Yes," she said in a benumbed voice.

"That's my girl." Reggie lowered his hand. His smile came right out of a Hammer horror movie, Priscilla thought. As scary as his punishing hand.

When he reached out to her, she flinched away. His smile only grew wider—even more ghoulish, she thought. He reached out again. She couldn't move. The hand that struck her now gently caressed her face. "You'll do fine."

Priscilla forced herself to endure his touch. He slowly took his hand away. The ghoulish smile remained in place. "You might ask me to stay the night," he said.

"Get out," she said.

"Okay, you're upset right now." Reggie started for the door. He opened it and was about to step over the threshold when he stopped and looked back at her. "I am sorry I hit you, Priscilla. I hated to do it. But if I have to, I'll do it again—worse next time."

"Just leave me alone."

"Sweet dreams, Priscilla. I will be in touch."

She waited until she could no longer hear Reggie's footfalls before burying her face in her hands, sobbing quietly in case he was still in the hallway.

CHAPTER TWENTY-SEVEN

Help!

A dark figure chased her across a moonlit field, quickly closing in. Ronnie Kray used a pair of pliers to yank out her fingernails. And Daisee Banville, in all her naked glory, kissed her passionately.

Priscilla jerked awake, finding herself in her own bed, discovering that the nightmares were just that—except for the part where Daisee was naked and kissing her. That was kind of interesting. She wasn't going to think about what it might mean.

She lay back feeling quite distressed—not surprising given the events of the previous evening—and seriously considering the idea of spending the rest of her life in bed with the covers pulled over her head. A very attractive prospect at the moment.

Eventually, she forced herself to get up and face the day.

After reviving herself in the shower, she spent time cleansing and massaging her face and blow-drying her pixie crop. She rummaged through the overstuffed chaos of her closet, trying to decide on the outfit with which to excite the world today.

She chose the Emilio Pucci minidress swirling with colour and accessorized with turquoise pantyhose and her treasured white Courrèges go-go boots. The addition of black eyeliner, frothy eyelashes, pale lipstick and—*voilà!*—she was Twiggy. Well, not *quite* Twiggy, a somewhat fuller Twiggy perhaps.

A cup of coffee added to her growing sense that she was at least somewhat human. How could anyone wish to harm the sweet-looking young woman in a trendy summer dress reflected back at her in the bedroom's full-length mirror? You would want to kiss such a woman—Daisee flashed into her mind to punctuate the thought. Certainly, you wouldn't want to harm her in any way.

Would you?

Unfortunately for her, not everyone felt the same way. Reggie Kray could break into her apartment with the ease available only to the criminal class, kiss her, kill her and then stop off for a pint at the Blind Beggar. No big deal for Reggie.

Daisee, a comparative novice in these matters, knowing that Priscilla had spotted her *in flagrante delicto*, would simply have her fired as part of the bargain she would strike with her husband to salvage their marriage and avoid scandal. No big deal for Daisee either.

Yes, when it came to the young woman in her bedroom mirror, so fresh and innocent and vulnerable—a young woman somewhat full of herself, if she was being honest—it was all a very big, destructive mess she had better find a way out of, and fast!

What about help from the Gossip's Bridle Club? she wondered as she dumped what was left of her coffee into the kitchen sink. Yes, they would try their best and there was no question about their loyalty. But Olivier and Gielgud were so easily distracted by arguments over who got the better reviews for *Hamlet*, and it was only a matter of time before Noël, lovely and supportive friend though he was, would retreat to sunnier digs in Jamaica. As for the police, she could take bets on either Charger Lightfoot or Nipper Read as to who might have her in handcuffs first. Her money right now was on Nipper Read. As far as she could see, there was no help to be had from either copper.

That left—and she hated to even think about this—a certain ink-stained, hungover ruffian named Percy Hoskins. She went over to the phone and picked up the receiver.

"I thought you weren't talking to me," he said when he came on the line.

"I never said that," she responded.

"Aha," he said. "That means you must want something."

"It could be that. Or maybe I hadn't heard from you for a while and thought I'd call and see how you're doing." Not particularly close to the truth, she thought. Brushing lightly against it.

"Liar," he said.

"That's no way to speak to the woman you say you love."

"My God," Percy said in amazement, "you really do want something. Come on, out with it."

"There is one thing." Well, there was no getting around it, was there?

"I knew it!" Percy crowed. "Honestly, you are so predictable, Priscilla."

"There *is* the argument that we use each other."

"An argument I don't buy, but never mind. Tell me what you want."

"Supposing I had a licence number and I wanted to know who that number was registered to. Would you be in a position to get that information for me?"

"What would be in it for me?"

"The lasting appreciation of the woman you keep insisting you love." Lasting for at least a day or so, Priscilla thought.

"I will need more."

Bugger, she thought. Aloud she said, "What do you want?"

His chuckle was lascivious.

"Don't even think about it," Priscilla said, but in the name of survival and England—maybe. Providing there was absolutely no other choice.

"Dinner at the very least."

"I could agree to that," Priscilla said. Relieved or disappointed she was getting off so lightly? Perhaps a bit of both.

"And you pay," Percy added.

Priscilla pondered if she would ever meet a man who wasn't in some way out to blackmail her. She decided the answer was no.

"All right," she said.

"And dinner can't be at the Savoy."

The Restaurant was the last place she wanted to be seen with Percy Hoskins. "Agreed," she said firmly.

"That's more like it," he said with satisfaction, seeming to think he had actually gained something. "Tell me what's on the licence plate."

She read it out to him.

"Incidentally," Percy said after he had taken down the number, "did I tell you that they spiked my Pierre Trudeau story?"

"No, you didn't," said Priscilla noncommittally.

"He left town early, the rumour being that his people wanted to avoid possible scandal."

"Is that so?" Priscilla replied, even more noncommittally.

"Concerning the women he was sleeping with in London."

"I wouldn't know anything about that." When in fact she knew far too much.

"Yes, I thought not," Percy said. "I'll get back to you."

He hung up.

"Bastard," she said to the receiver.

Trouble Always Rings Twice

Priscilla hit the waiter button as soon as she arrived at 205. As if by magic, Karl appeared minutes later with coffee on a silver tray and a morning smile on his face. Coffee and Karl's smile—now she could persevere through anything. Even Susie's inquisitive looks and the jarring ring of the telephone. Priscilla eyed the phone as it continued to ring, fearing that if she answered, she would have to deal with a furious and vengeful Daisee Banville.

"Do you want me to get it?" Susie called from the other room.

"I've got it," Priscilla said. She swallowed hard and picked up the receiver.

"It's me," Diana Dors said breathlessly.

Relieved, Priscilla said, "Diana, I've been worried about you."

"For now I'm okay," she said.

"Where are you?"

"I'd better not say, but I wanted you to know that I'm safe."

"Listen, all sorts of people are looking for you, including the police."

"And the Krays, I would imagine," Diana added, as though that was a foregone conclusion.

"Yes, I'm afraid so. Reggie broke into my flat last night. He's angry, saying that Ronnie is not in the film you gave the police."

"Yes, I'm sorry about that, Priscilla."

"You must go to the police, Diana. Tell them what happened to you in that garage. They will protect you."

Diana gave a derisive snort of laughter. "Are you serious? They won't protect me. Reggie has a copper working for him. I go to the police and I'm dead."

"You're not talking about Superintendent Read, are you?"

"Nipper? No, he's a bastard, but he's not bent, like some of the others. But Reggie's got someone on the inside, close to Nipper, who tells him everything. As soon as I go anywhere near Nipper, Reggie will know, and I'm dead."

"Superintendent Read says he is determined to bring down the Krays," Priscilla argued. "Once they're in prison, we're both safe. And whether we like it or not, we can help him achieve that."

"Nipper doesn't know the Krays the way I do. They don't go down so easily." She paused and then said: "Let's meet Saturday night. I'll be out in the country. A party I host from time to time. When you get here, I'll give you the film—the real film—that Reggie and Ronnie are looking for. That should take the pressure off. How's that?"

"Where?"

"Sunningdale, a village outside London. Orchard Manor is the house you're looking for. Shrubbs Hill Lane. You won't have any trouble finding it. Eight o'clock."

"Are you sure that's the safest thing to be doing right now?" Priscilla asked.

"As long as you don't tell the police. That would only upset a lot of people who don't wish to be upset."

"What about the Krays?"

Diana issued a derisive laugh. "Yeah, well, don't tell them either. Are you on?"

"I suppose so." Why was she agreeing to any of this? she thought. Because there wasn't a lot of choice.

"Wear something smashing that shows off those endlessly long legs." Diana's lowered voice sent an unintended shiver along her spine. "I can't wait to see you."

Then the line went dead. Priscilla hung up the receiver feeling...what was she feeling? An interesting combination of thoughts, she decided, one of them being...anticipation? Something like that, she had to admit. But trepidation, too.

Priscilla picked up her cup. The coffee had gone cold. She hated cold coffee. She hated her life. She hated her phone ringing because it brought only bad news.

The phone rang again. And again.

"Do you want me to pick that up?" Susie called from the other room.

Priscilla took a deep breath and picked up the receiver.

"What the devil are you doing?" Percy Hoskins, in full agitated flight.

"In the hour or so since we last spoke I've haven't had a chance to be up to much of anything," Priscilla said, surprised to hear from him so soon.

"Better not to talk on the phone," Percy said. "Meet me at the usual place in half an hour."

He hung up before Priscilla could tell him she wasn't going to meet him anywhere. Her head had begun to ache again.

Susie appeared in the doorway, looking distraught, as usual. "It's Mr. Banville."

"What about him?"

"He's on the other line. He wants to speak to you."

"Tell him I'm out," Priscilla said. "Tell him I'll call him back."

"It's Mr. *Banville*."

"Susie!"

"Yes, all right, fine! You don't have to yell!" Susie flounced away angrily.

Priscilla held her head between her hands, reminding herself that it was not the end of the world.

It only seemed like it.

The usual place was a bench amid the lush green of the Victoria Embankment Gardens facing the memorial dedicated to the English reformer Henry Fawcett, walking distance from the hotel. Even so, Percy had beat her there and was slumped on the bench, looking even rougher than usual, bleary eyes focused on the bronze plaque showing Henry Fawcett's heroic profile in three-quarters view above a dolphin spouting water into a basin.

"Ah, Henry, poor Henry," Percy lamented. "In his photographs, he looks haunted, a wraith, his eyes closed as if to shut out the world. Yet here was the defender of Darwin's theory of evolution, supporter of women's suffrage, the inventor of parcel post, the enabler of the telephone kiosk. How did we, his descendants, pay him back for his good works?"

He took bloodshot eyes away to focus accusingly on Priscilla. "I will tell you how. His descendants produced beautiful, deceitful women to charm and seduce honest, hard-working, pure-at-heart journalists like myself. Thus did Henry die in vain."

"Except for the telephones in those delightful red boxes," Priscilla said, joining Percy on the bench. "That's not such a bad legacy, I would say."

"You would say that," grumbled Percy. "A great man's legacy reduced to a pay telephone."

For a couple of moments, neither of them spoke. They were alone in this section of the gardens. Priscilla could hear the twitter of birds. Not often could she hear the twitter of anything while Percy was around.

"You seem very upset, Percy. What deceitful women are you referring to?"

"The kind of woman who would think nothing of telling me lies and leading me on," Percy retorted.

"Is any woman in particular leading you on?" Priscilla's eyes were dancing mischievously. She couldn't help enjoying this.

"The world is full of such women, I've discovered. In fact, at this moment, I happen to be sitting on a bench beside one."

"Hardly," Priscilla said.

"A woman who is up to something that she's not telling me about."

"I'm not up to anything that would interest you, put it that way." Not exactly true, but best to hold Percy off for now.

"Then why did you want to know the name of the person who owns a certain licence number?"

"Did you get it? The woman you supposedly love more than life itself is asking."

"The licence is registered to a man named Terry O'Hara. Does that name mean anything to you?"

"Should it?"

"It should indeed," Percy announced with satisfaction, understanding he had information and thus power over her. "This is why I wonder what you are up to, Priscilla. Terry is the younger brother of Major Jack O'Hara, your security chief at the Savoy."

"You're not serious."

"I am serious." Percy was looking even more satisfied with himself. "I did some checking on our friend Terry. Turns out he, like his brother, is ex-military. He now runs a small security firm that provides protection for London's posh set, including, I hear, Antony Armstrong-Jones."

"Lord Snowdon."

"Princess Margaret's off-again-on-again husband. I'm told Tony and Terry have become fast friends. Catting around town together."

Even extending their catting to Chipping Campden, Priscilla thought.

"Which brings me to the question of why you would be interested in Terry O'Hara. Or do you have your eye on his pal Tony?"

"Now you're being nasty." Except that's exactly what she had on him, albeit for other reasons than Percy might suspect.

"Or accurate," Percy countered.

"Obviously I had no idea until this moment who Terry O'Hara is."

"Unless you are impressed by his car. He drives an Iso Grifo."

"What's that?"

"A very expensive Italian sports car. They only make a few thousand of them each year."

"Just what I'm looking for. Rich men who drive Italian sports cars."

"What about the not-so-rich men who *don't* drive Italian sports cars?"

"Not interested," Priscilla pronounced. Not *that* interested, Priscilla amended silently. Interested on occasion.

Percy began sulking. Honestly, he could be a big baby at times, thought Priscilla.

She thought she had better say something to bring him back a bit. "Look, I'll tell you what this is about but you must promise to keep your mouth shut, and, more important, not print any-thing."

"Then this *is* something I might want to write about." The big baby was gone. The shifty-eyed Fleet Street reporter was back.

"You might, yes. But you can't. It's my job if you do."

"Better to not say anything. My journalistic instincts might get the better of me."

"Yes, I keep forgetting you would sell your first born for a good story."

"Are you kidding? I'd *give* my first born away for the story."

Priscilla was on her feet, dismissing any previously sympathetic thoughts. "You truly are a bastard."

"You keep saying that." Percy was smiling.

"I keep being reminded of it."

Priscilla started marching away along the gravel path.

"Aren't you going to thank me at least?"

Priscilla came to a stop, paused, then wheeled around grim-faced and returned to the bench.

"You've come back," Percy announced with ill-disguised glee. "You realize that you are wrong and wish to apologize."

"I need Terry O'Hara's address."

Percy's grin widened. "Ah, but that wasn't part of our original agreement, was it?"

"Percy," Priscilla said impatiently. "The address—*please*." She marvelled at his ability to always regain the upper hand.

"Rather posh, I would say—Dove Mews, Belgrave Square. Number eleven."

Stay Away from Terry O'Hara

His Highness, the Rajah of Faridkot, Harinder Singh, trailed by his quartet of bodyguards but with no wives in sight, burst into the Front Hall. As he started across to the lift, he caught sight of Priscilla. He immediately came to a stop. His bodyguards tensed, as though hired assassins might leap from the Resident's Lounge and attack their master. The rajah, by contrast, seemed unconcerned about much of anything. He blessed Priscilla with a satisfied smile.

"We have been to see Her Royal Majesty, the Queen," he announced.

"Isn't that marvellous?" Priscilla said, praying that was the correct response upon hearing important news from a rajah.

"She was at Buckingham Palace," the rajah added.

"Apparently, she lives there," said Priscilla.

"She served us tea."

"And were your wives with you?" Priscilla inquired.

Harinder Singh looked horrified by the notion. "Of course not." The horror turned to puzzlement. "Why would you ask such a question?"

"Forgive me, Your Highness," Priscilla said quickly. "I can't imagine what I was thinking."

"You are a curious woman, Miss Tempest." The rajah inspected her as if deciding whether or not to have her banished from his kingdom. "But you are attractive," he stated with great certainty. "There is no doubt of that."

Priscilla managed a "Thank you, Your Highness," while visions of becoming the rajah's fourth wife danced fleetingly in her head. Draped in priceless jewels, naturally.

Without another word, the rajah was off, apparently having spent enough time with the common folk.

Across the way, Major Jack O'Hara, the very model of an authoritative security chief in a double-breasted navy blazer, was watching Priscilla with what she imagined was a critical eye. He looked vaguely alarmed as she approached.

"Words with one of our foreign guests, Miss Tempest." The major made it sound as though that was not a good thing at all.

"The rajah was telling me about his tea with the Queen," Priscilla reported.

"Bully for Her Majesty," Major O'Hara said with a sneer. "What can I do for you, Miss Tempest? I am a busy man."

"Yes, I can certainly see that," Priscilla offered sympathetically. "With royalty such as the rajah staying with us, one has to stay on one's toes, I imagine."

"Precisely. One never knows what certain guests will get themselves up to. A trained eye can often foresee future problems by studying their comings and goings—getting a head start on possible trouble, as it were."

"And with that trained eye of yours, who are you watching this afternoon, Major, if you don't mind my asking?"

Major O'Hara nodded across the lobby. "I've had my eye on that chappie right there."

Priscilla followed his gaze across the hall to where Hans Kringelein was seated in the Resident's Lounge reading the morning's edition of the *Times*.

"That's Mr. Kringelein," Priscilla said.

Major O'Hara gave her a look of surprise. "You know that fellow?"

"I met him briefly when he checked into the hotel. He's a retired waiter from Germany."

Major O'Hara did not appear assuaged. "I don't know. There's something about him. Doesn't fit in somehow."

"My sense from meeting him is that he is an elderly gentleman, anxious to experience a taste of the luxury he provided others over the years," Priscilla explained, hoping to head off the major badgering poor Mr. Kringelein. Hardly the sort of guest who would cause trouble.

"I suppose I must take you at your word, mustn't I?" As though the last thing the major wanted to do was take any words from Priscilla.

"By the way," she said, pivoting toward the subject she actually had in mind. "I was at a party the other night and met your brother."

O'Hara looked at her sharply. "My brother?"

"Terry. Is that his name?"

"Yes," said the major coldly. "I believe it is."

He *believed* his brother's name was Terry? Priscilla thought. Not exactly the response she expected. Aloud she said, "He seemed like a nice enough gentleman."

Major O'Hara said nothing in response.

"He said to say hello," Priscilla added.

"I doubt he said anything of the sort," Major O'Hara replied brusquely.

"In fact, he did," Priscilla said insistently.

"You should know, Miss Tempest, my brother and I do not get along. In fact, we have not spoken for several years. If he said anything at all about me, I doubt that it was very pleasant."

"I'm so sorry to hear that," Priscilla said, somewhat taken aback.

"I've learned it's best to stay clear of him, Miss Tempest," Major O'Hara continued. "I advise you to do the same."

"The Earl of Snowdon likes him." Thrown in to see how he might react.

What she got was an angry glare. "How would you know that?" the major demanded.

Priscilla fumbled for something to say. "I suppose Terry must have mentioned that they are friends."

The major was distracted by something over Priscilla's shoulder. "Is that Nipper Read?"

Priscilla turned to see Superintendent Read crossing the Front Hall. Nearby, she noticed Hans Kringelein look up from his paper and do a double take at the sight of Read.

"It *is* Nipper," said Major O'Hara."

"You know him?"

"A friendly acquaintance, I would say. I wonder what the dickens the head of the Murder Squad is doing here. The Skye Kane investigation, I suppose, although I hadn't heard he's involved."

"Yes, that could be it, all right," Priscilla said, suspecting Nipper Read's presence had nothing to do with Skye's murder.

"I should have a word with Mr. Banville," O'Hara said. He nodded stiffly at Priscilla. "Good day to you, Miss Tempest."

Priscilla watched the major strut off. Her attention was drawn across the hall as Kringelein got up from his chair, dropped the paper and hurried away.

Superintendent Read, smiling happily, was already seated near a nervous-looking Susie when Priscilla entered 205.

"Were you expecting Superintendent Read?" Susie's voice broke a bit as she asked the question.

"I don't think you were, Miss Tempest," Read said, rising from the chair. "But I'm sure you have a minute or two for me."

"Of course," Priscilla said. "Why don't you step into my office?"

"Most kind of you," Read said. He went past into Priscilla's office. She came in behind him and closed the door.

"Listen, you can't keep doing this, Superintendent," Priscilla said angrily once she was seated in the safe zone that was the space behind her desk. "You were noticed coming into the hotel. You are placing me and my job in jeopardy."

"I do this because you do not keep in touch, Miss Tempest. What's more, given your reticence, I suspect my phone calls would not be returned either."

"Perhaps my *reticence*, as you call it, has something to do with the fact that you're supposed to be protecting me, but I'm not feeling at all protected." Priscilla had found exactly the right fierce tone she needed when dealing with Read.

"And why is that?" The superintendent did not seem at all disturbed by her accusation.

"It might have something to do with the fact that when I got home last night, Reggie Kray was in my flat."

Now that got to him, Priscilla noted with satisfaction. Read's smile evaporated; he looked abruptly concerned. "What was he doing in your flat?"

"He was very upset because I gave him the wrong film. Further, he suspects that the film did not come from Diana Dors, but from you."

"That's impossible," Read said.

"Believe me, it is entirely possible," Priscilla asserted. "You gave me your word that only the two of us would know about our relationship—you promised me that. But somehow Reggie knows."

"I have no idea how that could have happened." For the first time, there was a note of uncertainty in Read's voice.

"Well, it happened. Did you know you gave me the wrong film?"

"It wasn't the *wrong* film, necessarily," Read said carefully. "It was simply a film that did not contain the footage Ronnie is after. However, in fairness, we didn't know that either until it was too late. I'm afraid Miss Dors has taken advantage of us both."

"Does she have the real film or do you?"

"If such a film exists, she still has it," Read admitted. "Has she been in touch with you?"

Priscilla decided it was best to not admit to anything. She shook her head. "She's much smarter than I am. Faced with your incompetence, she's not waiting around for the Krays to come after her. Instead, wisely, she has made herself scarce for the time being."

"Then you don't know where she is?"

Priscilla thought of Diana's party invitation then shook her head again. "Even if I did, I'm not going to tell you, knowing that anything I do or say will likely get back to the Krays."

"I can ensure that won't happen."

"No, I'm afraid you can't," Priscilla said.

"I'm so sorry you feel that way." Concern was clearly etched on Read's face. He had not been expecting any of this, Priscilla decided.

"I don't have a lot of choice, Superintendent. So far you've done nothing but get me into more trouble than I ever could have imagined."

There was an unaccustomed sombre expression on Read's face as he rose to his feet. "You're wrong about me, Miss Tempest. You were in trouble the moment you were unwise enough to approach the Krays. You may not think so right now, but I am the one person who can get you out of that trouble."

Read moved toward the door. "Incidentally, I don't believe you're telling me everything you know about Miss Dors. If you are in touch with her, I suggest you convince her to give up the real film and co-operate with us so that we can bring charges of kidnapping and assault against the Krays."

"At this point, I don't think she trusts anyone, certainly not the police," Priscilla said.

"I leave it to you, Miss Tempest. You may be the one person who can persuade her to see things in a different light."

"Tell me something..." Priscilla said, deciding she might as well try to get information out of a policeman who kept demanding information from her.

Read came to a halt at the door. "If I can," he said.

"You know our Major O'Hara, I understand."

"Jack?" Read looked vaguely surprised. "A bit, yes."

"What about his brother, Terry? Do you know him?"

Read allowed a placid smile, signalling that the question had put him on more familiar ground. "Terry, now there's a piece of work for you. How will my knowing Terry be of any help to you?"

"Tell me about him," Priscilla said. "He runs a security firm, I'm told."

Read stepped away from the door. "That's what he says, but it's not what he does."

"Then what does he actually do?"

"If you listen to the scuttlebutt, you would say Terry's a bit of a player around town."

"What does that mean?"

"He's come in contact with police for running illegal gambling establishments. We've never been able to make anything stick with Terry, but we continue to have our eyes on him, much to Jack's embarrassment. He and Terry haven't spoken for years."

"What about Antony Armstrong-Jones?"

Read hesitated before he said, "I'm not sure what you're getting at."

"Do you know if he and Terry are friends?"

"I don't, but then the Earl of Snowdon moves in some pretty dark circles. I suppose it's possible." He paused before he added, "Is there something you'd like to tell me?"

"No," Priscilla replied. "Curious, that's all."

"A piece of unsolicited advice, Miss Tempest. You're in enough trouble as it is. Whatever you are curious about, do not get involved with Terry O'Hara."

Right, Priscilla thought as Read went out the door. Don't get involved with Terry O'Hara. Good advice. Unfortunately, where getting involved with men was concerned, she had a long, miserable history of not following good advice.

The Care of Moonshadow Euonymus

The old stables at Dove Mews had been transformed into cozy two-storey flats that opened directly onto the street. Flower boxes festooned with white petunias decorated the upper floor. A perfect picture dappled with afternoon sunlight.

A young woman leaned out from the second-storey window at number eleven, catching Priscilla, stationed across the street, by surprise. Model-slim with honey-coloured hair in a ponytail, the woman was watering the petunias with a large yellow watering can. She noticed Priscilla and waved. "Are you lost?" She shielded her eyes from the sun as she gazed down.

Thinking quickly, a startled Priscilla called back, "I was looking for Sloane Square and wandered into this neighbourhood. It's quite lovely. I didn't know about it."

"Something, isn't it?" The woman withdrew from the window and a couple of minutes later came out the door, still holding the watering can. "I never knew what a mews was until I moved here." She stood at the curb, seemingly eager to chat. Priscilla, recovering from the blow of being so quickly discovered on her first stakeout, was glad to oblige.

"You sound American," Priscilla said.

The young woman stepped off the curb and crossed to Priscilla. "From California—Los Angeles." By now, the young woman had crossed the street. "I'd never been to London before my boyfriend lured me over here. What about you? You don't sound English."

"I'm actually Canadian," Priscilla said. "Although I've been here for a few years now. It appears you are new to all this."

"I've only been here a few weeks but so far it's been wonderful. My name's Karen, incidentally. Karen Hollander."

"Priscilla Tempest," said Priscilla.

"And you really are Canadian?"

"Most definitely. And should I forget, someone is certain to remind me. I like it here but I'm always going to be the stranger in a strange land."

"That's two of us, I suppose—two strangers in a strange land. I'd shake your hand except mine are smeared with potting soil. I don't suppose you know anything about moonshadow euonymus?"

"I don't even know what that is."

Karen jerked a thumb in the direction of number eleven. "Those green and blotchy gold potted shrubs."

"Right," said Priscilla, narrowing her eyes to get a look at them. "I suppose you water them."

"They are supposed to be low maintenance but I don't know…" She allowed the sentence to trail off.

"How long are you staying in London?" Priscilla asked.

Karen issued a merry laugh. "I see. If I'm leaving town I shouldn't worry about the shrubs?"

"I didn't mean it quite like that."

"I'm afraid London and the shrubs have me," she said with more laughter. "At least I hope they do."

"What were you doing in Los Angeles?"

"You know how it is: If you live in LA you must be either an actor or a screenwriter—or both."

"Let me guess. Actress?"

"I was *trying* to be an actress. In point of fact, I made more money modelling and managing an agency."

"Are you going to be acting here?" Priscilla asked, wondering how the supposedly questionable Terry O'Hara fit in with this charming woman.

"I'd like to, or maybe management. I definitely want to do more than water the flowers and shrubs. We'll see." Once again, she shaded her eyes for a closer look at Priscilla. "What about you?"

What about her? Lie or tell the truth? "I work in public relations." The handy half-truth, suitable for dangerous gangsters or Americans worried about moonshadow euonymus.

"Sounds fascinating."

"*Trying* is the word I use a lot too," Priscilla said with a rueful laugh.

"From the sound of things, it doesn't seem like a whole lot is different over here."

"I'm afraid not."

"For now, all I have to please is my boyfriend and the flowers. The flowers are easy."

"And the boyfriend?"

"He's a little more complicated. But we're muddling through." She looked at the watering can she was holding. "I'd better get back to the watering. He's going to be home soon. We're going out this evening."

"He works here in London?"

"Security." She dropped her voice. "Very hush-hush. Or so he tells me. One of the complications."

"Then I'd better not ask too many questions," Priscilla said with a smile that was meant to reassure. "I don't want to get in trouble with someone in security."

"It's been great talking to you, Priscilla," Karen said. "Listen, if you don't mind, would you like to give me your number?

Maybe if you're not busy some afternoon we could get together for a coffee—or tea as they say over here."

"Let's make it coffee," Priscilla said. "I don't like tea."

Karen made a face. "A kindred spirit—neither do I. One of the things I worried about moving here. Was I somehow going to have to learn to drink tea?"

"You can escape it—barely," Priscilla said with a grin. "But you do spend a lot of time politely saying no."

Priscilla took a notepad and pen out of her shoulder bag and scribbled her home number. She tore out the page and handed it to Karen.

Karen put down her watering can and took the notepad and pen from Priscilla. "I think this is right," she said as she wrote, "the numbers are so different over here."

"Everything is different over here," said Priscilla. Including, Priscilla thought to herself, the mysterious bloke whose flowers you end up watering.

As she started off along Dove Mews, an exotic-looking sports car passed by in the opposite direction. Was that an Iso Grifo? She stopped and turned to see the car pull to a stop at the curb and a dark-haired man jump out. Karen embraced him.

Arm in arm, Karen and the man Priscilla imagined was Terry O'Hara disappeared into number eleven.

The watering can remained on the street.

Two Coppers in a Pub

Inspector Lightfoot collected two pints at the bar as the after-work crowd quickly filled Finch's, the inspector's pub of choice when he needed a pint. Or two. Nipper Read had managed to secure a table in a quiet corner at the back.

"Much appreciated," he said as Lightfoot joined him and set down the beers.

"Not at all." Lightfoot had pulled out his pipe and a tobacco pouch and laid them on the table beside his beer. "Do you mind if I smoke?"

Read actually did mind, but since just about everyone else was puffing away on something and a pall of smoke filled the pub, he could hardly object.

As Lightfoot stuffed tobacco into his pipe, he said, "Well, Superintendent, what brings us together today?"

"I was curious as to how you are coming along with this showgirl murder case," Read said.

"How are we coming?" Lightfoot played the question back in order to buy the time it took to get his pipe lit. He added more blue-grey smoke to the air before he said, "As it happens, I just spent an afternoon sweating out this Merrick chappie."

"The New York theatrical impresario. He still looks good for this?"

Lightfoot shrugged noncommittally. "We stopped him getting on a plane bound for New York, thinking he might be trying to escape. Claimed he was leaving because he was told by his solicitors that he had been exonerated. That was not the case. Then through his solicitors he assured us it was all a misunderstanding. That led to the afternoon's session. He swears he is innocent, of course."

"But?"

Another shrug and a puff on his pipe. "According to the medical examiner, Miss Kane was strangled around 12:45 in the morning. Merrick says he was in bed asleep at that time. He says he was alone so there is no one to confirm the truth of his statement."

"So not much of an alibi."

"The other point against him: He was staying at the Savoy, therefore could more easily strangle Miss Kane and then return to his room undetected. Anyone else would have had to enter the hotel. Such persons were more likely to have been noticed by a member of the night staff."

"Unless it was another guest at the hotel," Read suggested.

"Yes, we thought of that. What with the presence of some sort of Indian potentate and his large entourage, the hotel was fully occupied that night. But no one else stands out as a possible suspect."

"What about Miss Tempest?" Read asked.

Lightfoot, through a haze of pipe smoke, looked surprised. "You're still thinking of her, are you?"

"I am thinking of Miss Tempest and her association with the Krays."

Lightfoot removed the pipe from its comfortable corner in his mouth. "What? Back to our theory that Miss Tempest somehow conspired with the Krays to murder Skye Kane?"

"That's going a little too far," Read acknowledged. "But I am increasingly undecided as to the part Miss Tempest is playing in all this. She now strongly suggests that someone inside my squad has been compromised and is feeding information to the Krays."

"You don't think that's possible?"

"I find it highly improbable. My team has been thoroughly vetted. Therefore, I have to ask myself: Is Miss Tempest trying to throw us off the track with such allegations? I don't know, but I wonder. As I wonder about Miss Diana Dors."

"How does she fit into this?"

"Diana Dors was jealous of her younger rival, Skye Kane. Did she enlist the Krays to murder Miss Kane in her dressing room after the show? Did Miss Tempest facilitate that murder by making sure the killer or killers could access the hotel and the dressing room?"

"So you are coming around to that line of thinking."

"Let's say I keep coming back to it."

Lightfoot busied himself puffing hard on his pipe. The noise of the pub closed in around them.

"This theory—and it is only a theory for now," said Lightfoot, tiring of his pipe and picking up the thread of the conversation. "It does set aside Mr. Merrick as a suspect, and it places the Krays at the heart of it."

Read gave a quick nod, and added, "I simply ask you this, Inspector: Do you truly believe one of America's most successful and high-profile theatrical impresarios would risk everything to murder a woman in the hotel where he is staying?"

"If it is a crime of passion, and I believe it most definitely is," Lightfoot was leaning forward intently, "then to that I would say yes. As we both know, when it comes to affairs of the heart, men, rich or poor, successful or abject failures, are capable of just about anything, certainly murder."

Read sat back, as though repelled by Lightfoot's onslaught.

Lightfoot puffed contemplatively. "Tell you what," he said finally, "let's do it this way. Allow me to continue my pursuit of the Mr. Merrick angle while you keep an eye on Miss Tempest and see where she leads you. Does she take you to Miss Dors and the Krays? At the end we could both benefit from pooling our resources."

"Yes, I like that," Read acknowledged. "It's a plan. I have no objection, as long as whichever avenue takes us both over the finish line. With any luck, you solve a murder and I bring the Krays to the justice they so richly deserve."

"Here's to that," said Lightfoot, raising his pint.

"Indeed," agreed Read as he raised his.

Hello, David!

"Mr. Merrick has been calling for you," Susie announced as soon as Priscilla walked into 205. "Also, Mr. Banville."

"Who sounded happier?" Priscilla asked, a weak attempt to delay the inevitable.

"Neither of them sounded at all happy," Susie said miserably. "But Mr. Merrick did phone from his suite and he sounded quite distraught. He's there now."

"I'm not sure how I feel about going up there alone," Priscilla said.

"Perhaps the prospect of Mr. Banville would be more appealing," Susie suggested. Cattily, Priscilla thought. It was at moments such as this that Priscilla wondered if Susie had her best interests at heart.

"Mr. Merrick it is," Priscilla decided.

Susie managed a sort-of smile.

Steeling herself for the coming storm, Priscilla entered the Front Hall. Was she to spend the rest of her life steeling herself for coming storms? She was beginning to think so.

"Miss Tempest!"

Hans Kringelein waved to her from the Resident's Lounge. Setting aside his copy of the *Times*, he rose and hurried across the hall to where Priscilla waited. His face was alive with delight. "I just wanted to say *guten tag.*"

"And *guten tag* to you, Mr. Kringelein. How are you doing?"

"I am at the world-famous Savoy so how is it possible for me to do badly?"

"I'm delighted to hear that, Mr. Kringelein."

"Please, you must call me Hans."

"Ah, but you see, Mr. Kringelein, we at the Savoy must always address our valued guests formally."

"My goodness, Miss Tempest. I do not know how valued I am but at this moment I do feel very important."

"That's the idea, Mr. Kringelein."

"If you don't mind my saying, Miss Tempest, when I saw you enter the hall, I thought you looked lovely as always, but also...preoccupied? Do you mind if I ask if you are feeling unwell?"

"That's very kind of you, but I'm fine," Priscilla replied. If only he knew the truth, she mused. "It's a busy time at the Savoy, as always, ensuring that significant guests such as yourself are properly cared for."

"A tired old waiter from Itzehoe is feeling very well cared for, Miss Tempest. *Vielen dank.*"

"My pleasure," Priscilla said, shaking his hand. "Let me know if I can be of any further service to you."

"You are most kind." He gave her a formal little bow.

She felt Kringelein's eyes on her as she proceeded to the red lift. What a curious little man, she thought as the lift rose to the fifth floor. But at least he was enjoying himself at the Savoy, which was more than she was currently doing.

Reaching Merrick's suite, she drew a deep breath before knocking on his door. There was no answer. She knocked again and then again. Finally, a weak voice came from inside. "Go away!"

"It's Miss Tempest, Mr. Merrick. You wanted to see me."

The door opened a crack. An eye peered out at her. "Are you alone?"

"Yes, sir."

The door opened further to reveal Merrick in an embroidered silk robe, looking dishevelled and distraught. "Come in, please." His eyes were wild with a combination of fear and suspicion. If David Merrick had been the powerful, demanding, complaining guest before, there was no sign of any of that now.

The window drapes had been drawn. Dishes and platters full of barely touched room-service meals lay on trays and carts. A dining table was piled with scripts and books. Merrick, his hands plunged deep into the pockets of his robe, wandered about, disoriented, seeming to have forgotten Priscilla was present.

"Mr. Merrick..." Priscilla said worriedly.

He ceased his pacing. "You know the police stopped me getting on a plane? Can you believe that? They hustled me off and then dragged me to Scotland Yard. Questioned me for hours. *Hours!*"

"Yes, I heard," Priscilla said.

"My solicitor finally arrived and forced them to release me, but they won't let me leave town. The bastards really think I killed that woman."

"I understand there are a number of suspects," Priscilla said, attempting to be conciliatory.

"Yes, but they think *I* did it. *I* killed her. Jesus wept, I didn't. I'm innocent. But no one believes me."

He stumbled over to an armchair and slumped down on it, shaking his head. "I don't know what to do. I'm afraid to leave the room. I'm ruined. Everything I worked for—gone!"

He punctuated this statement by burying his head melodramatically in his hands. Against her better judgment, Priscilla was actually beginning to feel sorry for him. If Merrick was a killer, he was certainly a very distraught killer, not to mention a fine actor.

"What can I do to help, Mr. Merrick?" she heard herself say.

Merrick raised his head, focusing bleary eyes on her. "This may sound crazy, but you're the only person around here I feel I can trust. You at least listen to me. Everyone else...Everyone looks at me as though I have the blood of that woman on my hands."

"I'm sure that isn't the case."

"It is! They all think I did it." He threw himself against the back of the chair. "God, I'm finished! It's over!"

"What did you tell the police, Mr. Merrick?"

He gave her a despondent look. "What did I tell them?" He stopped, hesitating, as though battling with himself about what to say next. "That's the thing, okay? It's what I *didn't* tell them that's driving me crazy."

"What didn't you tell them?"

His despondency was replaced by a speculative expression, the gambler—or the savvy Broadway producer—assessing the risk before showing his cards. "Can I trust you?"

"You said yourself that you can."

"You say you want to help me, right?"

"If it's possible, yes," Priscilla said.

Merrick turned away abruptly, as though speaking to someone else. "A lie..." Uttered in such a low register that Priscilla wasn't certain what she had heard.

"What?"

"A *lie*," Merrick said in a louder voice. "I told the police a lie."

For the first time, Priscilla realized Merrick might actually have something of value to offer. "What did you tell them?"

"I told them I was in bed asleep when Skye was murdered. That wasn't true. I was here in my room. Drinking. Angry with Skye—angry with myself for losing my temper. I dozed for a time and then the telephone woke me up, everything in a blur. It must have been late when I answered. It was Skye..."

"Skye was calling you?" Was he lying? Or was Merrick level-ling with her?

Merrick nodded. "She sounded strange, said she had taken something. I'm not sure what. She said she felt really strange. She had finished the show at the Cabaret and was in her dress-ing room. 'Come down,' she said, 'I have to see you. You must help me...'"

"And is that what you did?" Priscilla asked. "You went down to her?"

"I almost didn't. I was drunk and tired and angry. She was a bitch, playing me. One minute she didn't want to have anything to do with me. The next, she's on the phone begging me to come to her. To hell with her, I thought. But then the next thing I knew I was taking the elevator to the ground floor. There was no one in the lobby."

"No one at the desk?"

"Not that I saw, no."

"Then what?"

"I stumbled around, found my way into the dining room. I'd been backstage once before to meet Skye so I sort of remem-bered how to get to her dressing room. That's where I found her. I mean, that's where I found her body."

"Skye was already dead?" Priscilla asked.

Merrick nodded. "At first I thought whatever she had taken had knocked her out. I was angrier than ever. She calls me, I come down to her, and she's like... Then I realized that she wasn't breathing... she was dead. It crossed my mind that she had overdosed. I didn't think of anyone murdering her."

"What did you do then?"

"The sight of her sobered me up enough to realize that sim-ply by being there it would look bad, that I could be in a lot of trouble. That's the last thing I needed, being found in the

dressing room of a young woman I barely knew who had overdosed. A world of trouble."

"You left her there?"

"If I was a better person, I would have stuck around, tried to
help. But I'm not that better person, okay? I'm sorry, but I'm not."
Merrick spoke in a defensive voice. "I panicked, no other word
for it, and got the hell out of there, back upstairs to my room."

"And no one saw you?"

Merrick was silent for a time. Then he said, "One person..."

"Who? Who saw you?"

"I don't know. Later, I wondered if I had seen anything at
all, thought maybe I was hallucinating. But I believe there was
someone in the Restaurant as I passed by on the way to the dressing rooms. A shadow, not much more than that...but someone..."

"A man or a woman?"

"Must have been a man. Big, blurry and indistinct. A man,
not a woman."

"What time was this?"

"I have no idea—late. Early in the morning, I don't know..."

"Why didn't you tell any of this to the police?"

"Because if I'd admitted I found her body and did nothing, in
their minds that would put me at what turned out to be a murder scene and thus make me more of a suspect than ever. They
don't believe me now. Changing my story, telling them something else, would only make it worse."

"But the person—the man you saw in the Restaurant—he
may have been the killer."

"What difference would it make? The police would think I
was lying."

"Then I guess the question is why should *I* believe you, Mr.
Merrick?" Was he a killer, creating an alibi that he was trying to
draw her into?

Merrick cast his gaze back to Priscilla. His eyes burned bright. "Because I'm spilling my guts to you, okay?" he said, speaking with a desperate intensity. "Look at me, for God's sake, do I look as though I'm lying? I'm at my wit's end. I'm confiding in you, okay? Taking a chance, telling you things I probably shouldn't. But maybe you can use this, somehow let the police know there was another man—the actual killer."

So that was it, Priscilla thought. Merrick couldn't talk to the police without incriminating himself. But she could, and so exonerate the producer—at least that appeared to be his mad reasoning.

"What do you think?" Merrick asked, pressing.

"I doubt they will believe me either," Priscilla said. "I would have to change my story and say I was in the Restaurant and saw someone. Which would only serve to confirm suspicions they already have about me."

"They don't suspect you—they suspect *me*."

"Let me think about it, see if there is a way to deal with this," Priscilla offered. "Are you quite sure you saw someone?"

"Yes, Jesus Christ Almighty, I saw the killer. I *saw* the goddamn killer!"

CHAPTER THIRTY-THREE

Priscilla Is on Notice

As she approached the general manager's office, Priscilla knew what she *could* tell Clive Banville. It was very much a question of what she *should* tell him.

And what she should tell him, she concluded a moment before facing the malignant El Sid, was absolutely nothing.

Anything else and the hot water in which she already found herself would become scalding.

Sidney drew her out of her reverie with one of the smug, you're-finished-sweetheart looks he loved to deliver.

"He's waiting for you," he noted, in the same tone Marie Antoinette would have heard just before the blade dropped.

She found Banville seated, frozen at his desk. Moreover, and much more worrisome, instead of being at least somewhat welcoming—which she might have expected, given the confidence he had shared with her—he looked as though she was the last person in the world he wanted to see.

"There you are, Miss Tempest. As usual, I've been trying to get hold of you. Without success, I might add."

"Sorry, sir," Priscilla said, thinking it best not to attempt to explain where she had been as yet.

"I find your tardy responses to my requests for meetings most irritating."

"Yes, I understand, sir. But I've been busy with the, uh, situation you asked me to look into for you."

Instead of reassuring Banville, her explanation caused him to look more unhappy and annoyed than ever. "Yes, yes, that situation." He waved a dismissive hand. Not a good sign at all, Priscilla thought. "That is why I've been anxious to reach you. In regard to our previous conversation, I may have...over-reacted."

"Sir?"

Banville engaged in more of the throat-clearing she had heard the other day. "I've had an opportunity to speak to Mrs. Banville and she assures me that there is no reason for me to be concerned."

Except Priscilla knew there *was* reason for Banville to be concerned.

"Miss Tempest, are you listening to me?"

"Definitely, sir," Priscilla replied, forcing herself to refocus.

"I am soon to return to our home; therefore, it will not be necessary to look further into these scurrilous rumours that have been going around—rumours Mrs. Banville assures me are no more than that, possibly fuelled by HRH the Princess Margaret as a result of the falling out between Mrs. Banville and herself."

Priscilla, not knowing what to say in response to this, remained silent as she tried to wipe out the image crowding her head: Daisee Banville naked on a sofa with her lover.

A lover who almost certainly was Lord Snowdon.

"Miss Tempest!" Banville's shattering voice was at an angry pitch. "I have the distinct feeling you are not listening to me."

"I am indeed, sir," Priscilla answered quickly. "Then it is your wish that I discontinue further inquiries?"

"That is correct." Banville hesitated, poised behind his desk, suggesting he was trying to decide what to say next. "Unless..."

"Sir?"

"Unless you have uncovered information that you would like to share."

"About what, sir?" Priscilla said, stalling.

"For God's sake," Banville snapped angrily. "You know damned well what I'm talking about. These rumours. Did you find that there was any truth to them?"

Priscilla had trouble swallowing before she managed to answer. "No, sir, I didn't."

Banville studied her, his face full of suspicion. "You are sure about that?"

There was a wild moment when Priscilla might have told him the truth. But in a flash that moment passed. "Yes, sir."

"Then that will be all for now, Miss Tempest."

"Very good, sir." Priscilla started for the exit. Banville's icy voice stopped her.

"Miss Tempest..."

She turned to him.

"A reminder that this remains between the two of us and is not to go any further than my office."

"Of course."

"And another thing, Miss Tempest."

"Yes, sir?"

"I must tell you I am not pleased with your tardiness. Therefore, I am putting you on notice. The next time I call for you, you will come promptly, without delays or excuses. Am I making myself clear?"

"Quite clear, sir."

"Good day to you, Miss Tempest."

Banville lowered his head, busying himself with the far more important papers on his desk as Priscilla exited, choking back her anger at being so summarily dismissed.

"What the devil is going on?"

In the corridor outside the Place of Execution, Priscilla found herself face to face with a furious Major O'Hara. Was there anyone in this hotel who wasn't angry with her?

"I'm sorry, Major, what did you say?"

"I ask—no, I *demand* to know what's going on between you and Mr. Banville, not to mention a very upset Mrs. Banville."

"What makes you think anything is going on?" Priscilla made her best attempt at a puzzled expression.

"Summonses to Mr. Banville's office. Secretive meetings about which I know nothing. Calls from a distraught Mrs. Banville, asking me what I know about events transpiring between the two of you."

"Whatever is going on, Major—and I am at liberty to say that nothing is *going on*, as you put it—it's none of your business."

"If it affects the security and reputation of this hotel and the wife of our general manager, it is most certainly my business," huffed Major O'Hara.

"Nothing I've said to Mr. Banville has anything to do with the security of this hotel," Priscilla shot back.

"What about Mrs. Banville?"

"If you have any questions about Mrs. Banville, you should address them to Mr. Banville or, better yet, Mrs. Banville herself."

"I'll keep that in mind after she finishes with you."

"What are you talking about?"

"Mrs. Banville. She's waiting in your office." Major O'Hara looked almost gleeful as he added, "Your time here has been short, Miss Tempest. Rest assured you will not be missed."

Yes, Priscilla thought as she headed toward her office, there was no doubt in her mind about that.

The Perfect Mrs. Banville

Feeling dizzy and slightly nauseous following confrontations with both Banville and Major O'Hara, horrified at the prospect of meeting Daisee Banville, Priscilla wasn't paying attention and thus was nearly run down by the small army moving across the Front Hall. Harinder Singh, the Rajah of Faridkot himself, was on the move once again, this time accompanied by his three wives, who were trailed by a dozen retainers and the omnipresent bodyguards.

As he came abreast of Priscilla, he stopped. His retinue stumbled to a halt around him. "Miss Tempest. Here you are yet again."

"So good to see you, Your Highness."

"You retain your position at the press office, I assume."

"Yes, most certainly." For the time being, anyway, Priscilla thought.

"You are aware that I do not wish to speak to the press while I am in London."

"I am, sir."

"Even though I recently met with Her Royal Majesty, the Queen."

"Tea with the Queen," confirmed Priscilla, wondering where this was going. "I remember. Most impressive."

"But no press."

"None. No."

"Except perhaps the *Times*."

"The *Times*?" Priscilla reminded herself that she really had to learn to stop sounding as though she was confused, even when she was very confused.

"The *Times* of London. Do you not know it?"

"Yes, certainly," replied Priscilla. "Do I understand you to say you would be willing to speak to the *Times*?"

"Perhaps."

"I would be happy to look into that for you, Your Highness," Priscilla said. "If that's what you would like me to do."

"See to it," he said curtly. "Now we are off to Van Cleef & Arpels to purchase a necklace."

The rajah walked briskly away, heading toward the front entrance. His retinue, caught off guard, sprang to life and hurried after him.

Susie was in full panic mode, making the frantic hand signals that warned of big trouble ahead as Priscilla entered 205.

"Yes, I know," Priscilla said. "I'll deal with it, but I want you to get hold of Godfrey Smith at the *Times* and see if he might be willing to do an interview with the Rajah of Faridkot."

"I thought the rajah wasn't talking to the press."

"He's not. But he wants to talk to the *Times*. See what you can set up."

"Right-o," said Susie.

Priscilla took one of her deepest breaths before entering her office.

Sure enough, as Major O'Hara had so gleefully predicted, trouble this afternoon was represented by Daisee Banville in all her immaculate glory; perfection polished to the point where she seemed to generate her own light as she sat on the sofa with long legs crossed, looking for all the world like the Cheshire Cat, satisfied that the canary had been swallowed.

"Mrs. Banville, what a pleasant surprise," Priscilla managed as she closed the office door.

"Did you tell him?" Daisee demanded, followed by what to Priscilla looked like the most diabolical of smiles.

"I don't understand," Priscilla said, feigning innocence. "Tell who, what?"

"You are a bitch," Daisee said calmly. "Did you really think for a moment that you were going to get away with this shit?"

"I'm not trying to get away with anything," Priscilla said, forcing herself, against all her better instincts, not to flee the office.

"You didn't tell him, did you?" Daisee was on her feet, waves of Hermès Calèche adding to the glow spreading around her; a beautifully constructed force of nature whose perfection could not be marred by the minor flaw that was her nasty smirk.

"There is nothing to tell," Priscilla said.

"Tell him anything you like," Daisee snarled. "Do you think he would ever believe you, anyway? Do not kid yourself, Priscilla. He believes me. He believes anything I tell him. He doesn't want to lose me. Therefore, he believes me. He will always believe me because if he doesn't, the marriage is over and he is ruined."

"Good for the two of you," Priscilla said, keeping her voice level, "I'm happy that you have been able to work things out."

The force of the slap Daisee delivered sent Priscilla staggering back. It crossed her mind that until now she had managed to get through her young life without anyone slapping her. The delivery of two blows in a single week had changed all that.

"Who do you think you are?" Daisee hissed. "You come snooping around in my personal life, break into my house, and then have the nerve to comment on my marriage?"

Her voice rose angrily. "You're finished here, you must know that. The final nail went into your coffin when you stuck your nose where it doesn't belong. I want you out of here, do you understand? If you won't go voluntarily, I will devote every breath to making sure my husband fires you. And he will. Believe me."

That did it for Priscilla. To hell with it. To hell with everyone. If Daisee wanted to make threats, fine, she could make them right back.

"First of all," Priscilla said in a voice that surprised her with its strength, "if you ever hit me again, I will beat the crap out of you—and believe me, I'm Canadian, I can do it. Secondly, you had better hope that I don't lose this job. Your husband suspects you've been revenge-fucking Princess Margaret's husband, and I'm pretty sure that is the case. Truly, you should do everything in your power, Mrs. Banville, to make sure that I *keep* my job. If I were you, I would quickly decide to become my biggest supporter. Inside the Savoy, I am no threat to you at all. I am the soul of discretion. Outside, well, then I'm outside, aren't I?"

Daisee looked as though she was about to explode. Her eyes blazed with fury, her mouth making curious twisting movements as though preparing to spit bile. But instead, she turned, opened the door, and flounced out past a slack-jawed Susie.

With everything swirling in a dizzying blur, Priscilla managed to reach her desk. Somehow there was safety there, refuge from the battering storm. She took deep, restorative breaths, trying to ignore the burning pain running up and down the side of her face. Susie appeared in the doorway. "A nightmare!" Susie announced. "I'm not even going to ask how you are. I can plainly see there is a problem."

"I'm fine," Priscilla insisted.

"What was *that* all about? I mean, good God..."

"A misunderstanding, that's all," Priscilla said, working to recover her equilibrium, the professional calm of the good Savoy employee.

"That was quite a misunderstanding," Susie observed.

"It's over. We get on with things. And we keep quiet, understand?"

"Yes, definitely. Mum's the word and all that. But we are going to lose our jobs, aren't we?"

"Not today," Priscilla said. "Today, like I told you, you are going to phone the *Times* and pitch an exclusive interview with the Rajah of Faridkot."

"Then tomorrow we lose our jobs?"

"Ah, tomorrow," Priscilla said. "Nothing is ever certain about tomorrow, is it?"

"Not around here," Susie said, looking mortified. "Definitely not around here."

CHAPTER THIRTY-FIVE

The Gossip's Bridle Club Reconvenes

Larry Olivier was late for a second emergency meeting of the Gossip's Bridle Club, once again called by the club's newest member, Miss Priscilla Tempest. Gielgud insisted that they meet in the American Bar so he could be more comfortable and enjoy something other than red wine.

"A Buck's Fizz, that's what you need," Noël suggested after they had settled into their usual corner. Around them, the tables were filling with the after-work crowd, in need of a little glamour and a stiff cocktail.

"I want a decent gin and tonic, thank you very much," Gielgud insisted. "Incidentally, where's Larry? Why couldn't he make it?"

"He's been busy hammering out the new season at the National—he says," answered Noël. "Although I believe there is a certain actress that has caught his lascivious eye."

"Sex is simply no excuse for missing a meeting of the club, even if it is an emergency meeting," Gielgud said, flagging a waiter.

They were interrupted by a harried Olivier as he trundled across the bar. Heads turned in delighted recognition as he passed. There was a smattering of applause.

"Oh God, we are never going to hear the end of this," Gielgud groaned.

Olivier was beaming by the time he sat down. "So sorry," he announced, glancing around, rewarding his admirers with a quick smile that managed to incorporate both embarrassment and appreciation. "Honestly, I'm no more than a humble thespian. The applause. The adulation. It's all too much."

Gielgud rolled his eyes.

"Trouble at the National? Or a talented young actress in need of words of advice from a humble thespian?" inquired Noël.

"No trouble and no young actresses, alas. Merely a dentist running late."

"You've arrived in time for Priscilla to tell us why she has called this meeting," said Noël.

"First of all," Priscilla said. "Thanks to the three of you for once again agreeing to meet on such short notice."

She took a deep breath and then proceeded to spill out the details of how a distraught Banville had called her into his office and revealed that he and his wife had separated, and that he suspected she was having an affair—and how, to Priscilla's dismay, he had asked her to use her sources to find out if there was any truth to rumours that her lover was Antony Armstrong-Jones.

Then suddenly, she told the other club members, that all changed.

"Now," Priscilla continued, "I have been told in no uncertain terms that he and his wife have reconciled. He has been convinced by Daisee, Mrs. Banville, that she is not having an affair and has ordered me to cease any investigation that might reveal that she is."

"In the meantime, were you able to uncover evidence that Mrs. Banville was being, shall we say, indiscreet?" Gielgud asked.

Priscilla hesitated long enough to cause Olivier's eyes to light up. "Aha! You *did* uncover something! Do tell, please!"

At that point the waiter arrived with their drinks—Buck's Fizzes for Priscilla and Noël, the gin and tonic for Gielgud. "The

1945 Château d'Yquem for me, if you please," Olivier said to the waiter.

The waiter did not blink an eye. "Very good, sir."

"Good God, Larry, that's a dessert wine," announced an appalled Gielgud.

"I happen to like it," countered Olivier peevishly.

"Tell us what you found," Noël said to Priscilla once the waiter had departed. His anticipation was such that he ignored his drink—highly unusual, to say the least.

"Let me put it this way," Priscilla said. "She was definitely with someone."

"And how do you know that?" Noël pressed.

"Because I saw them together," Priscilla said with certainty.

"But who?" Noël asked. "Who was Mrs. Banville 'together' with?"

"That's the problem. I couldn't make out the man's face."

"Then you don't know for sure if it was Tony Armstrong-Jones?"

"No. Not for certain. But I'm pretty sure he was with Daisee at her cottage in the village of Chipping Campden—"

"What the devil were they doing out there?" Gielgud asked.

"We know what they were doing," Noël said. "What else does one do in Chipping Campden?"

"As I left, Daisee spotted me," Priscilla went on.

"Oh dear," said Olivier.

"However, I did manage to get the licence number of the car she and her lover arrived in."

"And did you then find out who the car is registered to?"

Priscilla nodded. "A man named Terry O'Hara. I believe he was waiting outside."

"Did he see you?" Gielgud inquired.

"He chased me across a field, but I managed to get away from him."

"You said his name was Terry O'Hara?" Noël was leaning forward intently.

"Does that name mean anything to you?"

The playwright's eyes lit up. "This fits in with what I've been hearing from a source at Buck House."

"You still have sources at the Palace?" asked Olivier in disbelief.

"Indeed I do, dear boy. That old pile is full of Princess Margaret's detractors. They like nothing better than to vent their petty complaints about the princess and her very common husband, Mr. Armstrong-Jones."

"What are these sources of yours telling you?" asked Gielgud.

"Among their many concerns is the rather sketchy quality of a number of Lord Snowdon's friends. Particularly a gentleman named"—and here he shot a sharp glance at Priscilla—"Terry O'Hara."

"And pray tell, who is this Terry O'Hara?" Olivier asked. "I've certainly never heard of him."

"That's because, Larry, you do not frequent London's illegal gambling clubs," Noël explained. "If you did, you would know that Mr. O'Hara runs several of them."

"And he is a good friend of Lord Snowdon," added Priscilla.

"And this is the fellow you saw with Mrs. Banville?" Gielgud asked.

"It was Terry's car," Priscilla said, "but I think he was outside, keeping a lookout while Tony Armstrong-Jones was in the cottage with Daisee."

"Still, it is all rather a waste of time," remarked Olivier. "If your boss doesn't want you snooping around then what is the point?"

"Larry, this *is* the Gossip's Bridle Club," admonished Noël. "We *wallow* in gossip for gossip's sake. Our newest member has provided us with the finest quality. Princess Margaret's husband hobnobbing with a shady gambling club operator and possibly sleeping with the wife of the Savoy's general manager. Gossip, I would argue, doesn't get much better than this—and, I might add, there is more!"

"More?" Gielgud's eyebrows performed a delighted dance.

"The palace is lately in an even greater tizzy because our Mr. O'Hara has imported a girlfriend from Los Angeles—a woman known to run a high-end escort service in that city."

"Karen?" The name came out of Priscilla's mouth as an explosion of surprise.

The men regarded her with amazed expressions. "Don't tell me you know this woman," Noël said.

"Karen Hollander, if it's the same woman. I met her outside Terry O'Hara's place on Dove Mews."

"Soliciting?" Gielgud asked.

"Watering flowers."

Gielgud's noble face fell. "How disappointing."

"How did she strike you?" inquired Noël.

"As someone you would imagine watering flowers. She did not strike me as a woman in charge of an American escort service."

"You certainly have gotten around lately, haven't you, my dear?" observed Noël.

"But as Larry rightly points out, to what end?" Priscilla allowed herself to vent her frustration. "My snooping has only landed me deeper into Mr. Banville's bad books than I was before. Daisee just attacked me in my office. She is furious, naturally, even more determined than ever to see the end of me at the Savoy."

"All the more reason why we must solve the murder of Skye Kane," said Noël. "Once that is accomplished all else will be forgiven—and forgotten."

"We know damned well who the killer is," Gielgud pronounced.

"Do we now?" Noël's eyebrows reached new heights of skepticism. "Pray tell, Johnny, you mustn't keep us in suspense. Who is the killer?"

"There is no doubt in my mind that it is the Abominable Showman himself, David Merrick."

"I would have agreed with you earlier," Priscilla put in. "But now I'm beginning to have my doubts."

"How so?" Gielgud asked.

"I spoke earlier to Mr. Merrick. He seemed genuinely upset—an emotional wreck in fact. He swears he is innocent."

"What else would you suppose a killer would say?" Gielgud argued. "Merrick wouldn't concede he ever had a flop show, let alone admit that he killed someone."

"He has confessed to me that he was at the murder scene," Priscilla went on.

"I rest my case!" interjected Gielgud.

"Hold your horses, Johnny." Noël turned to Priscilla. "This is an amazing revelation. If he didn't kill Skye, what was his reason for being in her dressing room?"

"He said he had been drinking in his suite when she called and wanted him to meet her. When he got there, he told me, Skye was already dead. He said that he saw someone in the Restaurant, a man he thinks was the killer."

"A likely story," pronounced Olivier. "I mean, Johnny is right for once—how could he say anything else?"

"He's afraid that's what the police will think. That's why he is reluctant to come forward. Instead, he asked me to go to them."

"He's trying to frame you," Gielgud pronounced authoritatively.

"Johnny's got a point, Priscilla," Olivier said. "I'd be very careful about becoming involved with anything Mr. Merrick might ask of you."

"I do believe I need another Buck's Fizz," said Priscilla.

The waiter arrived with Olivier's Château D'Yquem. Noël summoned another Buck's Fizz. The crowd in the bar had begun to thin, enabling Priscilla to spot Hans Kringelein coming in the door. In the elegant atmosphere of the American Bar, he certainly stood out in his wrinkled grey suit and bow tie. She waved to him. Kringelein moved hesitantly forward, slightly crouched, as though entering a minefield. Unlike Olivier, he turned no heads as he made his way to where Priscilla was sitting.

"Miss Tempest," he said, "I thought that was you. What a pleasure."

"Mr. Kringelein, are you looking for someone? Meeting someone here?"

"My goodness, no. I look for no one. I am alone. I merely wanted a peek at what I have been told is a very famous bar at the Savoy."

Priscilla turned to the others. "Do you mind if Mr. Kringelein joins us? I would say he is the most interesting guest currently staying with us."

"Then, dear boy, by all means, you must join us," Noël said to Kringelein.

"Are you sure I am not intruding?"

"Not at all, Mr. Kringelein," Priscilla said. "Please sit down."

"This is very kind of you," Kringelein said, lowering himself into a chair.

Priscilla introduced Noël, Olivier and Gielgud. Kringelein eagerly shook their hands without appearing to recognize any of them.

"Mr. Kringelein has retired from his profession as a waiter at—you tell them where you worked, Mr. Kringelein."

"I was at the Dithmarscher Hof, the finest hotel in Itzehoe, not far from Hamburg," he explained shyly.

"I know the hotel—I have stayed there," announced Noël. "Lovely. Excellent service. Wonderful food. Who knows, Mr. Kringelein, we may have met. Your name does sound familiar. I wonder if I've heard it before."

"There are many Kringeleins in the world."

"Are there really?"

"But enough of me," Kringelein said. "What of you gentlemen? Please tell me what you do." He turned to Noël. "Mr.—I believe it is Coward?"

Noël appeared slightly taken aback. "What do I do? Let me see…" He seemed to ponder this for a time, blowing smoke rings into the air as he did so. "I have often asked myself that very question. As near as I can make out, I scribble down the words that occur to me from time to time. And then I go out and try to persuade people to read them back to me."

"This is quite unusual work." Kringelein seemed equally taken aback. "Do you mind if I ask what such work pays you?"

"Not nearly enough, I'm afraid," Noël said.

Kringelein next addressed Gielgud. "And you, sir?"

"At the moment, sadly, I am an unemployed actor."

"And Mr. Oliver…what of you?"

"I'm sorry, it's *Olivier*," the actor corrected, rather huffily.

"My apologies. Mr. Olivier."

"What am I, you ask?"

"Please," said Kringelein.

"I am the western world's greatest living actor," Olivier answered, wine in hand.

"Oh for heaven's sake, Larry!" Gielgud was rolling his eyes in exasperation. "That is too much, even for you."

"It happens to be true," Olivier retorted defensively.

"Good God in heaven," declared Gielgud.

"Come on, what's the use beating around the bush about it? This man might as well know who he's sitting beside."

"I do very much appreciate it," Kringelein put in eagerly. "And I am so sorry at my ignorance. We do not get news of world-famous English actors in Itzehoe."

Gielgud heaved a resigned sigh. "What brings you to the Savoy, Mr. Kringelein?"

"As I have told Miss Tempest, after serving the rich for so many years, I decided I would like to experience, for a short period of time, what it is *like* to be rich. What better place to do this than at the Savoy, the greatest of all European hotels?"

"Wonderful," said Noël. "Can we get you a drink, Mr. Kringelein?"

"Perhaps a Coca-Cola."

"Nothing stronger?"

"Oh no. You see, I do not drink alcohol."

Priscilla's Buck's Fizz arrived, and a Coca-Cola was ordered along with another gin and tonic for Gielgud.

"You know I just had the most marvellous experience," Kringelein announced.

"Do tell," said Noël.

"A real maharajah right there in the Front Hall with his three wives and a large entourage. I have never seen anything like it. Three wives! Apparently, he was returning from Van Cleef & Arpels where he is said to have purchased the most expensive piece of jewellery: a necklace containing thirteen emeralds. Can you imagine? Thirteen *emeralds*. Such wealth!"

"I didn't know there were still maharajahs around," Gielgud said.

"Right here in this wonderful hotel!" exclaimed Kringelein.

"In today's modern world the rajah is fast becoming an extinct breed," observed Noël, taking on the mien of Professor

Coward. "But they do continue to thrive in hotels like the Savoy. Personally," he added impishly, "I never stay as a lodge-a unless I know there's a rajah."

As the others groaned in horror, a server brought more drinks. Kringelein eyed the Coca-Cola apprehensively. Noël lifted his flute. "Tell me, Mr. Kringelein, you have served the rich and now you live among the rich. What have you concluded about the rich?"

For a moment, Kringelein seemed at a loss for words. "Before I say anything," he said when he finally spoke, "I must ask: Are any of you at this table rich, by chance?"

"Noël is filthy rich although he will never admit it," said Gielgud.

"My dear boy," Noël protested, "by the time the taxman finishes with me, I'm out on the street with a tin cup."

"As it happens," Gielgud said, "I am an actor and by definition actors are as poor as church mice." He lifted his glass. "I'm lucky to be able to afford a gin and tonic—or two!"

"I'm afraid I'm no better," Olivier admitted with a sigh. "The National Theatre doesn't exactly line my pockets."

Priscilla said to Kringelein, "I think you're in safe company when it comes to airing your views on the rich."

"The thing about the rich—they are...*stinken*!" The declaration silenced everyone momentarily. Then all three men burst into laughter.

"You mean stinkers," said Noël.

"Yes!" agreed Kringelein. "Stinkers! All of them!" Kringelein then raised a warning finger, "However, I must tell you that after staying here at the Savoy, I have decided it is better to live among the stinking rich than to serve the stinking rich."

"Well put, sir," Gielgud said.

"As I have observed many times over the years—" Noël began.

"Perhaps too many," interrupted Gielgud.

"As I have said," the playwright continued, "we're all made the same, though some more than others."

Kringelein was about to pick up his drink when his attention was drawn toward the entrance to the bar. A tall woman in her fifties wearing a broad-brimmed hat stood looking around. Kringelein abruptly appeared nervous. "Yes, I am so sorry." He stumbled to his feet. "I must leave you now. It is most imperative."

"Is something wrong, Mr. Kringelein?" Priscilla asked.

"No. An appointment I forgot about, that's all. *Danke, danke*—oh dear, I nearly forgot. My Coca-Cola. I must pay for my Coca-Cola."

"Not to worry, it's on the Savoy," Priscilla said. "Are you sure nothing's wrong?"

"Yes, yes." And away he hurried. Priscilla noticed the tall woman in the broad-brimmed hat was gone. A moment later, Kringelein was too.

"That was all quite strange," Noël offered.

"Yes, it was," Priscilla agreed.

"The rich may indeed be stinkers," added Gielgud, "but retired waiters from Itzehoe are most curious."

And even more curious, thought Priscilla: the retired waiter who knew no one but who seemed to know a tall, slim woman in a wide-brimmed hat.

"That name, Kringelein," Noël mused. "I've heard it before. But where?"

The Proposition

Fortified by the two Buck's Fizzes, which helped speed her recovery from Daisee Banville's assault, Priscilla returned to the tranquility of 205. It was not so tranquil, however. As soon as she was in the door, her phone started to ring.

She glared at the ringing telephone. It reminded her of a screeching child. She should never answer phones—or have children—she decided. The champagne fuelled her determination not to pick up the receiver.

But the child kept screeching remorselessly. There was only one way to stop it. She yanked up the receiver.

"Hello, is this Priscilla?"

"Yes, it is," Priscilla reluctantly admitted.

"Hi," the voice said cheerily, "it's Karen Hollander calling. Do you remember me? The American lady watering the flowers?"

The madam operating a high-end California escort service? Priscilla immediately thought. "Yes, of course," she said into the phone.

"How are you?" Karen asked.

"I'm very well, thanks," Priscilla said, somewhat nonplussed by Karen's call. "Do you mind if I ask how you got this number?"

"This is the number you gave me. Should I not have called?" Karen asked anxiously.

"No, no, it's fine," Priscilla answered hurriedly. In her haste, had she inadvertently scribbled down her direct line at the hotel rather than her little-used home number?

"I hope I haven't done something wrong," Karen said.

"Not at all. I'm glad to hear from you, Karen. I was just thinking about you as it happens." Talking about your sketchy boyfriend would be more accurate, she thought.

"I'm wandering the streets of London feeling slightly lost. I called on the off chance you might be free for a drink."

"Uh, yes, I could do that."

"Wonderful!" There was excitement in Karen's voice. "You know where I've always wanted to visit, having heard so much about it?"

"Where is that?"

"The Savoy Hotel. How does that sound?"

That did not sound good at all. "I'll tell you what," Priscilla said, recovering quickly. "Tonight, the Connaught would be more convenient for me. They've got a nice bar and it's a little quieter than the Savoy."

"Sounds great," Karen said enthusiastically. "Shall we say in an hour?"

"It's in Mayfair. Can you get there?"

"I'll find it," she said confidently. "See you soon."

Great, Priscilla thought as she hung up. What was she getting herself into now?

The answer? More of what she had been specifically told not to get into.

Priscilla's biases naturally ran against the Connaught in favour of the Savoy, never mind that the two hotels were owned by the same group. The former Coburg Hotel had been forced to hurriedly change its German name at the outbreak of World War I and become the Connaught. This was the same year the Royal Family dropped their Saxe-Coburg-Gotha name and took refuge behind the House of Windsor.

The sombre, dark-wood lobby, the iconic teak staircase inlaid with gold leaf, the gilt-framed paintings, she disliked all of it. And then there was the pretention of the martini trolley, a tradition in the Connaught Bar. What was the big deal about serving drinks from a trolley?

Karen Hollander certainly seemed to appreciate the effort. As Priscilla approached, an attentive waiter presented Karen with the martini he had just prepared—with a lemon twist, Priscilla noted.

"Isn't this amazing?" Karen gushed. "A martini prepared right at your table. Would you like one, Priscilla?"

"Champagne for me, please," Priscilla said to the waiter, seating herself across from Karen.

The martini trolley waiter looked at Priscilla as though he had been betrayed by an interloper who had no place in this rarified atmosphere. "Of course, madam," he said frostily, pushing the cart hurriedly away as though to make an escape.

"Oh dear," said Priscilla. "I'm afraid I've broken some unwritten law of the Connaught jungle."

"Not to worry," said Karen, lifting her glass, "I love martinis. I can keep them busy all night."

This evening Karen looked less like the flower lady with a watering can and more the elegant American abroad in London, hair falling loosely to her shoulders, subtle mascara and pale pink lipstick, a classic tweed Chanel suit, fashionable yet restrained, no hint whatsoever of a woman working in the sex trade. Could Noël Coward be mistaken? Looking at Karen Hollander sipping at her martini, Priscilla could well believe he was.

"I hope I didn't spoil any plans you had this evening," Karen said, putting down her glass. She reached for her Chanel purse with the chain-link shoulder strap.

"No plans," Priscilla said. "What about you? Where's your boyfriend tonight?"

Karen made a face as she withdrew a pack of Du Maurier cigarettes. "Terry is doing what he's always doing—working. Do you mind if I smoke?"

Priscilla shook her head. "Remind me again what he does for a living."

"Did I not say something about it being very hush-hush?" Karen had withdrawn a cigarette.

"Excuse me, madam," said a waiter reaching over to light it for her.

"Thank you," Karen said, inhaling deeply.

"Well, that's what it is," she continued. "Or so he tells me. Investments. The City. He never says too much about his work."

"Funny," Priscilla said, "I do remember the hush-hush part of it, but as I recall, you said your boyfriend was secretive about being in the security business."

Karen took another long puff on her cigarette before she said, "Did I? Well, then it goes to show you how secretive he is, doesn't it?"

Priscilla's flute of champagne arrived via another waiter who appeared more resigned to the presence of someone who failed to drink martinis. Karen retrieved her glass with her free hand and raised it in salute. "To the mysterious men in our lives."

Priscilla raised her glass. "Far too many of those," she observed before taking a drink.

"You suffer from them too?"

"On occasion," Priscilla said with a laugh.

Karen finished her drink and waved for a waiter.

"Did you figure out how to take care of it?" Priscilla asked.

"Take care of what?" Karen looked perplexed.

"The moonshadow euonymus."

Karen's relief was palpable. "Right, I got you. Good news about that. They are pretty hardy as it turns out. You don't have to do much of anything. My kind of plants."

Terry O'Hara arrived with the return of the martini trolley. As Priscilla did her best to hide her amazement, he seated himself beside Karen, saying, "Looks like I got here at the right time."

"With the martini trolley," Karen said, smiling.

Terry waved to the waiter already at work on Karen's second martini. "I'll have one as well. Adnams Longshore. Four dashes of bitters, not three. No olive. Lemon twist."

"Very good, sir," said the waiter with an appreciative smile for a customer who knew his way around a martini.

"Baby, what a pleasant surprise," Karen said, leaning over to kiss Terry.

"I finished early, thought I'd pop by," he said. He glanced at Priscilla. A rather sexy glance, she couldn't help thinking. "You must be Priscilla."

"My good friend, Priscilla Tempest," Karen added. "Priscilla, this is Terry O'Hara, the mysterious boyfriend I've been going on about."

Handsome Terry, Priscilla immediately thought. That thick black hair curling artfully around a tanned and dimpled face, just the right amount of five o'clock shadow, blue eyes framed with long lashes, a full, almost feminine mouth now turned to a rather sensual—in Priscilla's estimation—smile of welcome. "Karen has been telling me about you."

What was there to tell? Priscilla wondered as she accepted his firm hand.

The waiter placed the two martinis on the table and asked Priscilla if she'd like more champagne. Better to keep a clear head, she thought, and declined.

"To everyone's good health," Terry said, raising his glass.

"To a new friend in London," Karen added.

"New friends," Priscilla said. New friends who are up to what? she thought.

"Excellent," Terry pronounced after sipping his drink. "They say they make a good martini here and what do you know, they actually do." He looked at Priscilla. "Sure we can't offer you more champagne, Priscilla?"

"Thanks, but I'm still nursing this one," she said, indicating her half-full flute.

"What have I missed?" Terry asked, placing his glass on the table. "What have the two of you been talking about?"

"The problems of mysterious boyfriends," Karen said.

"Oh?" Terry adopted an expression of innocence. "Do you have a mysterious boyfriend?"

"Definitely," said Karen. "But maybe that's part of the fun."

"I must say, I don't consider myself very mysterious," Terry said with a shrug. He looked at Priscilla. "What about you, Priscilla? Any mysterious boyfriends?"

"Not at the moment," Priscilla answered.

"What happened to them?" Terry asked the question much more seriously than she might have expected.

"Let's say I solved the mystery and moved on." As good an answer as she could summon on short notice.

"There you go," Terry said. "Maintaining a bit of mystery, maybe that's the key to a successful relationship."

"At least if you want to keep Priscilla interested," Karen added, smiling.

"Actually, Priscilla," Terry said with a studied casualness, "you and I have encountered each other before."

"Oh? How so?"

"Sort of encountered one another, rather." His voice was friendly, conversational. "I am the fellow who chased you into a meadow the other night outside Chipping Campden. Do you remember?"

Priscilla, speechless, could only stare blankly at the two of them. Remembering only too well the dark figure coming after her.

"What were you doing, Terry? Not protecting Tony again?" Karen scolded him. "You told me you weren't going to do that anymore."

"Tony's hard to resist. What can I say?" Terry addressed Priscilla. "Tony and Terry. It's an all for one, one for all sort of thing with the two of us."

"Boys being silly boys." Karen shook her head. "You see what I mean by mysterious, Priscilla? I'm never quite sure what Terry is up to with Tony. But they are always up to something."

Terry ignored her as he spoke to Priscilla, "I must apologize. I didn't mean to scare you and I was relieved to see that you got back to your car. What's more, I don't believe anyone inside the cottage was any the wiser."

Daisee Banville was certainly the wiser, Priscilla mused. But these two didn't need to know that. They didn't need to know anything—except they did.

"Still, it does beg the question," Terry continued.

"What question is that, baby?" asked Karen, dousing the cigarette she had mostly ignored.

"The question of what Priscilla was doing at Chipping Campden in the first place."

"Yes, that question," Karen agreed. "A good question."

"Priscilla?" Terry had cocked an enquiring eyebrow.

"What's this about?" Priscilla demanded, suddenly feeling trapped in the Connaught Bar and increasingly alarmed.

Karen placed her hand on Priscilla's knee, a gesture that served only to make Priscilla more uncomfortable. "I have to say I admire the way you deftly shifted our meeting away from the Savoy. Very clever."

"Why would you admire that?" demanded Priscilla.

"I suppose a desire to keep me in the dark about where you work."

"But as it happens, we do know where you work," Terry said.

"How would you know that?" Priscilla struggled to understand where they were going with this.

"I suppose it's thanks to our unexpected encounter in Chipping Campden. A Canadian bird in London lands a job at the city's most prestigious hotel, no one quite sure how she got it. Performance somewhat uneven. Constant job worries. You see?" Terry said with satisfaction. "We know a good deal about you."

"Now don't let Terry upset you." Karen leaned forward, oozing reassurance. "We don't want you being frightened or worried. We're to be friends, and the last thing friends do is hurt or intimidate one another."

"Karen is absolutely right." Terry also leaned in, his face flush with what to Priscilla's eyes looked like manufactured compassion. "We are here, Priscilla, to change your life. Change it for the better, but change it."

"And how will you do that?"

Now Karen's intensity was a match for her boyfriend's. "Priscilla, I've been very successful in the Los Angeles area providing entertainment services to a great many wealthy men who can't be bothered with the complications of relationships, or who are unhappy with the relationships they find themselves in. These men are in search of beautiful women with whom they can share a delightful evening's amusement."

"With my encouragement, Karen has decided to expand her operation to London," Terry joined in. "I believe there are opportunities here even greater than those in Los Angeles. There is an underserved international clientele with lots of money to spend in a city that, despite its swinging reputation, remains quite conservative and sexually repressed."

"I aim to change that," Karen continued. "I want to open this city up to its sensual potential, but to do that properly, Terry and I will need help."

"What? You want me to work for you? Sleep with visiting oil sheiks and American millionaires?"

The two broke into laughter. "I have no doubt that you would be in high demand, Priscilla," Karen said. "You are an intelligent, lovely woman, but no, that's not what we need from you—although I must say your idea is tempting."

"What we need, Priscilla, is what you can provide for us," Terry explained.

"And what is that?"

"Access."

"I'm not sure I understand," Priscilla said, beginning to understand only too well.

"There wouldn't be much to it," Karen said. "All you would have to do from time to time is provide us with the names of guests at the Savoy who might be interested in the sort of services that I can provide for them."

"In other words, you want me to pimp for you," Priscilla declared.

Karen's abruptly unhappy face marred her innate perfection. "I wouldn't put it in those terms. This is a high-end business, the best people, the most beautiful women. No one gets hurt. Everyone benefits."

"What's more," chimed in Terry, "you would do very well financially with this arrangement."

"A huge windfall for you—for all of us," added Karen.

Priscilla stared dumbfounded as Terry lit another cigarette for Karen. She blew a cloud of smoke in the air and then smiled at Priscilla. "What do you think?"

"I think you are both mad."

"Hardly," Karen said calmly.

"We're businesspeople, laying out a business proposition," Terry said.

"Tell me, how is Lord Snowdon involved in your...business?"

Terry waved a dismissive hand. "Tony is a charming friend and I've had some great times with him. Certainly he has helped me with valuable contacts, but that's as far as it goes. He is not involved in this."

"Except he's sleeping with the wife of the hotel's general manager."

"That's over—no small thanks to you," Terry advised. "In any event, it is not going to get in the way of what we plan to do."

"The point is," Karen said, "this is a workable business model that has proved itself to be very successful. In Los Angeles, I have a number of people similar to yourself who gladly provide me with information at five-star hotels, including the Beverly Hills, the Beverly Wilshire and the Beverly Hilton. This works, Priscilla. It works very well."

"Good for you," Priscilla said, gathering her shoulder bag, "but I'm not having anything to do with it."

"I'm afraid you are." Terry made the statement in a flat, certain voice.

"It would be wiser if you didn't leave just yet." Karen's hand was back on Priscilla's knee. Priscilla shoved it away.

"This is the ugly part we hoped to avoid," Terry said.

"It's not how we like to do things, Priscilla," Karen said quietly. "It really isn't."

"We are at the point where I must tell you we are backed by a fellow named Teddy Smith," Terry said. "The tabloid press tends to portray him as a gangster, but I prefer to see Teddy and his friends as businessmen. That's how they see themselves. However you wish to describe him, Teddy is a formidable partner in our enterprise. He does not react well when potential business associates disappoint him."

"I'm obviously new in town but, from what Terry tells me, we don't want to upset Teddy. Neither do you, Priscilla," Karen said.

Priscilla rose to her feet. Terry jumped up at the same time. His smile was not so easygoing as before. "Think about what we've offered. Take into consideration the downside of you not joining us."

"Think about this," Priscilla shot back. "You have your friends. But I have mine as well. My friends are Reggie and Ronnie Kray. And the Krays, to put it mildly, do not like it when their friends are threatened."

Terry's face went blank. "What are you talking about?"

"Reggie Kray is a very good friend," Priscilla said. "If I hear another word from you about this, if I am threatened any more in any way, believe me, Reggie will hear all about it."

Karen had joined Terry on her feet. "You've got the totally wrong idea about us, Priscilla."

"No," Priscilla said. "I don't think I have."

She couldn't be certain, but as she left the bar it looked as though Terry's face had turned a shade of grey. That gave her a certain amount of satisfaction.

CHAPTER THIRTY-SEVEN

The Avenging Kray

Reggie Kray sat in a dark corner of the Blind Beggar, away from the shabby lowlifes lined up along the bar, giving him the eye from time to time. Did they love him or were they figuring ways to kill him? Reggie mused. Probably they'd like to kill me, he concluded. Well, good luck with that. He drained what was left of his double whiskey and decided that he did not need another drink, that it would be better to call it a night. Then his brother arrived. The bar lowlifes shifted uneasily. It was one thing for Reggie to be in their midst, but Ronnie...you never knew about Ronnie.

"I just got off the phone," Ronnie stated, sliding in beside his brother. He stank of the aftershave Reggie hated. "Your bird has flown the coop at the Connaught but O'Hara and his bird are still there."

"Okay," Reggie said, pushing aside the whiskey tumbler so he could gather his cigarettes and rise to his feet.

"What do you want to do?" Ronnie asked, remaining seated.

"It's fine. I'll take care of it." Reggie used the back of his hand to clear lingering drops of whiskey from the corner of his mouth.

"You want some help?"

Reggie shook his head. "Like I said. I'll take care of it."

"I don't trust that bird of yours." Ronnie was frowning. "First the cops. Now this with the Teddy Smith bunch. What the hell?"

"Priscilla's fine. I got it under control," Reggie said impatiently.

"Do you? Where that bird is concerned, I'm not so sure."

"I repeat," Reggie said, his voice tight, leaning over his brother to emphasize the point. "I will take care of it."

"As long as you know what you're doing," Ronnie said.

"I *always* know what I'm doing," Reggie replied, straightening.

"What do you want me to do?"

"Make sure you don't shoot me on my way out," Reggie replied.

"Let me think about it." Ronnie cracked a smile.

Reggie made sure to keep an eye on his brother as he left the pub. You can never be too careful, he thought.

Reggie lucked out and found a parking spot down the way from number eleven, but even so he felt exposed sitting in the darkness, wondering what was delaying them, and thankful that it was a quiet neighbourhood, not many people around.

The odd dogwalker passed with little mutts straining at their leashes, determined to sniff every inch of concrete along the street. The dogwalkers, again thankfully, were invariably consumed with their dogs and paying no attention to the figure hunched in a parked car.

He began to relax.

Finally, the sleek grey Iso Grifo he had been on the lookout for flashed down the street. Immediately, he was jealous. He had heard about the Italian sports car, and now here it was in the hands of that right bastard, Terry O'Hara, arse-kisser for the Teddy Smith mob. The anger welled inside him. What was that tosser doing with such a beautiful car?

Well, he was about to fix that, wasn't he? Time Teddy got a lesson in who they should be talking to and who they shouldn't. Priscilla Tempest was most definitely off-limits to these bastards.

The Louisville Slugger baseball bat he had imported from America was on the passenger seat. He picked it up, waiting until the couple left the Iso Grifo and started toward him. Terry and his new bird, bathed in a streetlight's beam, were two good-looking people, Reggie couldn't help thinking as he got out of his Jaguar.

The couple briefly registered shock before Reggie slammed the bat into Terry's head, sending him reeling. The woman got half a scream out before he swung at her, narrowly missing as she ducked away.

Terry had somehow remained on his feet, his head bleeding, wobbling under the streetlight. Reggie used the bat to poke Terry in the stomach, sending him to the pavement. The girlfriend had begun to shout at him. He intended to shut her up—except the girlfriend abruptly became quiet and he noticed something in her hand.

A gun.

There was an instant to regret not considering the possibility of a gun, and then he was shot, once again. His last thought before he hit the ground was relief that it wasn't his brother this time.

CHAPTER THIRTY-EIGHT

Tear Up the Bedsheets!

Priscilla was cocooned, finally, in the safe harbour that was her flat, surrounded by the clothes she should have put away but hadn't; the piles of books she was going to get around to reading but hadn't; the dishes she should have washed but hadn't; the carpet with the red wine stains she hadn't been able to get out; the bed that wasn't made; the perfumes, the eyeliner pencils, the cream jars, the soaps, all the things strewn about the bathroom she meant to put away, but hadn't; the glorious comforting mess of everything.

And the silence. Ah, the silence! No one yelling and complaining; no demanding voices on the other end of a constantly ringing phone. No one threatening. No one trying to blackmail her. Or seduce her.

Peace! Quiet!

Priscilla flopped on the sofa and closed her eyes, luxuriating in the hush of her solitude, gathering the energy required to retrieve the chardonnay she vaguely recalled was in the refrigerator.

That would be nice, she thought, a glass of wine. Her mind was focused on the wine when she became vaguely aware of a sound disturbing her reverie.

A pounding. On the door.

Someone thumping on her door.

Damn!

Priscilla struggled off the sofa, not wanting to do anything but drink wine and make the noise stop. But the pounding—not knocking, *pounding*—continued.

Her intention was to open the door a crack so that the late-night intruder could be properly inspected. However, as soon as she turned the lock, the door banged open, knocking her back so that Reggie Kray could lurch in—adding, Priscilla couldn't help but immediately notice, more red to the wine stains on the carpet.

The pantleg of Reggie's bespoke suit was soaked in blood. He braced himself against the wall, his otherwise perfectly cut hair tumbling down over his sweaty forehead, his breath coming in ragged gasps. "I was in the neighbourhood...thought I'd drop around, say hello..."

"What happened to you?"

"What makes you think anything happened to me?" he gasped.

"Reggie, you're bleeding all over the carpet."

"Sorry about that," Reggie said. "Someone shot me."

"Again?"

He managed a smile. "Lately, I haven't had much luck when it comes to people shooting me."

Reggie staggered as far as an armchair and fell into it. He leaned over to inspect his leg. "Doesn't look too bad," he concluded. "Looks like the bullet might have grazed my leg." He squinted up at the hovering Priscilla. "Don't have any whiskey, do you?"

"You need to get to a hospital," Priscilla said.

"No hospitals," Reggie said with a shake of his head. "Just the whiskey."

"I don't have any whiskey. Vodka?"

"Does the trick."

Priscilla hurried into the kitchen and came back with a tumbler full of straight vodka as well as a couple of tea towels she had grabbed off the counter. He took the tumbler from her and gulped down its contents. "God, what a fuckup," he announced. "Listen, you have to lift my leg up."

"Your leg up?"

"Stops blood flowing from the heart to the wound." He pointed a shaky finger. "That chair over there. And I need a blanket."

She fetched the chair, then she lifted his leg up and slipped the towels beneath it.

"Careful." He grimaced in pain as she lowered his foot onto the chair.

She found a spare blanket in the bedroom closet and then helped him wrap it around himself. "That's better," he said.

Reggie seemed to force the strength needed to speak. "Now...apply pressure to the wound. Also helps stop the blood flow. Got something for that?"

"I don't know," she said. "Let me think."

Entering the bedroom, she tore up a bedsheet and then returned to the living room with pieces of it. She kneeled and used scissors to cut through the cloth of his trousers. "There goes a perfectly good suit," he groaned.

"From now on, you should remember not to wear expensive clothes when you get yourself shot," Priscilla advised.

"I'll keep that in mind," he said, peering down at the mess of his leg. "I don't think it's bleeding as much."

Back in the kitchen, she ran warm water into a bowl and found a clean cloth. She washed the blood from the wound as best she could before binding his leg with strips of the bedsheet.

"Not too tight," he said.

When she was finished, she poured more vodka for him.

"Tell me what happened," Priscilla said.

"The usual," Reggie said. "A woman..."

"A woman shot you?"

"The times are changing," he said in a weak voice. "In addition to the lads, I've now got to be on the lookout for birds with guns."

"Why did you come here?" Why not any other place in the entire world other than here? thought Priscilla sorrowfully.

"If I didn't know better, I might start to think you're not glad to see me..."

"What do you expect? When you show up either you threaten me or you're shot."

"Sorry, about this, luv. I needed a safe place and a phone. Your flat is the safest I could think of—and you've got a phone."

"I don't know how safe it is," Priscilla said. "The police know where I live, and they know about the two of us. If they're looking for you, it may not take them long to come here."

"Don't worry about the police. It'll be fine."

Anything but fine, Priscilla thought. A wounded gangster was in her flat, bleeding on an armchair that didn't even belong to her—it was the property of the Savoy, an institution that would certainly object to gangsters bleeding on their furniture.

But how to get rid of him?

"I have a phone," she said to him. "Do you want to call Ronnie?"

"Christ, no. Ronnie's no good for this." Reggie's words were fading into a slur.

"Reggie, you've got to get some help," said Priscilla, beginning to have nightmarish visions of a dead hoodlum in her flat.

"Scotch Jack. Get hold of Scotch Jack."

"Give me a number, Reggie. I need a number."

"Inside...coat pocket..."

She reached into his suit jacket and found the pocket-sized notebook with a grainy black cover that she had seen him write in outside the Blind Beggar. "Number's inside," Reggie mumbled.

She opened the notebook to pages of neat script in black-inked capital letters. She looked up from the notebook. Reggie had slumped down, closed his eyes, his mouth open at an odd angle, breathing gently. Sound asleep? Or dying in her armchair?

Damn!

She took the notebook into the kitchen, flipping through its pages.

From the other room, she heard Reggie groan and then start to snore.

Priscilla went to the pantry at the rear of the kitchen where she kept her Pentax camera. Thankfully, there was film in it. She positioned the notebook on the kitchen table, focused on the page and snapped a photograph. She opened to other pages—numbers, cryptic arrangements of letters—taking more pictures. There followed pages filled with phone numbers and addresses. One of the names was vaguely familiar—a member of parliament? She kept snapping pictures. Another somewhat familiar name, E. Burt, followed by the initials, S.Y.

Scotch Jack's telephone number was scrawled across the inside of the notebook's back cover. Below it, Reggie had printed the initials S.K.

It took a dozen rings before Jack finally picked up. "What?" he barked in a garbled voice.

"It's Priscilla Tempest," she said.

"What?" His voice had cleared a bit.

"Reggie has been shot."

"What?"

"Listen to me, Jack. Your boss, Reggie, has been shot. You must come and get him."

"Priscilla, is it?" Jack sounded as though he couldn't quite believe it. She could hardly blame him. She was having trouble herself believing any of this.

"Yes. Jack, are you listening to me?"

"How bad is it?"

"Reggie was shot in the leg. He says it isn't bad, but he's bleeding a lot. He should go to a hospital."

"*No!* Not a hospital. Jesus wept." The alarm in Jack's voice was palpable. "Where are you?"

"He's at my flat."

That brought silence on the other end of the line. "Jack? Are you there?"

"Okay, do your best to keep him awake until I get there. What's the address?"

"It's 37–39 Knightsbridge. Just please hurry," Priscilla said.

Off the phone, Priscilla placed the camera back in the closet and then carried the notebook into the living room. Reggie remained in place, his chest continuing to rise and fall with reassuring regularity.

She opened his jacket and replaced the notebook. Then she shook him. "Reggie," she said. "Reggie, wake up."

He grunted loudly but did not move. She shook him until, slowly, his eyes opened. "Wha?" he said.

"Reggie, you must stay awake."

He closed his eyes and began snoring again.

"You bastard," she said to him. "Don't you dare die in my living room."

He snored louder.

Scotch Jack got there so much later than expected that she had begun to worry something had happened to him. When Jack did arrive and saw Reggie slumped in the armchair, he turned pale. "Jesus wept," he repeated under his breath.

"You need to get him to a doctor," Priscilla said.

That seemed to bring Jack into focus. "Yes." He leaned forward to give Reggie a shake. "Hey, Boss... Boss..."

Reggie opened his eyes a crack, saw Jack and tried a smile that was more a grimace. "Get me out... of here..."

"I'm going to do that, Boss, right away." He threw Priscilla a quick glance. "Give me a hand getting him up."

Priscilla lifted Reggie's leg off the chair. A low growl of pain escaped from him and his eyes flashed open.

"Up we go, lad," Scotch Jack said, bracing himself to lift Reggie. Priscilla got under Reggie's free arm to help him to his feet. Together, Priscilla and Jack half-carried, half-dragged him across the living room to the door.

Just as they managed to get him into the hall, the door across the way opened and there stood Lady Agatha in a pair of striped pyjamas, her hair in curlers, her expression one of wondrous disbelief. "It's very late, my dear," she said in a reproving voice, addressing Priscilla.

"I'm so sorry, Lady Agatha," Priscilla said.

"If you don't mind my saying, this doesn't look very good, now does it?"

"A gentleman friend has had too much to drink," Priscilla said. "I'm sorry if we woke you."

"This really isn't acceptable," Lady Agatha announced huffily, delivering a final look that managed to express disbelief and disdain simultaneously before disappearing into her flat and slamming the door.

"She saw us," Jack said. "I'm going to have to kill her."

"What?"

"Just kidding." Scotch Jack's crooked smile was like a crack opening across his craggy face. "Come along, let's get the boss into the lift."

Outside, there was a further struggle with a comatose Reggie, Priscilla afraid that at any minute the police would arrive, demanding to know what she was doing propping a wounded gangster against a column while his underling ran to get his car.

But no police appeared by the time Jack returned, and they managed to squeeze Reggie into the rear.

Scotch Jack shut the passenger door and heaved a loud sigh. "There we go," he said with relief.

"Where will you take him?"

"A doctor we know is available for this sort of nonsense," Jack said. "I do believe we will pay him a visit."

"Do you have any idea who might have shot him?" Priscilla asked.

"The woods are full of suspects," Jack answered. "Did Reggie say anything?"

"A woman, he said. Someone who he wasn't expecting."

"That's how blokes like Reggie get shot. It's the people they don't expect."

Scotch Jack started into the car, and then paused to offer another of his craggy Quasimodo smiles. "You're a good woman, Priscilla," he pronounced.

Yes, sure, Priscilla thought. A good woman. An out-of-her-mind woman. Soon to be a dead woman at the rate she was going.

How to Dress for an Orgy

The next morning, Priscilla sat in her office at 205, not as concerned about wounded gangsters bleeding in her apartment as she was about what to wear to an orgy.

That is if the party at Diana Dors's Sunningdale address was actually going to *be* an orgy, she mused. If one believed the stories circulating, it could well be. But then who would start this orgy? And, most importantly, what should she wear? Presumably something removed easily. That is, providing one actually participated in the orgy. Which she had no intention of doing.

She was certain about that.

Pretty certain...

"Have you seen this?" Susie was in the doorway holding a copy of the *Evening Standard*.

"Seen what?" Priscilla said, forcing herself to stop thinking about orgy etiquette.

Susie placed the paper, open at page three, on the desk in front of her. The headline read:

COUPLE IN VICIOUS ASSAULT

Beneath a photo of Terry O'Hara, the story detailed how he and an unidentified female companion had been attacked outside his Dove Mews flat by a lone assailant armed with a club.

Terry had been hospitalized, suffering a concussion and a broken arm. The unidentified woman had been treated and released. Police had not as yet provided a description of the couple's assailant. They were asking any member of the public with information about the assault to come forward.

Yes, Priscilla decided, she could certainly come forward with information about a wounded gangster who had shown up at her door the same night Terry O'Hara was assaulted. But for now she was keeping her mouth shut.

And she decided to play it dumb with Susie. "Why are you showing me this?"

"Isn't the gentleman who was attacked Major O'Hara's brother?" Susie remained in the doorway holding the paper.

"How would you know that?"

"One hears things around this place. Is it true?"

"Yes, I suppose it is," Priscilla admitted reluctantly.

"That's so terrible!" Susie exclaimed. "Major O'Hara must feel so awful. Honestly, you can't walk the streets anymore."

Not as long as Reggie Kray is out there, Priscilla decided. He was almost certainly the club-wielding assailant. And here she was—what?—aiding and abetting a criminal? Was there not a law against that sort of thing? She could only imagine there was. Never mind the proper attire for an orgy. Better to concentrate on the fashions worn by inmates at Her Majesty's Prison Holloway. Wasn't that where they housed female miscreants such as herself?

Dimly, she became aware that Susie was speaking. "I'm sorry," Priscilla said. "What were you saying?"

"The rajah."

"Yes, yes, the rajah."

"One of his people was on the phone this morning, reminding us that the rajah would not do interviews while he is in London."

"I thought he wanted to talk to the *Times*."

"Except for the *Times*, his representative reminded me."

"You were going to get in touch with the *Times*, were you not?"

"I did, but I'm not hearing back from them."

"Try the paper again—and here's the hook: The rajah recently purchased the most valuable, emerald-encrusted necklace ever sold by Van Cleef & Arpels."

"Is that true?"

"He bought a necklace. Who's to say it's not the most expensive? Try it."

"Right-o," Susie said, taking the newspaper back.

"Also, while I think about it, we should be concerned about the rajah keeping such an expensive piece of jewellery in the hotel. Check with Major O'Hara, will you? See if he knows about the necklace and ask him if they're taking any special security precautions."

Susie nodded and then moved aside so Karl could make his entrance with coffee. Priscilla blessed his very existence and wondered how she would manage at Holloway prison without the waiter button and Karl's efficient service. She would simply have to learn to make do, that's all there was to it.

"You look rather stressed, madam. I trust the job isn't getting you down." Karl poured the cream into her coffee.

"I suppose I'm sitting here considering the usual things that preoccupy a young woman such as myself."

Karl finished pouring the cream. "And what things occupy a young woman such as yourself, madam?"

"Oh, you know, prisons and orgies."

"Indeed, madam, the usual things," Karl said dryly and made his exit.

With a cup of coffee in her, Priscilla began to feel better. She took a deep breath and picked up the receiver, forcing herself to make a phone call she had been considering since arriving at work.

It took some time to reach him, but finally the clipped voice of Detective Chief Superintendent Read said, "What can I do for you this morning, Miss Tempest?"

"I need to meet with you," Priscilla said.

"Very well. I think I can find a moment in the schedule at my office tomorrow."

"I'm not meeting at your office, and we need to meet in an hour."

"That's impossible," Read said.

"I think you'd better meet me," Priscilla stated flatly.

Read fell silent on the other end of the line. "Very well. Where?"

A grey and windy day, clouds descending in preparation for the coming rain—perfect for a clandestine meeting with a Scotland Yard detective, Priscilla mused as she leaned against the railing that kept miserable people like herself from jumping into the Thames. She felt very film noir as she turned into the wind, her hair blowing behind her, to watch the approach of Superintendent Read.

He was attired perfectly for the occasion, raincoat and a fedora, a restraining hand holding it against the wind.

"It's going to rain," he observed as he reached Priscilla.

"Then we had better hurry," Priscilla said.

"You're being very cloak-and-dagger, Miss Tempest." Read gave in to the wind and removed his hat, allowing his thinning hair to fly around his head, which lent him a somewhat comical air.

"I have a question for you, Superintendent," Priscilla said.

"I was hoping that in dragging me away from the office on such short notice you'd have information, but go ahead, ask your question."

"You work with a partner, do you not?"

"I do."

"Is his name Eugene Burt?"

Read looked puzzled. "Why would you ask that?"

"Nicknamed Buster?"

"Yes."

"How is it, then, that an E. Burt ends up on a list of names in a notebook belonging to Reggie Kray?"

Read squinted at her as though suddenly unsure who exactly he was talking to. "I'm not certain what you're getting at. And how did you come across this notebook?"

"Burt is on a list of names contained in Reggie's notebook," Priscilla said, ignoring Read's question. "Important names, I suspect—one of them I recognized as a member of parliament."

Priscilla didn't expect Read to jump up and down with joy but she thought he would be a little more vocal than he was being.

"Go on, Miss Tempest," was all he said.

"If I'm not mistaken," she said, hoping to nudge him a bit, "discovering your man's name in a gangster's notebook is not a good thing."

Read cleared this throat, directing his gaze to one of the passing barges on the Thames. "No, Miss Tempest, it is not good at all. Where is this notebook now?"

"Reggie has it."

"That's not much help then, is it?"

Priscilla reached into her bag and extracted the roll of film she had taken from her camera that morning. "I photographed the pages," she said, handing him the roll.

Read looked at it as though it was about to burn a hole in his hand. "Jesus Christ," he said.

"What scares me," Priscilla said, "is that anything I told you,

you may have told Buster Burt and that's how Reggie knows I'm talking to you. You've put me in grave danger."

"Where is Reggie now?"

"I have no idea. He showed up at my flat last night. He'd been shot in the leg."

"Shot again?" Read blinked with surprise.

Priscilla nodded. "That's exactly what I said to him. I suspect he attacked Terry O'Hara and his lady, Karen Hollander. There was no mention of Reggie in the papers, but I have to assume they shot him. Reggie said he had nowhere else to go, so of course he came to my flat."

"And what happened after he arrived at your flat?"

"Scotch Jack came and picked him up. Reggie refused to go to a hospital. Jack said they had a doctor who took care of these things."

Read's fist closed tightly around the roll of film. His face was grim, no sign of his previous merriment. He pocketed the film and then replaced his fedora firmly on his head. "When do you expect to hear from Reggie?"

"I don't *expect* to hear from him. For all I know, he's dead. I've given you this film, Superintendent, so that I don't have to deal with Reggie, and so that you will do something about your man and protect me from the Krays."

"Yes," Read said.

"What does that mean?"

"Let me handle Detective Burt." Read was businesslike. He could have been discussing a bank loan, Priscilla thought, rather than the next steps that might save her life. "I will have this film developed and see what we've got."

"There's something else," Priscilla said.

"Yes? What is it?" It was evident Read did not like the idea of Priscilla and "something else."

"Hans Kringelein. Does that name mean anything to you?"

Read shook his head. He looked almost relieved. This was the sort of question a policeman was used to dealing with. "I'm afraid it doesn't. Should it?"

"He's a guest at the Savoy. A retired German waiter, he says. But I don't know. There's something about Mr. Kringelein that doesn't quite ring true. Would you do me a favour and check to see if Scotland Yard has anything on him?"

"Yes, I suppose I can do that." He gave her a smile. "That is, if it puts me back in your good books."

"I wouldn't go quite that far." Priscilla couldn't help but give him a smile back. Old pals, helping one another, she thought fleetingly—well, no. She imagined being a pal of Superintendent Read would be very bad for her health.

Read had his notebook out. "What did you say his name was again?"

"Hans Kringelein."

"Let me see what I can come up with." He jotted the name into his notebook then closed it and looked at her. "Will you be around this weekend?"

"Why do you ask?"

"In case I need to get in touch with you."

"Well," Priscilla said, "as far as I know, I'll be busy attending an orgy Saturday night. But otherwise, I'm available."

Read's expression, Priscilla noted, reflected a mixture of skepticism and keen interest. "You're joking of course, Miss Tempest." He gave her a closer look. "Or are you?"

Remembering Diana Dors's warning about saying anything to the police, Priscilla allowed a catlike smile. "I'll let you know, Superintendent."

CHAPTER FORTY

Major O'Hara Is Angry

Priscilla, keeping an eye out for Hans Kringelein, crossed a Front Hall that, in midafternoon, was nearly deserted.

The pageboys at their stations did their best to keep the expressions of boredom off their faces. The clerks at reception and the Enquiry Desk fought to retain their usual attentiveness. The concierge pretended to be busy as he stifled a yawn.

There was no sign of Kringelein, but Major Jack O'Hara came steaming across the hall, looking as though he was ready to kill someone. As he neared Priscilla, she had the icy feeling that someone was her.

"Miss Tempest, a moment." A voice barely controlling its anger.

"Yes, of course, Major O'Hara." The major being perhaps the last person in the world she wanted to face. Nonetheless, she allowed herself to be led into the Resident's Lounge off the hall. It was deserted at this time of day. O'Hara closed the door, his face knotted in the angry expression he appeared to reserve only for her. "You have heard what happened to my brother." A statement, not a question.

"I saw something in the paper this morning, Major. I am so sorry. How is he?"

"You ask me about Terry and a day later he is savagely attacked!" Very much an accusation.

"What? You think I attacked him? That's ridiculous."

"Don't play with me, damn you! I know you've had something to do with this highly questionable American woman friend of his."

"How would you know that?" The delaying question to allow Priscilla a moment to come up with a good lie.

"Terry phoned me. Asking about you. I couldn't believe it. I don't hear from the blighter for years and then he phones me to ask about you of all people." The major seemed incredulous that anyone would make inquiries concerning an individual as insignificant as herself.

When she couldn't think of a good lie fast enough, Priscilla decided to try the truth—or a version of it. "Karen and I had coffee together, if that's what you mean."

"You had *coffee* together?" O'Hara was practically apoplectic, as though having coffee with Karen Hollander was unthinkable. "How would you ever end up having coffee with my brother's girlfriend?"

"What's any of this got to do with Terry and Karen being attacked?"

"Terry has just been released from Royal Brompton, but he suffered serious injuries. And who has been sticking her nose into whatever it is the two of them have been up to? You! For God's sake, what the blazes are you up to?"

"I don't know what happened to them." True, partially. "But I certainly had nothing to do with it." Also true. Partially. Priscilla longed to tell O'Hara that his brother had been attacked after he and Karen tried to blackmail her into helping them set up a call girl operation at the Savoy. Wouldn't that please Major O'Hara no end.

She bit her tongue.

"You have been the source of nothing but trouble ever since you arrived here, Miss Tempest," the major fumed. "Not only have you been implicated by police in a murder, but now I am certain you are somehow mixed up in what has happened to my brother. If it is the last thing I do on this earth, I will ensure that your time here comes to an end and that you are turned over to authorities so that they can deliver what I am certain will be your just desserts."

That tore it as far as Priscilla was concerned. What did she have to lose at this point? "What do you know about what your brother was up to with Miss Hollander?" she demanded.

"I have no idea," sputtered the major.

"You don't know that he's involved in a number of illegal gambling clubs in London?"

"As far as I know, he is in security," O'Hara didn't sound as though he believed that any more than Priscilla.

"That's a front for what he really does—and you damned well know it," Priscilla insisted.

"I know no such thing!"

"Do you have any idea what Karen Hollander does in America?"

"I know nothing at all about my brother's women."

"She operates a high-end escort service. She and your brother were planning to expand her operation in London. Their first stop was to be here at the Savoy."

"That's absolutely ludicrous!" the major sputtered.

"If you dare take any action against me, I will ask Mr. Banville to launch an investigation into what role you might have played in your brother's plan."

O'Hara's expression was one of abject horror. "Preposterous! My brother would never become involved in any such enterprise."

"Wouldn't he? From what I know, he definitely would. But he would need help—perhaps from you, perhaps from his close friend, Lord Snowdon. Why don't we have a talk with Mr. Banville, see what his views might be? But then we must be certain none of this gets into the papers, right Major? Think of the scandal if the press were to link the Savoy and Lord Snowdon, as well as yourself, to high-end prostitutes."

"You are a godawful bloody liar!" roared Major O'Hara.

"Am I? We will soon see."

"Liar!"

Major O'Hara stormed away. Priscilla inhaled deeply, all but certain that she had just made a lifelong enemy. Nothing much she could do about that, except perhaps she could have better managed her temper and her tongue. She took time to gather herself before re-entering the Front Hall. A wildly gesturing concierge confronted Major O'Hara. Nearby, the pageboys swirled in confusion. Staff members at reception were on phones. A cacophony of jumbled noise rose through the hall. Priscilla began to make out words: *Stolen... necklace... the rajah...*

The emerald necklace from Van Cleef & Arpels.

Stolen!

The Jewel Thief

"Have you heard?" Susie was agog as Priscilla came into 205.

"I just heard," Priscilla said. "Everyone's going crazy in the Front Hall."

"A thief somehow got into the rajah's suite and stole that necklace. While he slept!" Susie exclaimed. "Can you imagine? At the Savoy! What a nightmare!" Susie caught the distracted sheen in Priscilla's eyes. "Priscilla? Are you listening to me?"

"Always," Priscilla said absently, thinking that she did not want to be considering what she was starting to consider. It couldn't be...

Could it?

Out loud, Priscilla asked, "Did you ever get on to the major about extra security for the rajah after he bought that necklace?"

"I left him a message, but never heard anything back. I didn't think—"

The piercing sound of the ringing telephone interrupted Susie. She picked up the receiver, listened for a moment and then said to Priscilla, "It's Mr. Coward for you."

"Noël," Priscilla said into the receiver, "I'm afraid I can't talk just now."

"Won't take a minute, Priscilla. I've been thinking about your friend Kringelein."

"What about him?"

"His name, Kringelein. I haven't been able to get it out of my mind. Where have I heard that name before? Then it suddenly occurred to me. *Grand Hotel*, the novel by Vicki Baum! And the classic Greta Garbo film. Cheap entertainment but very popular."

"I'm not sure I understand," Priscilla said impatiently.

"Kringelein, don't you see? He's a character in the novel, a poor German waiter who comes to the hotel for a taste of luxury before he dies—much like our Herr Kringelein. What I now fear is that this man is an imposter of some sort."

"Shite!" Priscilla exclaimed. She hung up on Noël and then dialed the front desk.

"What are you doing?" Susie demanded.

"Give me Mr. Kringelein's room, please," Priscilla said into the receiver.

"I believe Mr. Kringelein has checked out," the operator said.

Priscilla replaced the phone, her heart beating faster as she hurried past an amazed Susie. "Where are you going?"

Priscilla flew out the door and dashed along the corridor into the Front Hall, looking frantically around. A familiar figure was disappearing out the revolving doors.

Racing out into the forecourt, past the doorman, Priscilla spotted Kringelein ahead of her. He gripped a small suitcase as he moved toward the Strand where a car was pulling to a stop. The tall woman was behind the wheel, her face mostly obscured by the same broad-brimmed hat Priscilla had seen in the American Bar.

"Mr. Kringelein!" Priscilla called.

Kringelein jerked to a stop. When he saw Priscilla bearing down on him, his face popped with surprise. "Miss Tempest. What's wrong?"

Priscilla was out of breath as she reached him. "I don't want you leaving, Mr. Kringelein."

"Whyever not? My niece is here to take me for a drive."

"You don't have a niece! You're a lonely German waiter from Itzehoe. There is no niece."

"This is ridiculous." Kringelein's eyes darted nervously. "What is wrong with you, Miss Tempest?" Passersby had stopped to watch the unfolding drama.

"You need to speak to the police," Priscilla asserted.

Kringelein looked confused. "The police? Why should I talk to the police?"

"Because a valuable necklace has been stolen," Priscilla said, improvising quickly. "The police are investigating the theft. They wish to speak to all our guests."

"Hans, please, you must hurry," the tall woman called from the car. "We are going to be late."

"I have to go, Miss Tempest." Kringelein's voice was edged with anger. "Please excuse me."

He started to turn away. Priscilla grabbed at the suitcase. "What's in your suitcase?"

Kringelein tried to pull away. "What are you doing? Are you mad? Let go of my suitcase."

"Mr. Kringelein! Give me the suitcase!"

"Leave me alone!" cried Kringelein.

He struck out at Priscilla, knocking her back. There were gasps from members of the small crowd that was gathering. Priscilla lunged forward and grabbed Kringelein's arm. "Stay where you are!" she shouted.

Again, he tried to yank away and when that didn't work, he swung the suitcase at her, yelling, "Help! This woman is assaulting me! Help!"

As she tussled with Kringelein, out of the corner of her eye she saw Major O'Hara burst through the onlookers. Before she had a chance to say anything, he dived at Priscilla and pulled her off Kringelein. "Miss Tempest, stop this!" he yelled. His face was twisted in fury.

"She attacked me!" shouted a distraught Kringelein. Horrified onlookers murmured assent. "This crazy woman attacked me!"

"She's out of her mind," called a young woman standing at the curb.

"Miss Tempest! What is the meaning of this?" Major O'Hara had lifted himself into the highest of high dudgeons.

Priscilla made a final, desperate lunge at the suitcase, catching Kringelein off guard. He lost his grip. The suitcase fell to the pavement, its latches springing open so that the lid flew up, sending its contents sailing into the air.

The rajah's necklace made a soft landing atop Kringelein's clothing, which had spilled across the pavement.

Detective Chief Superintendent Read had to kick up a fuss, uncharacteristic for him, but by the end of the day the photos from Priscilla's camera were on his desk.

Whatever reluctance Read had had about her claims evaporated as soon as he began to study the pages from Reggie Kray's notebook. Some names he didn't recognize but many he did, particularly the name of his partner, Detective Eugene "Buster" Burt. It was right there in Reggie Kray's carefully constructed block letters.

He'd had his suspicions about Burt, that was certain, but to see those suspicions confirmed in such stark fashion left him in shock. There was a knock at his door and Read made sure he covered the photographs before calling, "Come in."

Buster Burt stuck his eager young face into view. "Got a moment, Super?"

"Come in, Burt. What can I do for you?"

Buster Burt stepped into the room. He had his raincoat on. "Checking in to make sure all is well."

"Why wouldn't it be?" Read inquired.

"No reason, Super. You seemed a bit preoccupied earlier this afternoon, that's all."

"Is that the only reason why you're here, Eugene?"

Burt smiled sheepishly. "Hoping you'd let me clock out a bit early today. Wife and I are celebrating our anniversary this evening."

"Congratulations." Read forced the cheery smile expected of him in such circumstances. "Got something special planned?"

"Dinner out at our local, I expect," Buster said. "Nothing too special."

"Go ahead," Read said. "Enjoy your weekend."

"Sure you're okay, Super?"

"A lot happening at the moment, that's all, Eugene. Busy time."

"Anything breaking on the Kray investigation?"

"What makes you ask?"

Burt looked abruptly nervous. "I know you've got that Tempest woman working for us. Is she being helpful?"

"Jury's out, Eugene. We'll see."

"You have a good weekend, Super—and many thanks."

When the door closed, Read uncovered the photos and sat studying them, willing Buster's name to somehow disappear from the list in front of him.

It didn't. And his name in Reggie's notebook meant what it appeared to mean, no matter how many excuses Read invented.

He thought about Priscilla Tempest and the danger he had placed her in. She had said something about attending an orgy. Was she serious? Who knew what young women in London got themselves up to these days?

If there was something like that going on at the weekend, it was likely hosted by the elusive Diana Dors. It crossed Read's mind to alert Inspector Lightfoot: He could find out from Miss Tempest where the party was being held and get officers there to bring in Miss Dors for questioning.

But then he decided against it. No, he would let Miss Tempest loose. The woman was totally unpredictable. Left to her own devices, who knew what she might come up with?

Superintendent Read smiled, considering the possibilities.

How to Act at an Orgy

How does one act at an orgy?

The question was on Priscilla's mind as she steered her Morris Minor through the gathering dusk along the M3 toward Sunningdale, Berkshire.

Were you expected to throw off your clothes upon arrival? Or was there a period of ice breaking, getting to know your fellow orgy participants? And supposing the stranger you had just met wanted to have sex with you but you didn't want to have sex with that stranger? What happened then?

Can you say no at an orgy? Or does that rather defeat the purpose?

Or did everyone, once the lights went down, simply throw themselves at each other in the dark, giving and taking whatever was available?

So to speak.

Following the chaos that ensued after the arrest of Hans Kringelein, Priscilla very nearly wasn't able to get away at all. Everyone had been very complimentary, naturally. Although initially, despite the necklace spilling out of Kringelein's open suitcase, there was some doubt as to whether such an elderly gentleman could have carried out such an audacious theft.

Kringelein himself angrily denied any culpability, claiming the necklace had been planted in his suitcase. His puzzlement at being associated with a woman in a wide-brimmed hat was certainly convincing, particularly in light of the fact that the woman in question had vanished. Kringelein's sudden fainting spell was convenient, ending further questioning while he was rushed to hospital.

No one actually believed anything the old man said. However, his adamant denials brought on a fusillade of questions for Priscilla from Charger Lightfoot when he showed up at the hotel to lead the investigation.

She barely had time to scurry to her flat to get into an orgy-appropriate costume: purple velvet hotpants, paired with a sleeveless, low-cut beaded cerulean top—it tinkled as she walked—along with fuchsia kitten-heeled Mary Jane pumps. She debated adding a pair of dangly earrings to the mix, then decided against them in case they got lost in whatever fray she might become involved in. She topped off her out-for-an-evening-orgy look by smoothing on a slash of blue eyeshadow and then adding a set of wicked false eyelashes.

Definitely hot, if she did say so herself.

It was dark by the time she drove through the quaint village of Sunningdale, shuttered tight on a Saturday night, reminding Priscilla of Dylan Thomas's "black and folded town fast, and slow, asleep." From there it wasn't far to Orchard Manor.

A two-storey manor house at the end of Shrubbs Hill Lane, cars already parked in the drive and in an adjacent meadow. Had she arrived late to the party? Was everyone already inside, naked, and fornicating madly?

Priscilla parked in the meadow and then crossed to the drive. Lights burned in the windows fronting the house. Music wafted faintly from inside. What was the proper etiquette? Priscilla wondered. Did you knock on the door or simply walk in? She tried the doorhandle. The door swung open easily. In addition to the music, she could now hear the murmur of voices.

Well-dressed men and women clustered in a great room off the main hall, chatting and sipping drinks—the picture of a sedate Saturday evening cocktail gathering. A few couples eyed her with what could possibly be perceived as carnal interest as Priscilla made her way through the room. Diana Dors, iridescent in a pale ivory gown that matched her shoulder-length hair, lit up as soon as she saw Priscilla.

"You came," she said excitedly, embracing Priscilla. The feel of Diana against her, the heat and the scent emanating off that sumptuous body, made Priscilla feel...what? Possibly the flash of desire one should experience at an orgy.

Diana pulled back, eyes gleaming. "Let me get you a drink."

She led Priscilla to a bar that had been set up in the corner. A beautiful young woman in a black dress molded to her curves poured a flute of champagne.

On a nearby leopard-print sofa, a man and woman embraced. The woman's blouse was open to allow the fondling of her breasts. Perhaps it was not the usual Saturday night cocktail gathering after all, Priscilla mused.

"I'm so glad you've come," Diana said. Her hand stroked Priscilla's arm. The champagne warmed her. She told herself she had to focus on what she came for.

"The film," Priscilla said. "Please."

"There's no hurry," Diana said.

"I can't stay long."

Diana gave her a look. "Yes, you can."

Not far away, a couple approached a petite young woman and began to caress her. The two women kissed.

"Is this how it happens?" Priscilla said, eyes on the three hotly embracing one another.

"Happens or doesn't happen," Diana said. "It all depends on the mood you're in."

The mood on the leopard-print sofa had progressed to the removal of clothes.

Diana said, "How about you? What sort of mood are you in, Priscilla?"

"I'm not sure," Priscilla said truthfully. Her heart was definitely beating a lot faster than it had been before she got there.

"Come along." Diana took Priscilla by the hand. "Let me show you around."

A pair of bronze doors flanked by black marble panthers opened to an indoor swimming pool. Nude swimmers were backlit by an art-deco window. A man sat at the edge of the pool while his companion worked between his legs. Not far away a couple made love on a chaise longue.

"Everyone comes to these parties," Diana said. "Celebrities, professional athletes, even the odd politician."

"And the Krays." Priscilla made sure it wasn't a question.

"They won't be here tonight." Diana allowed a fleeting smile. "They sent you instead."

"Nonetheless..." Priscilla said.

"The film is upstairs. Follow me."

They went along a passage to a wide staircase that rose to the second floor. Priscilla followed Diana into a bedroom done in pink with a canopy bed and a sunken jacuzzi. A mirror ran the length of a wall. "Whenever there's a light in the other room, we can see in, but they can't see us," Diana reported.

"For instance, no one can see you and me." She stepped closer.

"I don't want this," Priscilla said in a weak voice.

"Yes, you do." Diana sounded very confident as she positioned Priscilla's face gently between her hands, kissing her deeply.

Whatever thoughts Priscilla might have had about what she did or did not want—and she was leaning toward the wanting part—ended abruptly when the bedroom door flew open. The man who stumbled in had black hair framing a darkly complexioned, youthful face. He wore a black leather jacket and ridiculously tight pants. His white shirt was open to the waist to show off his bronze chest.

Diana slowly brought the kiss to an end. "Alan," she said, calmly, her arms still around Priscilla. "Get out of here."

"That's no way to greet your husband, ducks." Alan stumbled over to the bed and with a loud sigh flopped down on it. "That's better," he announced. A wave of his hand was accompanied by a sleepy look. "Go ahead, don't let me stop the two of you. Continue with what you're doing. I am far too drunk and high to interfere."

"Who is this?" Priscilla asked Diana.

"My one and only probably failed to mention it," Alan said. "But she has a husband—and I'm *it*. Alan Lake, actor and drunk, not necessarily in that order."

"If I had a husband worthy of the name, believe me, I'd mention it," Diana sneered. "But as it is..."

"I'm absolutely snockered," Alan said. "Too much booze. Too many women to undress." He lifted himself up for a closer look at Priscilla. "Diana usually won't have anything to do with her guests. But I see she has made an exception tonight. Can't say as I blame her. Wouldn't mind taking a run at you myself."

"Alan, I mean it," Diana said angrily. "Get out."

Alan ignored her and spoke to Priscilla. "You must tell me who you are, ducks."

"I'm Priscilla Tempest. And I am not your duck."

"Yes, yes, the little duckling from the Savoy. A fellow suspect along with Diana in the untimely death of poor Skye Kane."

Alan fell back on the bed. "The Krays did it. That's what I think. Either that or that big buffoon who was so obsessed with her."

"What big buffoon was that?" Priscilla asked.

"Alan, shut up." There was a warning edge to Diana's voice. The lazy passion she had previously exhibited was gone, replaced by a sheen of anger.

"You see what happens," Alan said. "Diana wants me to shut up any time the conversation turns to the Krays and their minions."

"I want you to shut up and get out of here," Diana said.

"What's the bloke's name?" Alan's voice had become dreary. "Jack something? Whisky Jack?"

"Scotch Jack?" Priscilla said.

"That's it, that's the lovesick lad! Scotch Jack. Absolutely besotted with Skye. She played him for a fool, of course. But then Skye played all men for fools"—he cast a bleary glance at Diana. "Much like my lovely wife here. Except Diana is an equal opportunity player, women and men. Of course, maybe Skye was too. That would explain her hold over Diana—a hold I certainly don't have."

A scream of rage, an animal sound, erupted from Diana as she launched an assault on her husband, pummelling him with her fists, screaming for him to get out. Caught by surprise, Alan tumbled off the bed onto the floor. Diana took advantage and began kicking at him. Alan, nose bloodied, got to his knees as Priscilla pulled at Diana. "Diana, enough, that's enough."

"You bastard," Diana shrieked as Priscilla held her. "You bloody drunken bastard!"

She wrenched herself away and stormed from the bedroom.

Priscilla helped a groaning Alan regain his feet. "The woman is bonkers," he managed to gasp.

She helped him onto the bed. "You shouldn't be around her, sweetheart," he continued. "Bitch has the blood up tonight."

"Tell me about Scotch Jack," Priscilla said.

Alan eyed her suspiciously. "What's to tell?"

"Jack and Skye Kane," Priscilla pressed. "Tell me what you know."

"Like I said, he was head over heels for her. Consumed, you might say. Out of his dim mind, of course. Skye may have led him on a bit but she was no more interested in him than flying to the moon."

"What about you, Alan? Were you interested in Skye?"

"Who wasn't interested in Skye? That's the better question. Nights like this, all the possibilities at your fingertips. Hard not to indulge."

He inspected Priscilla lazily, taking her hand. "Like tonight, for instance. More possibilities. Those legs of yours..."

He jerked her toward him. She pushed him off. "No thanks."

"I should say something like 'you don't know what you're missing—ask Diana.'"

"I don't think that's necessary," Priscilla said acidly.

Alan fell back on the bed. "Ah, Saturday nights at the manor house...sometimes you hit...occasionally, a miss..."

As she left the room, Alan Lake had begun to snore, confirming her suspicion that she wasn't missing much at all.

Priscilla came downstairs to find the living room pretty much emptied out. Had everyone in an unexpected show of decorum retreated to the privacy of the manor's bedrooms? The couple making out on the sofa was nowhere in sight. A few strays lingered at the bar, a little drunk, a bit bored. They eyed Priscilla disinterestedly as she searched around for Diana.

She found the actress leaning on the balustrade on the wide terrace outside the sitting room, watching a naked couple on the lawn, bathed in moonlight.

"They're having fun, at least," Diana said as Priscilla stood beside her. She gave Priscilla a sidelong glance. "What did you do with Alan?"

"I left him sound asleep."

"Did he try to shag you?"

"He was the perfect gentleman."

Diana rolled her eyes. "I'm sure," she said wryly. "He's a right bastard, but I suppose he's my right bastard."

"I need that film, Diana," Priscilla said.

"Yeah, you do." Diana turned to her. In the moonlight, her hair was like white silk. "I have to keep in mind that's why you're here."

"Yes, but if I'm being honest, I was curious about what a real live orgy might be like," Priscilla conceded.

"Not enough oomph tonight, I'm afraid," Diana said. "Okay then. Wait here. I'll be right back."

Out on the lawn, the man rolled off his partner. The two lay motionless on their backs. Diana returned a few minutes later holding a reel of eight-millimetre film. "Here you are," she said, handing the reel to Priscilla.

"You're certain this is the right film?"

Diana nodded. "I'm sick and tired of this whole thing. It was Alan's idea in the first place. He thought the Krays would pay to get it back. It never occurred to him that they might prefer to kill rather than pay. It's a great deal cheaper. Take it, but do me a favour, will you?"

"If I can."

"Forget what Alan said about Scotch Jack and Skye. Alan is a blowhard. He has no idea what he's talking about."

"Are you sure about that?"

"Nothing happened between those two. Jack had a bit of a crush, that's all. Not a big deal."

"No?"

"David Merrick murdered Skye," Diana asserted.

"Not the Krays?"

Diana shook her head. "Skye was afraid of Merrick. She thought he was a jealous hothead who could go off at the most unexpected times." She indicated the reel in Priscilla's hand. "Get that back to Reggie or Scotland Yard or whoever it is you plan to give it to, and then we'll forget about it."

"I wish it were that easy," Priscilla said.

Diana leaned forward, kissing Priscilla softly on the mouth. "Memories of a night that might have been. Good luck, Priscilla."

Deciding she did not want to exit through the house, Priscilla went down the steps that led from the terrace. So much for attending an orgy, she thought. Kissed by a movie star and propositioned by a drunk. Not much more to it besides a reel of film that hopefully would put an end to her problems with the Krays.

Two men were walking toward her. She thought about telling them that they were late; the orgy, such as it was, had faded to an anticlimax—so to speak. As they drew closer, Priscilla saw with a start that one of the men was Terry O'Hara. A battered Terry O'Hara, a slightly limping Terry O'Hara. An unsmiling Terry O'Hara.

"There you are, Priscilla," he said.

Fearful, Priscilla took a step back, as though these two had abruptly become radioactive. "What do you want?" she demanded.

Terry indicated the burly young man with him. Dressed in a business suit with a shock of sandy hair, his companion had the plump face of a baby, except for the tiny black eyes and the nasty little mouth. An ugly baby.

"I believe I talked to you earlier about my friend Teddy Smith. I thought it was time the two of you met."

"Terry and Teddy, a couple of real pals." Teddy Smith said, somehow making the declaration sound threatening. "Terry's told me all about you, Priscilla." Which sounded even more threatening.

"Is that so?"

"That's definitely so," Teddy said. The mean little mouth had turned itself into a mean little smirk. "He says you're a friend of Reggie and Ronnie."

"That's right."

"I'm no friend of those two, and I don't much like people who are."

Priscilla found her throat constricting. "Get out of my way," she managed to say.

"Sorry, Priscilla," Terry said. "I tried to warn you."

Teddy's cherub face went blank suddenly as he moved toward Priscilla, attacking with his arm raised. She tried to jerk away, dropping her shoulder bag. Teddy Smith's arm whipped down. The searing pain of the striking blow triggered a burst of bright light that quickly extinguished into exquisitely velvet blackness.

Mad Teddy

The darkness was filled with the low hum of an engine.

The searing pain in Priscilla's head offered evidence of returning consciousness. She strained to raise her arms, discovering that she couldn't do it because her wrists were bound behind her. When she attempted to move, she banged against a hard surface. Her breathing exploded in ragged gasps, the claustrophobia making her feel as though she were suffocating. She cried out, her voice a hollow, useless echo in the enclosed space.

She forced herself to remain calm and understand that she wasn't in a coffin—her first thought. But then panic flared again: If this was not a coffin, could they have thrown her into a car's boot? No, she told herself, that couldn't be. Terry wouldn't do that to her, would he?

But hold on a minute, Priscilla thought. Terry was with his pal Teddy. And Teddy, with that ugly baby's face, appeared to be capable of just about anything, including dumping a helpless young woman dressed for an orgy into the boot of a car.

She must have lost consciousness again because the next thing she knew, they were slowing, turning and then coming to a stop. A couple more minutes and she heard the sharp click of a latch and the sky opened up.

Hands lifted her out roughly and set her down on wobbly legs, gripping her arms to keep her upright. "There you go, luv," a voice said. She became aware of a yard full of scrap metal surrounded by a high fence. The torn-up fuselage of a plane emblazoned with a Royal Air Force roundel lay like a dead animal amid masses of steel and iron.

Before she could take in much else, Priscilla was hustled across the yard through a wide archway. A light flared, illuminating piles of copper coils, steel bars and the crushed corpses of kitchen appliances stacked atop one another. The restraining hands let go of her. She teetered on her kitten heels, fighting to keep her balance. Other hands worked at her bonds, finally freeing her. She felt dizzy and nauseous. A hand reached out to steady her. "Easy does it there, girlie," said Teddy Smith. In the half light, Teddy's face had lost its baby-like qualities. It was a pale, wicked face, Priscilla decided.

"I have to sit down," she said, everything spinning.

"Yes, I'm sure you do," Teddy agreed. "But first we need you to help us out." He turned to Terry, who had now materialized out of the surrounding darkness. "Priscilla's going to help us. Am I right about that?"

"That's it, Teddy," Terry said. "I'm certain Priscilla is anxious to help us." His face was swollen and purplish, still showing the results of his encounter with Reggie Kray. Two disfigured ghouls in a garage full of junk, Priscilla thought. The nightmare was complete.

"Can't help you," Priscilla murmured.

"That's where you're wrong," Teddy insisted. "The film you received tonight. You hand it over to me and that's a great help."

Priscilla couldn't stand any longer. She collapsed to her knees. Terry's voice came from far away. "Did you hear what my friend Teddy just said? You want to help. Tell us what you've done with the film."

"Don't know what you're talking about."

"Here's the thing." Teddy's tone was infinitely reasonable. "Me and my friends, we're South London lads. We've tried our level best to get along with those bastards across the river in the East End. But, you see, Reggie Kray, he goes after Terry here, Terry and his lovely bird, and that does it as far as I'm concerned. Friends of mine, you see. Friends, incidentally, who offered you a great opportunity, which I understand you rejected."

"Karen and I tried to make her see reason," Terry said. "We did our best to make her understand you would not be happy to learn that she refused to co-operate."

"There you go," Teddy agreed. "I'm not happy at all. Fact is, I'm pissed."

"Did I mention what they call my friend Teddy?" Terry asked Priscilla. "Tell her, Teddy. Tell her what they call you."

"I don't hear it myself, but from what I'm told, they call me Mad Teddy." The baby's face had become sullen.

Terry dropped down to his haunches so that he was closer to Priscilla. "Mad Teddy's specialty is what he does with pliers." He looked up at Teddy. "Show her."

Teddy extracted a pair of pliers from his pocket and held them for Priscilla to see.

"That's it, Teddy," Terry acknowledged. He turned his attention back to Priscilla. "What he does with those pliers—he uses them to pull teeth." He chuckled. "You heard the expression 'like pulling teeth?' That's what Teddy does. It's like pulling teeth for him."

"Ronnie Kray...he uses pliers too." Priscilla's words came out with difficulty.

"Like hell," she heard Teddy exclaim.

"Only he pulls out your nails." She saw with satisfaction that this was having an effect on Teddy.

"Bastards," Teddy said. "They stole from me. Bugger!"

Terry didn't look happy either as he straightened up. "There you go, Teddy. What is it you have been telling me?"

"You can't trust the Krays," Teddy said.

"There's the proof for you right there. Although, I suppose there is another way to look at it."

"What's that?" Teddy demanded.

"You know, imitation being the sincerest form of flattery? Isn't that what they say?"

"Do they?" said Teddy. "I never heard that."

"What they say, for what it's worth."

Terry looked down at Priscilla. "I'm not sure what's worse, having your nails pulled or your teeth. Personally, I'd rather lose my fingernails. They will always grow back, right? But teeth? I don't think they grow back." He paused and waited for Priscilla to respond. When she didn't, he shrugged and offered the glimmer of a smile.

"I like you, Priscilla. But you've caused me a lot of pain. Karen too. Give me the film and we're square. I give you my word, you and your teeth will be safe."

Priscilla tried to say yes but, to her amazement, the word wouldn't come out. She had to be satisfied with moving her head up and down.

"Good," Terry said with satisfaction. "Let's have it."

"My shoulder bag."

Terry looked confused. "Shoulder bag?"

"It's in my bag."

"Where is your shoulder bag?"

"You must have it," Priscilla said.

"What are you talking about?" Terry knocked Priscilla over and then rolled her onto her back. His hand groped at her clothing. It occurred to Priscilla that when you are wearing hot pants, there are not a lot of places to hide a reel of film. Terry quickly realized that as well. "What the hell?" he said, his face twisted in anger. "Where is it?"

"It was in my bag...where's my bag?"

"Don't play with me, Priscilla," Terry said sternly. "Where is it?"

His fist was raised, poised to hit her when a voice called out, "That's enough, lad."

Terry jerked around, dismay pushing the fury off his face. Priscilla was able to lift her head enough to see the figure poised in the archway.

Scotch Jack, his bowler hat tipped at a rakish angle, held a short-barrelled shotgun in one hand, a revolver in the other.

CHAPTER FORTY-FOUR

Nobody Moves!

"Lads," Scotch Jack said, addressing Terry and Teddy. He was outlined heroically, Priscilla observed happily, in the pale light coming through the archway.

"In my hands tonight," Jack continued in a warning growl, "I'm holding a loaded twelve-gauge shotgun and an Enfield revolver."

Nobody moved. Teddy managed one of his ugly smirks, his small eyes glittering. "There you are then, Jack. Long time no see."

"I heard you were dead, Teddy," Jack replied.

"Everyone keeps telling me that, but as it happens, no thanks to the Krays, I'm still breathing."

"That's good to hear, Teddy. What you want to do now is keep it that way."

"Sure thing, Jack," Teddy replied carefully. "That's what I want all right."

"I need for the two of you to step back from Priscilla and do it now," Jack said. "You do anything else and it's the shotgun. Priscilla, please darlin', why don't you start toward me? Everything nice and slow now."

Priscilla began crawling toward Scotch Jack while Terry and Mad Teddy fell back a few paces, keeping their eyes riveted on Jack.

"We don't want trouble," Terry said carefully.

"Good for you, lad. Couldn't agree more." Jack eyed Teddy. "They still calling you Mad Teddy, Teddy?"

"That's what they tell me," Teddy acknowledged.

"What is it? You're so mad they got you kidnapping birds?"

"I do what's necessary, Jack. That's what they hire me for. But at least I'm an original. Not like you lot, imitating me."

Jack looked puzzled. "Think what you please, Teddy. But here's the thing. What it is you're after, Priscilla don't have it. Next time you kidnap a bird, make sure you don't leave her bag behind. Now I've got the film and that's the end of it."

Priscilla drew closer to Jack, managing to raise herself in time to see the figure darkening the archway. She cried out a warning that was interrupted by the sound of a gunshot.

Jack grunted and lurched forward so that Priscilla could get a look at Karen Hollander, the gun raised in her hand as she fired a second bullet into Jack. He dropped the Enfield revolver at the same time as he pulled the trigger on the shotgun. The blast reverberated loudly through the garage, pellets ripping into Teddy, sending him spinning backward.

Jack had the presence of mind to pivot around swinging the shotgun, its short barrel smashing into Karen's face before she could fire again. Screaming, Karen fell to the concrete, dropping the gun. Priscilla blindly grabbed for the Enfield and had it in her hand when Terry, shouting furiously, sprang at her. She fired. Terry stopped, thinking he must have been hit. As soon as he realized Priscilla had missed, he retreated.

Teddy Smith was lying on his side, his shoulder torn apart, howling in pain. Priscilla, holding the Enfield, expected Terry to resume the attack. But he stood still, as if anticipating a bullet. "Jesus," he said softly.

She backed away, holding the gun pointed at the two men. Karen was down on the floor, issuing sharp moans of pain. Jack was still on his feet but teetering uncertainly as Priscilla took his arm. "Let's go, Jack. I believe we're finished here."

"That we are, lass," Jack gasped. "That we are."

They backed out into the yard, Priscilla with the Enfield, Jack with his shotgun, ready in case Teddy or Terry decided to come after them.

It started to rain as they passed the remnants of the RAF fighter and went out into the rainswept street where Jack had parked Reggie's Jaguar. She leaned him against the hood. He had his back to her. "Need a minute." He was breathing heavily. A dark strain of blood spread across his jacket.

"Let me help you, Jack," Priscilla said. "I'll drive."

"Think that's for the best." Jack's breath was coming in heavy exhalations. "Get us out of here before those villains back there come to their senses."

Yes, thought Priscilla in a numbed state as she helped Jack into the passenger seat, perhaps it was high time everyone came to their senses.

Confession

Scotch Jack slumped against the passenger door, his Quasimodo face a ghastly white beneath the bowler hat that somehow had remained in place atop his head.

The rain came in gusts driven by a fierce wind, Priscilla straining over the wheel, trying desperately to see the road ahead through the opaque windscreen and wipers that appeared to be designed to clear as little rain as possible.

"Get onto South Lambeth Road and from there cross the river at Vauxhall Bridge," Jack instructed between gasps for breath.

"We've got to get you to a hospital," Priscilla said.

"Don't bother, darlin'. My insides is on fire. I'm afraid old Jack is about finished."

"No," Priscilla said vehemently. "I'm getting you help."

Jack didn't say anything. His breathing had become shallow.

"Jack? Are you listening to me?"

"Still here darlin', not gone yet."

"Jack, I want you to keep talking to me. Okay?"

"No problem there. Old Jack and his mouth. Blabbing away. What do you want to talk about, darlin'?"

"Skye Kane. Let's talk about you and Skye. How's that?"

"Ah, yes, yes, the lovely Skye. What of her?"

"I think I know who murdered her."

"There's a conversation to keep me awake," Jack allowed. His eyes were closed, his head lolling back.

"You were in love with Skye, weren't you, Jack?"

"What would make you think that?"

"Am I wrong?"

"Me and all the other lads, I suppose. She had that effect on men, yes she did."

"But you were different from the others, weren't you, Jack? You truly cared for her."

"Did I? Maybe I did, yeah. I don't know..."

"Because you did care, I imagine she must have hurt you badly."

"I cared, that's right," he muttered. "Cared too much. Silly...had me out of my mind, she did..."

Priscilla stole a glance at him. Jack's eyes fluttered shut. The bowler hat had dropped off to allow his head to rest against the seat.

"Cared for her a lot more than the others, I can tell you that; buggers were using her, filling her full of lies, particularly that bloody theatrical bloke."

"David Merrick."

"Bastard hit her. She refused him, wouldn't do what he wanted...hit her...She called me after it happened. Called me from her dressing room, wanting me to come to her, make sure he stayed away...get her away from there."

"You loved her," Priscilla said to him as she drove. "You cared. Wanted to protect her. That's why you went to her dressing room after the show. You wanted to be with her. You wanted to be sure she was safe."

"She was hurt. That bastard had hurt her."

"Tell me what happened, Jack." The rain was coming down even harder now, sheets slamming the windscreen.

The sound of the rain filled the car. Jack had fallen silent. Priscilla chanced another quick look at him. His eyes remained closed, his head back. She could see his chest moving up and down, but otherwise no breath appeared to be coming out of his opening and closing mouth.

Finally, he spoke slowly, in a whisper that Priscilla had to strain to hear. "I get there... and she's all cold and remote... tells me Merrick is coming for her. *Merrick*. The bugger assaulted her, for Christ's sake. She was going off with him. Couldn't believe what she was doing... going off with the bugger who hit her..."

"I imagine that made you very angry, Jack." Priscilla, holding her breath, waited for his answer.

But he went silent again. Priscilla pressed him: "Jack? You were badly hurt, weren't you? Feeling betrayed."

Jack managed to move his head up and down slightly. "I guess I lost it. I get like that sometimes, you see; a bloke pushes me too hard, someone takes advantage, takes something that rightfully belongs to me. I see red and the next thing..." His voice fell away into another series of dramatic exhalations. "Jesus save me, I'm not well..."

"The next thing, Jack?" Priscilla asked, speaking quietly, pushing gently. She kept her eyes on the road as she spoke, not sure where they were or where they were going. Simply driving through a black, rainy night, keeping Jack talking.

"I loved her..." he continued. "God help me I loved her so much... but where would it end? She was never going to be with me... impossible... I knew it... broke my heart... my bloody damned black heart..."

"You shouldn't have done it." She looked quickly over at him again. "You know that. You shouldn't have killed Skye."

"I felt terrible afterwards." Jack's voice had weakened even more, all but lost against the sound of the engine and the windscreen wipers and the rain beating hard on the car. "But that's what I've chosen in this cursed life of mine, isn't it? First kill came at eighteen. Bastard cheated me. He deserved what he got...After that, it wasn't so difficult. By the time I met up with Reggie and Ronnie I was a hard man, no doubt about it. A life of murder, that's what it's been. Blood on my hands...Kill or be killed, know what I mean? Law of the jungle...law of the sodding jungle."

"Jack, you loved Skye." The desperation was showing in her voice, as if she wanted him to call out his innocence, that his love was so strong, he could not possibly kill it off. Someone else must have murdered her, not the man who loved her more than anything.

But that was not to be.

"Shouldn't have done what I did...the damned killer inside me...I will pay in hell..."

Now there was only the shoe leather left, Priscilla thought morosely, the working out of the comings and goings that night. Aloud she said, "As you left Skye's dressing room, you nearly ran into David Merrick. True?"

Jack's head again moved up and down slowly. "Came close to finishing the bugger for hitting Skye like that. But I'd settled a bit by then, a little calmer...could think straighter, figured there was no time. If I was to get past this, I had to be gone from there."

"What about Reggie? Did he know? Did you tell him?"

"Told him everything. Had to tell someone...bottled up inside me, about to explode. He's a good lad, Reggie. I knew he'd understand that it was an accident, that I was seeing red in the way I see red when I'm betrayed. He understood, agreed that it was an accident, couldn't be helped. Good lad, said he'd take care of me. I was part of the Firm. That's what Reggie calls it, the Firm...Good lad..."

"And Diana Dors? What about her?"

"Diana, damned Diana!" Jack grimaced. "Foolish woman. Why she ever filmed Ronnie in the first place. She and her husband...the two of them, out of their minds...Unnecessary problems all around..."

"But Diana suspected what happened," Priscilla interjected. "She worried that you and Reggie might do something to her because of what she knew. So maybe she thought the film was her insurance policy."

"It was Reggie...he sent me tonight...make sure one way or the other we got that bloody film back from Diana Dors so Ronnie could rest easy and stop going on about it...not that Ronnie ever rests easy or ever stops...so I got the film and made sure you came to no harm. Did what I was supposed to do, like a bloke does when he's part of the Firm...Can I tell you something, darlin'? Would you mind?"

"No, Jack, tell me," Priscilla said.

"You're an all-right bird, in my estimation, I want you to know that. You walked into things with Reggie and you caught his eye. That's not always a good thing."

"As I've had to learn the hard way," Priscilla concurred. "Reggie says he likes you but then he'll gladly kill you. Not a good combination."

As soon as the words were out of Priscilla's mouth, it occurred to her that was probably not something she should say to the man who killed Skye Kane.

But Scotch Jack seemed unbothered. "I'm afraid you got yourself into a nest of killers, darlin'...I done what I could to protect you...tried my best..."

"Thank you, Jack. You saved my life tonight."

"Those buggers back there..." Jack opened his eyes and forced a smile. "We took care of them, didn't we, darlin'?"

"Yes, I guess we did," Priscilla said. But at what price? Priscilla thought. A woman dead because she said no. Blood spilled because a gangster was doing something he didn't want anyone in his gangster underworld to see.

What a price, indeed.

Jack was trying to sit up to get a better look out the windscreen. The rain had let up a bit. The wipers weren't quite so overwhelmed. "Now you're approaching Vauxhall Bridge, that's good..." Jack settled back. "You've done well, Priscilla. Yes, you have. You know who murdered Skye and lived to tell the tale. Well done..."

"I'm sorry it was you, Jack," Priscilla said. "I really am."

"Not as sorry as me, darlin'..." Scotch Jack closed his eyes.

"Jack?" Priscilla's eyes darted to him. He didn't respond.

By the time she drove across the bridge, Jack's chest had become still.

Damned Fine Work, Miss Tempest

"You should know that we have arrested Reggie and Ronnie Kray," Detective Chief Superintendent Leonard Read told Priscilla when they met in Priscilla's office Monday morning.

The meeting followed the drama and confusion that ensues when a distraught young woman shows up in hot pants and false eyelashes at a police station late at night, in the midst of a rainstorm, with a dead gangster in the front seat, a sawed-off shotgun on his lap and an Enfield revolver jammed in his belt. And a reel of film tucked in his jacket.

Priscilla, fighting hard to keep her wits about her in the face of a barrage of questions and a lot of hostile looks, had finally persuaded local officers to call either Inspector Lightfoot or Superintendent Read. Such was Priscilla's importance that both detectives had arrived at the police station and wasted no time whisking her off to Scotland Yard.

Hours of questioning had followed, accompanied by a few tears. There was initial resistance to the idea of Scotch Jack as Skye Kane's murderer. Lovelorn gangsters who murdered their lovers did not usually come wrapped in an ungainly body topped by a bowler hat. Finally, though, there was grudging acceptance that while dead men tell no tales, occasionally they leave behind a confession.

"Did you hear me, Miss Tempest?" Read drew her back to concentrate on that ever-cheerful face across the desk. The face whose bland cheerfulness was beginning to set her teeth on edge.

"I'm sorry, Superintendent," Priscilla said. "I should have offered you something. Would you like coffee? Tea?"

"No, thank you, Miss Tempest." He looked at his watch. "I'm due in court. I don't have much time."

"I understand," Priscilla said. "What was it that you were saying?"

"I was trying to tell you that we have arrested the Kray twins. This is rather a red-letter day for Scotland Yard and the Murder Squad, if I do say so."

"Well done," Priscilla said without enthusiasm. "Jolly good and all that."

"Yes, I must say it has been a long slog to the point where we could arrest those two early this morning."

"That might explain why I haven't heard from Reggie since Scotch Jack died."

"At the same time as we arrested the brothers, I am sad to report that we also arrested Detective Eugene Burt, along with several other officers who had been conspiring with the Krays."

"What did you arrest Reggie and Ronnie for?"

"The murders of George Cornell and Jack McVitie."

"The gangsters you told me about earlier."

"That's right," Read said with a thin smile. "Ronnie gunned down Cornell at the Blind Beggar. We believe Reggie shot McVitie in the head in a basement flat."

"Then what I did for you had nothing to do with their arrests," Priscilla said.

"As it turns out, no," Read admitted. "But that's not to say we don't appreciate your efforts, Miss Tempest. After all, thanks to you, we now have the confession of the late Jack Dickson, better known to one and all as the villain Scotch Jack. Inspector Lightfoot is most pleased—and relieved, I have to say. There was an immense amount of pressure on him to solve that crime."

"What about Karen Hollander and Terry O'Hara, who are responsible for Jack's death?"

"Missing, on the run—but we are actively seeking to bring them in, along with Teddy Smith, also on the run."

"You know, of course, that Terry is the brother of Major Jack O'Hara, our head of security?"

"Yes, I feel very sad for Jack. Spoke to him earlier. He's most upset."

"I'm really sorry to hear that," Priscilla said. "I tried to get in touch with him, but I understand he's taking some time off."

"Additionally," Read continued, "thanks once again to your efforts, the jewel thief Max Gerhardt, who you know as Hans Kringelein, is in our custody. I understand the Rajah of Farid-kot, Mr. Harinder Singh, is most appreciative."

"What about his accomplice?" Priscilla asked.

"An Austrian woman named Brigitta Haas. They have worked together for years. There is a warrant out for her arrest. Incidentally, it may interest you to know that Gerhardt used the alias Kringelein, drawn from a character in that most famous of all hotel-set novels, *Grand Hotel,* written by Vicki Baum."

"Yes, I found that out, finally," said Priscilla. "Or, more accurately, I was told by a good friend."

"Damned fine work on your part, Miss Tempest." Nipper Read's bland face beamed with admiration.

"I have to say that I can't quite shake the feeling that despite everything, Inspector Lightfoot would just as soon I was among those headed for prison."

"I do think you are wrong," Read said. "I believe Charger quite likes you. It's just that he's a reserved, pipe-smoking English policeman, a breed not often given to showing their true feelings."

"How about you, Superintendent, do you also like me?"

That brought on another of Read's cheery smiles. "I do indeed, Miss Tempest. You are, I would say, an intelligent, resourceful woman. Quite the amateur sleuth, if you want to know the truth."

"The sleuth you almost got killed over a reel of film that in the end no one cares about."

"In fact, after viewing said film, it really is difficult to tell whether it's even Ronnie. I doubt it ever would have been much use to anyone."

"Great," said Priscilla ruefully.

"This is one of those situations where you never know until you know."

"The least you could do for me, Superintendent, is make sure my name doesn't get into the papers."

"There is no reason why you should be implicated in any of this, unless an enterprising reporter comes after you. Should that happen, we will do our best to steer him away." Read rose to his feet. "Again, you have my thanks and the thanks of my colleagues at Scotland Yard." He offered his hand.

Priscilla took it reluctantly. "No offence, Superintendent, but I hope we don't have to run into each other ever again."

"No offence taken." He bathed her with a final cheery smile. "However, you never know, do you?"

"No, Superintendent, I suppose you never do."

Read started away and then paused. "Incidentally..."

"Yes?"

"How was that orgy you attended?"

"Not much to it, I'm afraid," Priscilla said glumly.

"There never is, is there?"

Priscilla looked at him. "You've attended orgies, have you, Superintendent?"

Read just smiled and continued on his way.

Midday in the Savoy's Front Hall, the rich checking out so that the richer could check in. It had been pointed out many times, Priscilla reflected, that if you did not have money, lots of it, you were unlikely to be a guest. Instead, you served those who did have it, anonymously delivering the impeccable service expected. And doing so quietly and discreetly.

Priscilla had to concede that while she continued to be one of those servants, lately she had been neither quiet nor discreet, and certainly not nearly anonymous. She had consorted with notorious London thugs, had been kidnapped, and, yes, to be fair, had foiled a theft and solved a murder. But was that enough to save her job?

She had her doubts.

The Savoy, after all, had not hired her to stop thieves or solve murders. Then there was the vengeful Daisee Banville. Who knew what kind of poison she might be enthusiastically pouring into her husband's attentive ears?

Preoccupied with agonizing over her future, Priscilla nearly missed the departing Rajah of Faridkot, trailed through the Front Hall by his three wives and his entourage. Priscilla could have sworn the rajah cast a glance in her direction, but it was no more than that. If he had any idea what she had done for him, he gave no sign of it. After all, who was she but an anonymous servant? It was her job to foil any jewel thief who might steal a guest's emerald necklace. That's what she was there for, was it not? No thanks needed.

"He doesn't give a damn about you." Abruptly, David Merrick was standing next to her.

"Excuse me, Mr. Merrick, what did you say?"

"The rajah, or whatever he is. I hear you're the one who caught the thief who stole his necklace. Is that true?"

"All in a day's work here at the Savoy," Priscilla said.

"I was in the press office looking for you," Merrick said.

"I was just on my way in." She noted the passing porters laden with Merrick's luggage. "You're leaving us, are you?"

"And none too soon," Merrick said.

"Yes, given what has happened, I'm sure you're glad to see the end of London for a while."

"I wanted you to know, Miss Tempest, that I'm not such a bad fellow. I admit I was not at my best with Skye Kane. I regret that, I truly do. I understand from the police that you played a part in finding the real killer. You lifted the cloud over me that could have destroyed my life. I wanted to make sure I stopped to thank you."

"Your words are much appreciated, Mr. Merrick. Really. But how would you like to do me a favour?"

Merrick looked somewhat taken aback. "Sure. What can I do for you?"

"You can say nothing but nice things about your time at the Savoy. And you can promise me that when you come back to London, you will stay with us."

Merrick gave her the sort of dark look that persuaded Priscilla he would never return. But then, suddenly, he broke into a wide smile that made him look like her kind, sweet uncle. "I will come back, thanks to you," he said. "But I warn you: I'll be as difficult and demanding as ever."

"We would expect nothing less," Priscilla said.

"I was going to say something like stay out of trouble but, from what I understand, you and I suffer from a similar shortcoming. Neither of us can stay out of trouble for long."

"I hope you're wrong, Mr. Merrick."

"I don't think I am, Miss Tempest." He gave her a nod. "Take care of yourself."

Priscilla couldn't help but heave a relieved sigh as Merrick followed his retinue of porters out the front entrance.

Perhaps there might be hope yet, she thought, entering 205.

Then she saw the stricken, tear-stained expression as Susie turned beseechingly to her. "Oh God," she said.

"Susie, what is it? What's wrong?"

"I'm afraid we really are going to lose our jobs."

"What makes you think that?"

"Because Mr. Banville wants to see you—immediately!"

Priscilla groaned inwardly. *Doomed!*

CHAPTER FORTY-SEVEN

"Call Me Tony"

El Sid regarded Priscilla with the smug satisfaction she associated with *les tricoteuses*, the hags who sat knitting at the guillotine while the heads rolled. "You may go straight in," he said, his tiny eyes agleam with anticipation of the horrors to come.

Clive Banville's expression, as Priscilla entered into her doom, was one of mere disapproval rather than the highly anticipated show of anger. "There you are Miss Tempest. Difficult to track down as usual." Spoken in a nonjudgmental manner, Priscilla noted hopefully.

Banville turned to a short, very handsome man with thick brown hair, dressed casually with the sort of bright kerchief around his neck you seldom saw inside the Savoy. He jumped up from the sofa where he had been seated at the far end of the office. "Priscilla, have you met my friend, Antony Armstrong-Jones, Lord Snowdon?"

"No, I haven't," Priscilla said, trying not to look too flummoxed by this unexpected turn of events.

She willed herself not to think about the tanned smoothness of his skin, which so nicely emphasized the blue eyes she swore sparkled, as he said, "Please, call me Tony." He took her hand, at the same time producing the bright, alluring smile that only added to his attractiveness and undoubtedly had swept Princess Margaret off her feet.

"Tony was gracious enough to drop by the office today," Banville was saying. "I thought it high time the two of you met."

Tony continued to hold onto Priscilla's hand and keep that smile in place as he said, "Clive, you failed to tell me how lovely Miss Tempest is."

"Please," Priscilla heard herself saying, "call me Priscilla." She immediately kicked herself. Too much too soon, she decided.

"Priscilla it is," Tony said, reluctantly dropping her hand. The smile held in place. "But only if you call me Tony."

What was she supposed to say to that? Nothing, she ordered herself. Just smile.

Which she did.

"I'm very pleased to inform you, Miss Tempest," Banville was saying, "that Lord Snowdon, Tony, has agreed to take a series of photographs set around life here at the Savoy."

"That's...wonderful," Priscilla said, having trouble with the word "wonderful."

"I'm very much looking forward to it," Armstrong-Jones said, keeping his eyes firmly on Priscilla. "The Savoy is a great hotel. I'm determined to capture that greatness on film."

"Quite," said Banville. He addressed Priscilla. "To that end, Miss Tempest, I want you to work with Tony, show him the ropes. Do you think you can do that?"

"Yes, of course," Priscilla said, gulping out the words. Was she mistaken or was that an anticipatory gleam in Lord Snowdon's very blue eyes?

"Should be great fun," he said. "Can't wait to get started."

"Any idea when you will start?" Priscilla asked.

"As soon as possible," Armstrong-Jones answered. "We can work together to come up with some sort of schedule so that I don't disrupt life at the hotel too much."

"There we go, then," pronounced Banville, looking particularly satisfied as he shook Armstrong-Jones's hand. "So glad we can come to this arrangement."

"I am, too," Armstrong-Jones replied. He turned to Priscilla. "I'll walk you out."

"Go ahead you two." Banville gave them a blessing smile.

They exited together past a morose El Sid, undoubtedly disappointed to see that Priscilla still had her head on her shoulders. They stepped into the silent corridor. Priscilla turned to Armstrong-Jones and said, "I have a question—Tony. If you don't mind."

"Not at all."

"Between the two of us?"

Armstrong-Jones grinned. "Absolutely."

"What was that all about in Mr. Banville's office?"

His expression was a combination of amusement and puzzlement. "Whatever do you mean?"

"You've just received a plush assignment from the Savoy."

"I have indeed," said Armstrong-Jones cheerfully.

"Forgive me for even suggesting it, but I can't help but wonder if this assignment might have been given in exchange for leaving Mr. Banville's wife alone."

Armstrong-Jones leaned closer. "If I said I haven't the faintest idea what you're talking about, would you believe me?"

"No."

He seemed unperturbed. "Look at it this way." He paused to flash one of those devastating grins that Priscilla always told herself she could easily resist in men, but then never could. "It could be simply that Clive had a brilliant idea and he has hired me to transform that idea into reality. If I'm allowed to blow my own horn, I have to point out that I'm considered an excellent photographer. Renowned, some might say. If it goes the way we all hope, I will add credit and prestige to this hotel. Not such a bad thing, no matter the circumstances that brought me here."

"It could be that, I suppose," Priscilla said, all too aware of his closeness.

"Then again," Armstrong-Jones went on, "it could be I've heard from certain sources that you're quite a hot girl and so naturally I was anxious to meet you."

"Daisee told you that?" If that was the case, there are snow-balls in hell, Priscilla thought.

"At this particular moment, I can't quite recall names. But in any event, my sources were absolutely right. I'm looking forward to working with you, Priscilla. Very much looking forward to it."

His hands touched her waist. "Working very closely together..."

Armstrong-Jones took his time about moving his lips in the direction of her mouth—a man certain he could get away with what he was about to do. And sure enough, she allowed him to kiss her. Her mind filled with a lot of gibberish she couldn't quite grasp. Then a warning voice finally broke through the noise to argue against what was currently happening.

She drew away and slapped his face.

Armstrong-Jones looked vaguely surprised before that dazzler of a smile made a comeback. "Well done," he said. "I deserved that. We're going to get along just fine." As he started off along the corridor, he called back to her. "Lovely to meet you, Priscilla. I will be in touch."

Oh God, Priscilla thought. Oh, Lord Snowdon!

"You don't mean to say he actually kissed you?" Noël Coward, striking an uncharacteristically flabbergasted note, set aside his Buck's Fizz. A meeting of the Gossip's Bridle Club had been called to order in the American Bar.

"He did in fact kiss me," agreed Priscilla.

"What did you do?" inquired John Gielgud.

"If I told you I didn't stand for it, I would be telling a fib," Priscilla said. "However..."

"However?" Olivier's eyebrows had reached record heights.

"I did slap his face."

"Good for you!" pronounced Olivier, his eyebrows lowering to show determined support. "Cheeky blighter!"

"Was it a good kiss?" Gielgud inquired.

"I didn't have a great deal of time to judge," Priscilla said after taking time to consider the question. "Still, I have to admit it was not a *bad* kiss, as kisses go."

"But you think this photo assignment is nothing more than a payoff for staying away from Banville's wife?"

"That's what I accused him of," Priscilla said.

"My God, you said *that* to Lord Snowdon?" The monarchist in Olivier had found voice.

"I'm afraid so."

"How did he react?" Gielgud looked faintly amused.

"With delight. And he seemed pleased when I slapped him."

"A bounder!" Olivier declared.

"I am looking determinedly on the bright side," Priscilla went on. "This morning I had convinced myself that I would soon be out on the street. This evening, somewhat to my surprise, I am still employed at the world's greatest hotel."

"But for heaven's sake, why would your job ever be in jeopardy?" Gielgud sounded aghast. "If it hadn't been for you, Skye Kane's murder might never have been solved."

"I suppose there is a case to be made for the view that if Priscilla hadn't been so clever, David Merrick might have spent the rest of his life in Wormwood Scrubs, thus saving both American and British theatre from his ravages," Noël suggested.

"And let us not forget that Priscilla also thwarted the theft of a priceless necklace from the hotel," piped up Olivier.

"A marvellous job of thwarting," Gielgud said.

"I might add that I had a little something to do with the apprehension," Noël put in.

"Says the man who thinks he won the war," added Gielgud.

"We are quite a team, I would say." Noël beamed with pleasure at Priscilla.

"Gentlemen." Priscilla raised her champagne flute. "Let me say that the one very good thing to come out of all this is my membership in the Gossip's Bridle Club. It is an honour to be part of such charming company. Thank you all for taking me in and helping me out during these difficult times."

Gielgud and Olivier grinned with pleasure. Noël raised his glass. "To the contrary, my dear, the honour is ours. Why, with you as a member we now have murder, mystery, sex and gangsters to discuss."

"Otherwise," said Gielgud, "we'd be listening to Noël prattle on about his missing knighthood."

"While I remind Johnny of his disaster directing the London production of *The Glass Menagerie*," put in Olivier.

"It was not *that* bad," Gielgud responded sourly.

"And, as I must constantly remind the two of you," Olivier went on, "while Noël lusts for it and Johnny settles for it, I received my knighthood back in 1947. Furthermore, I have it on the best authority that, as has often been speculated, I am indeed soon to be named a lord."

"Lord Larry, God help us," said Noël with a groan.

"I want you all to know that such a high honour will not change me in the least."

"How could it?" Gielgud said. "You're already impossible."

"For now, let us put our differences aside." Noël raised his glass in salute. "To Priscilla, Princess of the Savoy, who has saved us from ourselves!"

"Priscilla! Princess of the Savoy!" chimed in Olivier and Gielgud.

The Price of Love

Feeling a little sad and drained following the adjournment of the Gossip's Bridle Club, Priscilla returned to her office to collect her things before heading off to her lonely flat where she would sit with a glass of wine and feel sorry for herself.

Susie had left for the day. That probably explained how Percy Hoskins got into her office. He was arranged in all his rumpled glory on her sofa with a beer.

"You're not supposed to be here," she said, unwilling to concede that she might be a little bit glad to see him.

"I've come to be with the woman I love," Percy said, going so far as to sit up now that Priscilla had arrived.

"To drink free beer is more like it," Priscilla said.

"There is that," Percy acknowledged. "But in addition to the beer, it could also be that I felt compelled to be here because, after all you've been through, you must be feeling a bit knackered and could use some fascinating company to take your mind off your many problems."

"I have only one problem and he's sitting here on my sofa drinking hotel beer," Priscilla said. "And among the many things he is not, he is definitely not fascinating company."

Percy was on his feet. He smelled of beer and aftershave, not exactly an irresistible combination. Quite resistible in fact.

But still...

"Come on, Priscilla, be nice. You know you're glad to see me."

"I have no idea what you're talking about."

"Yes, you do." Percy's mouth darted toward hers. She ducked away. "What's the matter?"

"During the workday, the Savoy does not allow its employees to kiss members of the press."

"Let me try to understand the hotel rules," Percy said. "These rules do not allow you to kiss a reporter who loves you. But they do allow you to sleep with Canadian prime ministers. Have I got that right?"

Her eyes widened. "You know!"

"Of course I know," Percy said, knowingly. "It's my business to know."

"Then why didn't you—?"

"Why didn't I use your name in the story everyone was trying to track down? Maybe it was because I care for you and didn't want you to lose your job."

"Because otherwise you would have no source at the Savoy," Priscilla suggested.

"That may have crossed my mind," Percy conceded.

"I knew it. You couldn't care less if I did sleep with the prime minister—although I am not saying I did," Priscilla maintained resolutely.

"You did sleep with him. I have it on the best authority."

"Bollocks," was as close as Priscilla could come to a denial.

"However, being the generous fellow I am, I'm willing to put our little disagreement aside, knowing you are anxious to help me with the latest rumour that's flying around."

Priscilla eyed him narrowly. This was not going to be good at all. "What rumour are you talking about?"

"That Lord Snowdon has been paid a great deal of money to photograph life at the Savoy in return for staying away from the general manager's rather promiscuous wife."

Priscilla's eyes widened. "You bastard! Once again you're try-ing to use me."

"No, no," Percy protested. "But until I succeed in convincing you that you love me, I might as well use the time to squeeze information out of you."

"I don't love you," Priscilla protested.

"Yes, you do," Percy countered. "You simply don't realize it yet."

"That is certainly news to me," Priscilla stated. "How could anybody in their right mind love you?"

"The question of a right mind is a conversation for another day," Percy deflected. "For now, tell me about Lord Snowdon."

"How's this," Priscilla responded. "If I agree to kiss you, will you stop asking me questions?"

"Is that the price of love?" Percy feigned disbelief. At least it looked to Priscilla that he was feigning disbelief.

"A bargain, if you ask me," she said.

"I might agree to pay that price—if you finally have that din-ner with me that you promised."

"You really, truly are a bastard, you know that?"

"Undeniable. But that aside, are you going to kiss me or not?"

The telephone on her desk began to ring, as though warning of the danger involved in kissing Percy Hoskins.

"Don't pick that up," Percy admonished.

Priscilla picked it up.

"Priscilla." The voice on the line sounded far away.

"Yes?"

"Priscilla, it's Pierre Trudeau calling. *Comment ça va?* I've missed—"

Priscilla slammed the receiver back onto its cradle. She looked at Percy.

"About that kiss..." she said.

314

Guests of the Savoy

The Right Honourable Pierre Trudeau, the charismatic bachelor who took London by storm, remained Canada's prime minister for nearly sixteen years except for a nine-month period when the opposition Conservatives briefly defeated his government. Mr. Trudeau stepped down as prime minister in 1984 after a reflective walk in a snowstorm. At the age of fifty-one, he married twenty-two-year-old Margaret Sinclair. Their marriage lasted for six stormy years. One of their three sons, Justin, grew up to become Canada's twenty-third prime minister. Mr. Pierre Trudeau died in 2000 at the age of eighty. He never again attempted to get in touch with Miss Tempest.

Miss Diana Dors, the former Diana Fluck, acted in a series of mostly forgettable films throughout the 1970s. She did a great deal of television, including playing the lead role in a situation comedy for two seasons. She maintained her notoriety in the press, hosting sex parties with her husband, the actor Alan Lake. Sued for back taxes and forced to declare bankruptcy, Miss Dors became a popular TV guest in her later years, speaking candidly about her many misfortunes, even giving advice to the lovelorn on a morning television show. Miss Dors died of cancer in 1984 at the age of fifty-two. In the autumn of that year, after burning all his wife's clothes and suffering from depression, Mr. Lake, at the age of forty-three, used a shotgun to kill himself.

Having been cleared of any involvement with the death of Miss Skye Kane, Mr. David Merrick continued to pursue a busy theatrical career. Through the late '60s and '70s, he produced a steady stream of plays and musicals, winning Tony awards for his productions of *Rosencrantz and Guildenstern are Dead* and *42nd Street*. Married six times, he suffered a stroke in 1983 that impaired his speech and left him unable to walk. He died in London in 2000 at the age of eighty-eight. Although his brush with the law did nothing to change his irascible and combative personality in the following years, it should be noted that when in London, Mr. Merrick always stayed at the Savoy.

Detective Chief Superintendent Leonard Ernest "Nipper" Read not only outsmarted but also outlived most of the London hoods he brought to justice. By the time he retired in 1977, Superintendent Read had solved every murder he ever investigated, except for one. A boxer as a young man, in his later years he pursued his love of the sport in various official capacities, including as vice-president of the World Boxing Association. In 1991 he published an autobiography titled *Nipper* (it was later reissued as *Nipper Read: The Man Who Nicked the Krays*). Covid-19 ended Superintendent Read's life in April 2020, one week after his ninety-fifth birthday.

In 1969, the Kray twins were convicted of murder and given sentences that specified no parole for at least thirty years. At the age of sixty-one, Mr. Ronnie Kray died of a heart attack in the Broadmoor Hospital, a high-security psychiatric hospital. An older brother, Mr. Charlie Kray, died at the age of seventy-three on the Isle of Wight while serving a twelve-year sentence. Mr. Reggie Kray outlived them both. Finally given a compassionate release after being diagnosed with cancer, Mr.

Kray died little more than a month later at the age of sixty-six. Mr. Reggie Kray never again tried to contact Miss Tempest—although she could not help but wonder from time to time why he didn't.

There always has been uncertainty as to the fate of Mr. Teddy Smith—Mad Teddy, as he was known. Mr. Smith was thought to have been murdered at the insistence of the Krays, with whom he'd had a falling out. However, many years later, stories began to circulate that he was alive, an old man living in Australia, where he supposedly died of cancer in 2006.

Despite his friendship with the Krays and a rumoured affair with Teddy Smith, not to mention all sorts of scandalous escapades, Mr. Thomas Edward Neil Driberg, well-known journalist, influential Labour politician, High Anglican churchman, an openly gay man at a time when it was illegal, and an alleged Soviet spy, miraculously managed to escape any retribution for his sometimes notorious behaviour. In fact, before his death at the age of seventy-one in 1976, he was granted a peerage and introduced in the House of Lords as Baron Bradwell. Known as a self-absorbed liar and braggart who could not be relied on to keep any secret, Mr. Driberg was proof that if you were well connected in the British establishment in those days, you could get away with just about anything—and end up a baron.

Sir John Gielgud and Lord Laurence Olivier, undaunted by encroaching age, continued to pursue busy careers on stage and screen. Mr. Noël Coward finally became Sir Noël in 1970. Priscilla, along with Messrs. Gielgud and Olivier, attended the party at the Savoy celebrating his knighthood. The Gossip's Bridle Club continued to hold regular meetings, tasked as often as not with lending a helping, supportive hand to their newest member, Miss Priscilla Tempest.

As for Miss Tempest, what can—or should—be said about her, other than to report that despite her repeated assurances that she would, she could not seem to stay out of trouble. Management at the Savoy placed her on notice regularly and continued to view her with a combination of suspicion and amazement. Internal management memos from the time reveal a reluctance to fire her because, to quote one of those documents, "Miss Tempest appears to know too much about where the bodies are buried."

ACKNOWLEDGEMENTS

Ghosts of the Savoy

Seated on a banquette in a corner of the Savoy Hotel's iconic American Bar, sipping one of Priscilla's Buck Fizzes, the celebrated ghosts of the hotel's legendary past swirl around. The 2022 Savoy is a sleek, modern, beautifully run hotel in the midst of twenty-first-century London. Yet reminders of its glamourous past are everywhere present. Lining the walls along the corridor outside the bar are autographed photos of various celebrities that include Gary Cooper, Humphrey Bogart and Lauren Bacall. Noël Coward peeps out from a glass case. A bronze bust of the famous playwright and longtime Savoy habitué is also on prominent display.

Off the Front Hall, in the Thames Foyer, beneath its dramatic glass-domed atrium, the Savoy's traditional afternoon tea is served as a pianist tinkles the ivories in the gazebo that dominates the room. Patrons nibble at a selection of dainty sandwiches and homemade scones—with clotted cream, naturally—surrounded by lush portraits of Ava Gardner, Alfred Hitchcock, Marlene Dietrich and Frank Sinatra, long-gone guests of the Savoy—the past very much a part of the hotel's present.

That dazzling past is what fascinated us writing *Death at the Savoy* and now its successor, *Scandal at the Savoy*. One of the pleasures of visiting the contemporary hotel is discovering that the era in which we have set the novels has not been forgotten but is in fact celebrated.

ACKNOWLEDGEMENTS

In writing *Scandal at the Savoy*, we had a lot of help getting the past just right.

Kathy Lenhoff, longtime first reader, provided encouragement and gave us hope. London editor Ray Bennett brought us down to earth again with his gentle suggestions and insights, while eagle-eyed forensic closer James Bryan Simpson got the novel into the shape needed for being shown to a wider world.

Pam Robertson not only came up with the title, but once again sharpened her pencil to oversee the editing for Douglas & McIntyre. What Pam didn't straighten out, Caroline Skelton did. By the time the editorial process was complete, the two authors couldn't help but notice a better novel had emerged. Finally, artist Glenn Brucker once again found an original way to bring Priscilla to life on the book's cover.

Back at the American Bar, the small circular glass-topped tables, ornamented with tastefully shaded lamps, are occupied by the early evening pre-theatre crowd. The murmur of conversation fills the room as white-coated waiters serve cocktails on silver trays. Among the patrons, there are no signs of the rich, famous and aristocratic who once crowded the bar. But that's all right. In the subdued light of the American Bar at night, the ghosts of the Savoy are very much present. They exist on the walls and in memory.

And thanks to everyone who worked so hard on the book, they are captured forever in the pages of *Scandal at the Savoy*.